Flames
on the Sky

The Turquoise Legacy, Book Two

by

Linda LaRoque

Flames on the Sky: The Turquoise Legacy, Book Two

Cover Art by *Kim Mendoza*

The Wild Rose Press
PO Box 706
Adams Basin, NY 14410-0706
Visit us at www.thewildrosepress.com

Publishing History
First Faery Rose Edition, 2009
Print ISBN 1-60154-582-7

Published in the United States of America

Madison felt as if she'd traveled to the Twilight Zone.

Lilly's claims were preposterous, but, she couldn't deny what she'd seen on the cliff face or the dreams.

"Yes, you need to tell me about the dreams. They started at the time you received the necklace, right?"

Madison nodded. "How did you know?"

"I assumed the ancient Elders would haunt you, but when Lonan called yesterday, I knew so for a fact." Her smile was sympathetic. "Tell me about them."

Lilly's eyes lit with excitement as Madison talked. When she finished, the older woman leaned back and closed her eyes.

Lonan's brow was furrowed, his mouth pinched. "What did you mean when you said, 'You are the one'?"

She pierced him with an intent look. "Did not Madison say you were the very image of the warrior in her dream? The prophecy requires that someone from the past, which is you, son, be chosen to be Madison's protector." Lilly turned to Madison.

Oh, no. I don't think I want to hear this. She held up her hands and shook her head. "No—"

"Yes, Madison, with hair of fire, whether you like it or not, the Gods chose you, someone from the future, to find the third stone and reunite the twins with the mother stone. Together, you two will find a way to consign the evil one to the pit below mother earth where he belongs."

Reviews for *Flames on the Sky*

"A compelling, heart-stopping adventure through the magical folklore of an extinct Native American tribe while simultaneously introducing today's western tribal culture with gripping precision... chock full of fiery romance, unseen twists and endless intrigue...without doubt a top shelf keeper!"

~Author Sky Purington

"Cross Indiana Jones with THE HAUNTED MESA...[This] is truly a magical tale that will keep you guessing until the end."

~Skhye Moncrief; www.skhyemoncrief.com

"A thought-provoking journey into the mystery surrounding the Anasazi, experienced through the eyes of a modern young woman."

~P. L. Parker www.plparker.com

"Rich with history and ancestry...a well-written, suspenseful story that's descriptive and well researched. I thoroughly enjoyed this book. A+"

~Carrie Destler www.CarrieDester.com

Reviews for *My Heart Will Find Yours*:

"A wonderfully twisted time-travel tale!"

~Terry Spear, Heart of the Wolf, www.terryspear.com

An entertaining, fantastic read!...unexpected twists and loveable characters... wit and snarky attitude... readers won't be disappointed!"

~Katie Reus http://www.katiereus.com/

"A wonderful Western time travel...unexpected plot twists... fast paced and compelling."

~Laurel Bradley, Author, A Wish in Time, Crème Brûlée Upset, www.laurelbradley.com

"A wonderful story of compassion, loss and triumph. You won't be disappointed."

~Carrie Destler www.CarrieDester.com

Dedication

To Lee, Crea, and Terran
for their continuous support and constant prodding
to get this story just right.
Thanks, ladies.

Acknowledgements

Research for *Flames on the Sky* was a total joy. I'd read Kathleen and Michael Gear's *The Visitant* and other novels about the Anasazi. The mysteries surrounding them intrigued me. Then I visited Mesa Verde and was awed by its grandeur, beauty, and history.

The first book of The Turquoise Legacy, *My Heart Will Find Yours,* was finished and work on *Flames On The Sky* began. In November of 2007, my husband and I toured Chaco Canyon to see if I'd gotten the layout correct. I'd made a few wrong assumptions about the canyon, but nothing of great importance. Basically, the roads inside the park are paved instead of dirt. The road leading into the park was unpaved and as rough, if not rougher than I'd been led to believe. My husband described it as a washboard.

Something about Native American historical sites calls to me. I don't know if it's that tiny tab of Cherokee blood in my DNA or what. It doesn't matter what nation of people, but their history, their customs, their love of nature and the earth reaches inside me and grasps my heart. During a ceremonial dance in Oregon, I was so moved I struggled to stem the flow of tears.

Though *Flames On The Sky* is fiction, I hope I've given the Four Corners region, the Indian Nation, and Chaco Canyon the respect and honor they deserve.

Happy reading!
Linda

References used for *Flames on the Sky*

Online References
1. Chaco Culture, National Historical Park:
   http://www.nps.gov/archive/chcu/chacoan.htm/
   http://www.nps.gov/archive/chcu/museum.htm/
   http://www.nps.gov/archive/chcu/sacred.htm/
2. Una Vida:
   http://www.colorado.edu/Conferences/chaco/tour/v
   ida.htm/
3. Chaco Canyon New Mexico. The Center of the Anasazi Culture:
   http://www.fortunecity.com/victorian/rothko/140/
   chaco.html/
4. Destinations Along the Turquoise Trail:
   New Mexico Mountain Bike Adventures
   GORP
5. Pueblo Bonito: Turquoise Trade Capital:
   http://www.kstrom.net/isk/art/beads/bonito.html/
6. Turquoise Mining History:
   http://www.cerrilloshills.org/mines/turq01.htm/
7. Tri-Cultural Use of the Cerrillos Mines:
   http://www.cerrilloshills.org/mines3cult.htm/
8. Spiritual Beliefs and Turquoise:
   http://www.jewelrysupplier.com/2_turquoise/turq
   uoise_spirituality.htm/
9. Turquoise—The Fallen Skystone:
   http://www.collectorsguide.com/fa/fa098.shtml/
10. Turquoise Necklace Facts and Beliefs, by Sam Serio:
   http://www.morninglightjewelry.com/ariticles_tur
   quoise_necklace_facts_beliefs.php/
11. Amber Legends:
   http://www.dragonflyamber.com/about_our_ambe
   r/amber_legends/
12. In Search of Shaman:
   http://www.goddess.org/cmhg/shaman.html/

13. Shamanism:
    Wikipedia
14. Phenomenon of the Vortex:
    http://www.angelfire.com/indie/anna_jones1/vortexes.html
15. Puebloan peoples:
    http://en.wikipedia.org/wiki/Pueblo_people
16. Zuni:
    http://www.crystalinks.com/zuni.html/
17. The Navajo People:
    http://library.thinkquest.org/J002073F/thinkquest/Navajo_people.htm/
18. All My Relations, Mitakuye Oyasin:
    http://www.trailtribes.org/pierre/all-my-relations.htm/

Prologue

New Mexico, November 1875

The morning sun cast a strip of light across the dirt floor of Spirit Warrior's hogan as it rose above the mountains he loved so well. The red cliffs were as important as each breath he took, a part of his soul.

Winter was here, the cold air making his bones ache with each step. He dropped the deer hide over the opening of his dwelling and added more sticks to his fire. With a sigh, he fell into the only chair in his small home. He had waited too many moons to pass on to his son the responsibility his family had been charged with, over eight hundred years ago. Now it might be too late.

Lone Wolf would be here in less than a week's time, but would Spirit Warrior live that long? The chest pains grew worse with each day. His only solace was Lone Wolf would know what to do with the small box on the table. His greatest fear was his neighbors would find him before Lone Wolf arrived, and as custom dictated, burn everything in his hogan.

With shaking fingers, he pressed one square on the intricate wooden box and it opened. He pushed the sand aside, lifted the clay bottle to ensure it wasn't cracked and the seal was still intact. *Ah, Nukpana, evil one, you are still securely bound for all eternity. May the gods protect your guardians, so that you remain cut off from Mother Earth's people forever.*

1

Assured that the package was secure, he carefully placed the vial back into the bed of sand, covered it, and closed the lid. The box in his hand, he stood, shuffled to his cot, and lay down. With his charge clutched to his chest, he pulled a blanket over his thin frame and closed his eyes.

Come, my son, I need you. A clawing pain racked his body. He cried out, the sound dying in a rasping gurgle. *May the ancient people forgive me if I have failed at my duty.*

Chapter One

Madison ran through the darkness, her legs churning as she flew across the packed earth, searching for anything familiar. The shrieks of her pursuers filled her with terror, making her press on. Her side hurt. She gasped for air. Her lungs burned. How much longer could she stay erect, running on the uneven canyon floor?

Worn beyond her physical capabilities, her legs collapsed, arms windmilling to slow her descent to the ground. As she hit the red clay and rolled, they were on her, poking, jabbing with spears. She screamed, and covered her head while drawing her knees to her chest.

A loud shout echoed over her tormentors' whoops of victory. They stepped back, allowing a large man through. Long black hair, twisted into a bun at the back of his neck, held colorful parrot feathers.

As he stood there, feet spread looking down at her, she saw a crudely made club tucked in the waistband of his loincloth. His bare chest, broad and well-muscled, bore numerous scars. One traveled across his abdomen and up to his ear.

He reached for her. She scurried back like a crab. The watchers laughed as they stepped in to stop her movement. Face grim, he shouted an order she didn't understand. When she didn't respond, he growled, and with one swoop of a large arm, grabbed her by the hair, jerking her to her feet.

She screamed in pain and terror.

He shook her like a rag doll. She closed her mouth, tried to swallow her sobs. It must have been

3

*what he wanted, because he grunted. Hand still
fisted in her hair, he thrust her forward, back to the
pueblo from where she'd just fled.*

*Their dwelling resembled the Big House at Mesa
Verde, except here, rather than hidden underneath a
rock cliff, the building backed up against rocky
mesas surrounded by level land.*

*Legs trembling, she struggled to stay on her feet.
This had to be a nightmare. She had no memory of
leaving her apartment. Please, God, let me wake up
now. Panic choked her, stealing what little air she
managed to inhale. Shaking, desperate, she struggled
to break free. Her captor stopped, and struck her on
the side of her head with his fist. She sank into
blessed darkness.*

*Madison woke to the smell of food. A naked child
squatted beside her, patting her face. She lay on the
ground, her hands and feet tied. Her arms ached
from being bound behind her back. Her head hurt,
her mouth was dry. When the little girl moved, light
from the sun pierced her brain. She cried out from
the pain.*

*Jabbering softly, the child ran to an Indian
woman stirring something over the fire, and pointed
toward her. Madison could only gape. Why, the
woman's buttocks were bare. Something like an
apron, made out of what looked like human hair,
gave her some modesty in the front, but the effect was
spoiled by her naked breasts. She snapped her mouth
shut and tried to look nonchalant as the woman
turned toward a curtained doorway and called out.*

*Her heart lurched and raced. She was crazy, had
lost her mind. Tears choked her as she lay in the dirt
sobbing.*

*The warrior from last night pushed the cloth
aside and appeared in the doorway. His angular face
was rigid, jaw clenched. As he drew near, he pulled a
wicked-looking knife from his waistband and bent*

4

toward her. She arched away in fear, but instead of stabbing her, he cut the binding on her feet. Amber eyes never leaving hers, he cut the bonds on her hands. She groaned in agony as needles pricked her limbs from lack of circulation.

Gasping for breath, she rolled her shoulders and worked to bring her hands around to her lap. She watched the man cautiously as she said, "Thank you."

He said something in his language, then lifted her from the ground by her upper arms. She screamed in pain, but at his growl of anger, she tried to soften her whimpers. People, all dressed in loincloths or aprons, gathered around to stare at her, chatting quietly as they pointed.

A shriek rent the air. Everyone froze. The group parted to allow an old woman to approach. Even the warrior backed away. If he was frightening, the hag was terrifying. A crone, a witch from Halloween, a zombie...she limped toward Madison, shaking rattles with one hand, chanting, as she brandished a stick.

She stopped directly in front of her, reached out, and touched her hair, eyes wide in wonder. Her breath smelled like something dead. Madison heaved, yet managed to quiet her offended stomach.

Cackling, the old crone laughed like a loon, showing off a mouth of rotten teeth, as she pointed from Madison's red hair to the fire. A murmur went up from the crowd. Small, pendulous breasts hung from her skinny body, black hair streaked with gray stood out on end in places, falling to her waist in the back. It was filled with knots and things Madison shuddered to think about.

The ancient woman turned back toward Madison and started jabbering and dancing. Then Madison saw the large blue stone hanging around the witch's neck. It was a beautiful piece of turquoise, not like anything she'd ever seen before. On impulse, she reached to touch the locket lying against her breast.

The old woman saw the gesture and, mumbling, shuffled back to stand in front of her. A wrinkled, dirty hand reached toward Madison's neck. She shrank away, trying to avoid her touch. But, it was too late. Chanting, moving from foot to foot, the crone yanked her shirt aside and saw the locket. In a fury, she jerked the locket from around her neck. Madison yelled, "No! It's mine..."

Gasping for breath, crying, Madison kicked and fought until her legs were free. She sat up to find her tangled sheets half off her bed. Moonlight cast the room in shadow. Furniture resembled phantoms of the night. She shivered as her gaze flicked around the room in fear, not knowing where she was. She'd been dreaming—again. The minute the thought registered in her brain, she snapped awake and recognized her bedroom in her small apartment in Houston, Texas. Sweat covered her body. Filled with relief, she fell back against the pillows.

The necklace! Hand shaking, she reached for the nightstand. When her fingers touched metal, she sighed in relief. The alarm clock read 2:00 a.m. She got out of bed and padded barefoot to the bathroom. The light blinded her for a minute, but her eyes adjusted as she turned on the faucet to splash water on her face.

Back beneath the covers, she couldn't sleep. Thoughts of the vision, the ancient civilization of people, haunted her. The face of the handsome warrior filled her mind, intruding on her thoughts at odd times. His amber eyes glowed like those of a wild animal.

Since the day her mother died, and she'd inherited the necklace, she'd had nightmares. Each successive one became sharper, more real, and took her deeper into the other world. The first time

Madison put the heirloom on, she felt connected, as if her soul had been looking for the necklace her entire life.

It had been six months now. Neither she nor her sister had known about the necklace, or the papers and pictures documenting the jewelry's history, or the lives of their ancestors. The records dated back to 1880. Their mother's lawyer explained as much as he knew when he read the will.

The dreams grew worse—they started the same, but went further and were more frightening. She shuddered to think what would happen if she had to live the nightmare out fully.

It was time she went to Mesa Verde. Maybe if she could determine where the turquoise originated, the hallucinations would stop. It was summer break. She'd just finished her PhD and deserved time off to go where she chose.

Madison got up and started packing. By 8:00 a.m., her car was loaded, including violin and family papers. Just before locking her apartment door, she remembered she needed to let someone at the Houston Symphony know she'd be unavailable to substitute. No one answered the phone, so she left a message.

At the curb, indecision clawed at her mind. Was she doing the right thing? Did it matter? She shook her head and laughed. Heck no! If the trip was a waste of time, at least she'd have a vacation. She got in her car and set out for Albuquerque. At the edge of town, she called her sister to let her know where she'd be.

Rosalie's voice vibrated against her ear. She'd never been known for having a soft voice. "Have you lost your ever lovin' mind, girl? You've never done anything unpredictable in your life."

Maybe it was about time she did.

****

7

For the thousandth time since Rita Santiago had found the box in 1975, she picked it up to study it from every angle. It had been in a pile of rubble of what appeared to be a burned out hogan. Though still blackened in places, she'd done her best to remove the stains. Where the true color of the wood shone through, it glowed with a patina obtained only by the touch of loving human hands.

She'd yet to find a way to open the thing. At times, she'd been tempted to crack it open with a hammer, to discover what was inside. Something always held her back—she didn't know what, couldn't describe it, but it was a force that made the hair on the back of her neck stand on end.

Perhaps that hesitancy had to do with the odd occurrences of the day she'd found the container—a little more than thirty years ago. That afternoon, she'd been a young woman, carefree, and beautiful. Her black hair glowed with health, her body strong from the hikes she and Luis, her young son, took in the hills near the small town where they lived, north of Albuquerque.

That day, she'd wrapped the box in a cloth and placed it in her apron pocket. As she and her son walked back to the car, she felt the thumps as it bounced against her leg, reminding her of its presence. The wind picked up and a dust devil whirled around, choking her with sand. She'd shivered at the strangeness of nature—dust devils developed when warm air on the earth's surface rose to meet the cooler air above. Instead of being warm, this air was icy cold.

Shaking off the memory, and the unease it produced, she set the wooden container back on the corner of the desk, hung her purse strap over her shoulder, and keys in her hand, picked up a large stack of magazines she planned to take to a nearby nursing home. Her grip slipped, and her keys fell onto the clay tile floor. Drat! It was 9:30, past time to leave for the museum. That's what she got for trying to do too much at one time. Her purse dangled to the front of her body. To be able to bend forward, she swung it back behind her hip. It hit the box, sending it crashing to the floor. Sand flew everywhere.

"Ah-ya-ya, what next?" She placed the magazines and purse back on the desk and went to her knees to examine, at long last, what the undersized crate contained. A small clay pot, a little smaller than her fist, lay broken amid the sand. Dark dirt, no, maybe it was ashes, flowed from the bottle. A nasty, rotten odor rose, clogging her nostrils and throat. Gasping, choking, she jerked back as she struggled to fill her lungs with clean air. Her head hit the hard tile floor. Everything went black.

****

"Criminey," Madison gasped. The stone was magnificent, just like the one worn around the crone's neck in her dreams. Madison's nose almost touched the glass as she peered at the robin's egg blue piece of turquoise in the exhibit case. About the size of her fist, a piece of knotted rawhide cradled it to wear around the neck. It sat on a piece of rustic copper sheeting with bright colored parrot feathers for accent, just like those the warrior wore in her dream. The hairs on the back of her neck stood up. She shivered.

Thrusting her nightmare to the back of her mind, she returned her attention to the wall behind the display. A mural of hills and canyons set against a New Mexico sky called to her, further tweaking her interest in the gemstone's heritage. The showing was titled "Skystone."

Her heart lodged in her throat as she clutched the locket she wore around her neck and rubbed the smooth stone embedded in the gold's surface. Her piece of turquoise was the same color as the one shown behind the glass.

Could this be where it came from? She snorted. *Don't be ridiculous, Madison.*

Upon closer inspection, she noticed the hairline crack down the center of the large stone. Where the break ended was a gap about three-eighths of an inch wide, and an inch-and-a-half tall, that diminished to a point. She was unable to tell the width or depth of the fissure from her vantage point. The space resembled a tiny pie wedge, the edges rough rather than neatly sliced.

She jumped as the man behind her loudly cleared his throat. She glanced over his shoulder to see she held up the line. Reluctantly, she moved on.

Before leaving the museum, she stopped in the gift shop and bought a book titled *The Legend of the Skystone* and several tourist maps. Tomorrow, she would drive up the Turquoise Trail to visit some of the old turquoise mines.

As she signed her credit card receipt, her locket fell forward. The clerk, an older woman, gasped. "Oh my, your necklace is lovely, dear. May I take a closer look?"

Madison held the gold and turquoise piece out so the gray-haired lady could study it more closely. Her blue eyes, trimmed by the red frames of her glasses, were sharp, inquisitive. In her mid-fifties, she was attractive, and though slightly wrinkled, bore her age well. In her youth, she must have been a beauty.

"The locket has been in my family for over a century. We've treasured it all these years."

"I can see why. The color is most unusual—rare in its purity."

Madison peered down at the locket. She thought it was unusual, as well as beautiful, but to have others think so reinforced her mind-set. "Do you really think so?"

"Oh, yes, I know so."

When she glanced up, the woman's hand grasped the necklace and pulled. Madison stumbled back, breaking her hold. "Ouch!" The heavy chain cut into the tender skin of her neck. She rubbed the area.

The clerk's face reddened. "I'm so sorry, dear, I didn't mean to tug, but my curiosity to see it more closely outweighed my good sense. I hope you'll forgive me."

Her explanation seemed reasonable to Madison. She'd often been over-zealous about an old book, or other item of interest, and found herself in an embarrassing situation. "Of course. No offense taken."

To ease the tension, she said, "This summer, I intend to discover where the turquoise came from."

Face still flushed, the lady straightened. "Is that so? Have you checked with a gemologist? A good one might be able to help you." She opened a drawer, and removed a card to hand to Madison. "This man is excellent. If he can't help, he'll know who can."

"Why, thank you. I'd intended to visit one, but your recommendation will save me time."

"Happy to help, young woman. Good luck."

****

Madison stepped out into the bright afternoon heat, grateful for New Mexico's lack of humidity. At home, the moisture would have tendrils curling around her face. Keeping the unruly red strands of hair tied at the base of her neck was a chore. A gust of wind lifted a loose wisp, brushing it across her mouth, but as she turned, the tendril moved back to join the riotous lot.

The gemologist's shop was in the next block, so she stuffed her purchases in her large shoulderbag. It wasn't the Dooney & Burke she'd wanted, but she couldn't justify spending that much on a purse. So, she'd opted for a cheaper look-alike. She set off down the street, the heels of her strappy sandals clicking on the sidewalk.

She wore a new outfit, a set she'd bought after her mother's funeral. The top was soft and clingy tangerine silk. It blended well with the lined, sheer, swingy print skirt. She liked the way it moved when she walked, making her feel feminine, a characteristic foreign to her.

For years, while in college, she'd dressed in jeans and tennis shoes—grubbies. Now that she'd graduated, her wardrobe had improved somewhat. She wasn't used to the clothes and new look. As she walked, she caught herself stealing glimpses of herself in the plate glass shop windows and thinking, *Who is that person?*

Downtown was filled with a variety of beautiful outdoor sculptures. In places, trees lined the sidewalk. Benches provided rest for the weary shopper or art lovers. Jewelry, pottery, and other artwork filled the shop windows. Madison wanted to visit each one, but forced herself to keep walking.

Unable to resist, she stopped in front of a window filled with jewelry, mostly in silver, with stones of turquoise, amethyst, amber, topaz, the list went on. Stepping back, she squinted up at the sign—Rico Santiago, certified licensed gemologist. A bell tinkled above the door as she went inside. Glass cases in a U-shape pattern filled the room, with another row running down the middle. Jewelry and gemstones gleamed under the spotlights.

As she made her way to the back of the store, Madison scanned the displays. She'd never owned expensive jewelry. Her only nice pieces were the locket and her great-grandmother Evans' amber earrings. She'd worn them today because they matched the tangerine blouse she'd worn with her floral skirt.

A young man approached. Dressed in a dark, expensive suit, white shirt, and gray tie, he smiled graciously, most likely hoping to make a sale "Hello, may I show you something?"

Madison straightened her shoulders and took a deep breath. "Yes, I'd like to see Mr. Santiago."

He frowned. "May I tell him what your visit is in reference to?"

"Yes, I'd like for him to analyze a piece of turquoise for me." She pulled the locket from the neck of her blouse and dangled it in front of him.

He gaped. "Yes, yes, of course. Come right this way."

She followed him to a back room, where an older version of the young man sat with a monocle over his eye, studying a white stone.

"Father, this young lady..." He turned back to her. "I'm sorry, I didn't get your name."

"Madison Evans."

"A pleasure to meet you. My name is Luis Santiago."

He turned his attention back to the man behind the desk. "Miss Evans would like your opinion on a piece of turquoise." He wrung his hands while the man continued with what he was doing. He cleared his throat. "It looks to be a very old piece, Father."

Smiling, she nodded. "Yes, it is, over a hundred years."

Finally, the old man raised his head.

"Miss Evans, this is my father, Rico Santiago."

She extended her hand. "Pleased to meet you, Mr. Santiago."

He ignored her gesture. "Sit down, young woman and show me what you've got. I don't have all day." He waved at his son. "Get back out front in case any customers come in." Face pinched at being dismissed so rudely, Luis turned and left the room.

Madison was embarrassed for the younger man.

"Well, I'm waiting."

Madison removed the locket and held the piece in front of him. "This is a family heirloom. I'm trying to find the source of this turquoise."

Now she had his full attention. He took it and peered at the stone closely through the lens. Several minutes later, his eyes pierced hers. "Where'd your family get the turquoise?"

"My ancestor, Royce Dyson, inherited the stone from his father. Though he wasn't the oldest son, he was chosen to be responsible for its safekeeping. They lived in Waco, Texas. From what I understand, the stone had been in their family for many generations."

"And how do you know this?"

"From his wife's journal, written in 1880. He had the locket with the stone made for her in 1873. It's been passed down to the oldest daughter in the family ever since." *Odd how, after being made into a piece of jewelry, it had passed on to the women of the family.* Where did that thought come from? Had she read something that unconsciously put the idea in her mind?

He rubbed it with his thumb as he glanced between her and the locket. "Hmmm. I'd say this piece most likely came from the Chaco Canyon area."

"Not one of the mines along the Turquoise Trail?"

"Well, actually, yes, it probably did come from one of the mines in the Cerrillos Hills north of Albuquerque, but the turquoise is too old and fine to be from the nineteenth century." He put the monocle back to his eye and studied it again. "My guess is that the stone was part of the earlier turquoise mined by the Chacoan Anasazi, probably around 1000 AD."

Realizing her mouth hung open, she shut it. She was stunned. "You think it might be that old?"

"It's possible. I'll need to run some tests to be sure." He opened a drawer, pulled out a plastic zip lock zipper bag, and dropped the locket inside.

Alarmed, she asked. "What are you doing?"

"I need to do some research and analysis before I can say definitely where this came from. I'll be through in a week or two." He zipped the bag closed, then began writing on the label with a felt tip pen.

"No," she said. "I can't leave the locket." An emotion she couldn't define told her not to let the locket out of her sight. It was probably ridiculous, but she couldn't ignore the sensation.

He frowned, his white eyebrows drawing closer together. "I promise I'll take good care of your family heirloom."

She held her hand out, waiting. "I'm sorry, I didn't realize you'd need to keep the necklace. I'm leaving Albuquerque tomorrow. I'm sure you understand." He put it in her palm. She opened her purse. "How much do I owe you?"

"Well, nothing, but won't you reconsider? I'd like to get some accurate data for you."

"Thank you, but no." She turned and exited the room, passing a middle-aged woman at the watch counter as she did so. She could feel Luis's eyes on her as she walked through the showroom, his customer apparently forgotten. When she crossed the street, she glanced back. Both men were at the door, looking at her. *Strange, very strange.*

****

Up at the crack of dawn, Madison dressed in another of her new multicolor skirts and a turquoise blouse. Today, she wore comfortable beige pumps instead of the high heel sandals she'd worn yesterday. She ate breakfast in the Denny's next door to the motel, and with a cup of coffee to go, got in her tan Saturn heading north.

The sedan was comfortable. Knowing her

penchant for spilling drinks, she'd spent the extra money to get leather upholstery. She wanted a sports car, but her practical nature wouldn't allow her to be frivolous.

By two o'clock, she'd visited the mine ruins along the Turquoise Trail, and seen Sandia Crest. She stopped in the quaint artsy town of Madrid—if the line of buildings could be called a town—to eat a late lunch. In one of the shops, she purchased a gold and turquoise bangle bracelet. The wristlet would go well with her locket. Since money was tight, it would be her only souvenir on this trip.

Madison studied the bracelet on her arm. Mama would be pleased she'd bought something to match the locket, and that she was using part of her inheritance for this trip. Not for the first time, she wondered why her mother had kept the diary and pictures secret from her and Rosalie.

It was almost four o'clock when she reached the motel in the small town of Sotol, just outside the national park. With a little attached carport, the building resembled one of the old tourist courts common in the 1950s along Route 66. Not that she was alive back then, but she'd seen the documentaries on television. Inside, the decor was rustic, decorated with a southwest theme, and comfortable. She'd be staying several days, so she unpacked, putting her suitcases and violin case in the closet.

Since she'd had a late lunch, it was too early to go to dinner. Shoes kicked off, curled up in the stuffed chair by the window, she returned to the pamphlet she'd been reading the night before. She opened the booklet to the picture of the Skystone and the legend surrounding it. Supposedly, around 1000 AD, while worshiping at sunrise, the stone, a piece of the sky, fell and landed at a young Anasazi man's feet.

With the stone, he performed amazing acts. He healed a variety of illnesses, became a powerful Shaman, and was respected, legendary in the country. The turquoise passed on to his son, who misused the stone's power, angering the gods. To exact revenge, they threw a lightning bolt from the sky. It struck him in the chest, killing him, cracking the Skystone. Two shards fell from the bottom. An eagle took them in his mouth and carried them far away. The rumor was that if the pieces were ever reunited, the power of the stone, if in the hands of evil, could cause great destruction.

The story was intriguing, but in Madison's opinion, that's all it was—a fable. Not that she didn't like a good fairy tale on occasion. Since she was right here where the scenario supposedly all took place, her interest was definitely tweaked. But, then, she couldn't discount her dreams. The images were so vivid, they couldn't be a figment of her imagination. Plus, the stone around the woman's neck greatly resembled the Skystone.

She closed the booklet and placed it on the nightstand. At the window, she fixed her gaze on the rugged desert bathed in a colorful sunset, the San Juan Mountains appearing blue in the distance. She wasn't very hungry, but knew she'd regret not eating something and hit the candy machine outside the office later. Thin, her metabolism was the type that burned calories fast. Her friends were jealous of her ability to put the food away and not gain weight.

The night clerk recommended a restaurant a few miles down the road. She could smell the spicy cuisine before she got out of the car. When her plate arrived, the smell of green chicken enchiladas had her mouth watering, but where were her refried beans? These were whole, very similar to the pintos Mama cooked. She shrugged. It wouldn't hurt to try something new. Used to Tex-Mex food, her mouth was on fire before she realized New Mexico fare was hotter than what she was accustomed to. To cool the heat, she washed the food down with beer. She left the restaurant feeling fine, not *too fine* to drive, but definitely relaxed.

When she flipped on the light in her motel room, she gaped in horror at the room's condition. Her hanging clothes were ripped off the hangers, drawers turned upside down, her luggage opened, the lining slashed. Even the mattress had been thrown off the bed.

Shaking, she backed out and ran to the front office. Her heels caught on the gravel and she tripped. As she hit the ground, her knees skidded across the sharp pebbles. She tried to soften her fall with her hands, but scraped them more as she scrambled to her feet and ran to the front desk.

The clerk called the police. Within fifteen minutes, an SUV drove up. Madison watched as a park ranger climbed from the vehicle. She couldn't see his face under the Smoky the Bear hat, but as he approached the office, she noticed his long-limbed stride and how he moved effortlessly.

Once inside the lobby, he removed the hat and she got a good look at him. He was above average in height, with short black hair and a strong jaw. When he turned toward her, she recognized his face. The warrior from her dream.

Chapter Two

Lonan didn't know what to think of the young woman crouched in the cheap vinyl office chair. Her print skirt reached her knees, revealing a pair of long legs ending in low-heeled pumps, not the strappy high heel sandals women wore today. The hem of her skirt was torn and bloody where she'd been badly scraped. She'd been sitting stiff as a poker when he came through the glass doors, but when he smiled reassuringly, she turned pasty white. He didn't consider himself handsome, but he'd never received a reaction like hers. She acted afraid of him, ready to bolt any minute.

A Navajo Police truck pulled up, followed by several patrol cars. Joe Redhawk unfolded his large frame from the truck. *Thank goodness.* Maybe he'd better let Joe deal with this woman.

Joe clapped him on the shoulder. "Hey, had a chance to talk to the victim?"

He turned so the woman couldn't see his mug. "Not yet. Check with the clerk. For some reason, she's spooked. When she saw my face, I thought she'd faint."

Joe's brow furrowed as he regarded the injured party. He turned back to Lonan and mumbled, "I've been trying to tell you, you're ugly." Though his words were mocking, his expression was serious as he approached the desk.

The clerk was anxious to help. "Officer Redhawk, her room has been destroyed."

"Got a team in there already, son, looking for clues. Have you got a first aid kit?"

19

The young man nodded and rushed to a back room, to return with the needed supplies. Joe handed the kit to Lonan, then turned to the young woman. "Miss Evans. This is Park Ranger Lonan Stone. While we talk, he's going to tend to your knees."

She said, "Okay."

Lonan turned an eye on Joe as if he were nuts, but his buddy ignored him. Lonan pulled a chair up in front of her. She watched him through lowered lashes as he opened the kit.

"Miss Evans, my name is Joe Redhawk. I'm an officer with the Navajo Police. Lonan being with the National Park Service, he and I often share jurisdiction."

She nodded and tried to smile. "Just call me Madison."

"Okay." Joe sat down beside her. "Why don't you tell me exactly what happened?"

"Happened? All I know..." She jumped. "Ouch, that stings."

Lonan didn't look up. He was being as careful as possible. Getting gravel and dirt out of a wound tended to hurt. "Sorry, it can't be helped. Try to concentrate on Joe's questions."

"I left to go to dinner." She glanced toward the clerk. "He suggested I try the restaurant down the road, and save the diner for breakfast in the morning."

Lonan had to agree with the kid. They fixed a good breakfast next door, but that was about all. "When I got back, my room had been ransacked."

"Anything missing?" Joe had his pen poised above his pad.

She bit her lower lip to still its trembling and shook her head. "I didn't take time to look, I...turned, ran." She shrugged. "It just doesn't make any sense. I don't have anything of value with me."

Lonan applied large, square bandages to her knees. "Let me see those hands." She extended them, palm up. The soft skin was scraped, but didn't appear to be as bad as her knees. "I'll just clean these and apply antiseptic. Don't think you'll need bandages."

She held unmoving as he worked. "Thank you."

"You're welcome." It appeared she'd decided to relax around him.

While Joe stood at the counter, talking with the clerk, Lonan asked, "When I first arrived, you gaped at me as if you'd seen a ghost. Do I remind you of someone you fear?"

She shrugged. "I don't know why I acted that way. I apologize."

"No need for that. We're here to help you, so feel free to tell us if you're trying to get away from someone." Lonan wasn't sure he believed her story. She'd definitely reacted to his appearance. Mistaken identity, he guessed.

Her blue eyes rounded, she shook her head.

Joe returned with a key. "You'll stay in another room until we get yours processed. In the morning, we'll need you to check to see if anything is missing."

Lonan took her arm, grateful she didn't flinch, to help her stand. She wobbled for a minute, and then steadied herself.

"Will you be all right by yourself? We can get someone to stay with you if you want."

"No, no, I'm fine. Had a fright, that's all."

She didn't look fine. Her already pale complexion appeared bleached of color.

"We'll get you something to sleep in, and your toothbrush."

"Wait, I'll get her something." The clerk escaped to the back room. He emerged with a *Welcome to Chaco Canyon* T-shirt and a travel set with toothbrush and paste. "It's the least we can do. Sorry

21

for the damage to your things, Miss Evans. We have insurance if you need to make a claim."

Madison took the items. "Thank you."

In her room, Joe's people were sweeping for clues and dusting for prints. They entered the room right next door. As soon as they were inside, Madison dropped to the bed.

"Before we leave, we have a few additional questions," said Lonan. He hated bothering her more, as she appeared on the brink of collapse, but they needed information. He sat in one of the chairs around a small table. Joe took the other. He motioned to him. "Joe, you go ahead."

"Why are you in New Mexico, Miss Evans?"

She sat on the side of the bed, shoulders slumped, head down. At his question, she looked up. "I'm here on vacation, the first one I've had in six years."

Most people he knew would've had at least one vacation in that period of time. By the looks of her clothes and her car, she wasn't destitute. Of course, appearances could be deceiving.

Lonan asked, "What's your occupation?"

She squinted at him in inquiry. He rephrased the question. "What do you do for a living?"

"Nothing right now."

Uh, oh. She's on the run for some reason—ex-husband, boyfriend...

"Actually, I've been in school all these years, working odd jobs to get by and pay my bills." She sat up straighter. "I just earned my PhD. As soon as I return home, I'll look for a permanent position."

Hmmm, impressive, and her reason made sense. He'd not had any vacation time while in college, either. "In what did you get your degree?" Lonan asked.

"Shakespearean literature, with a minor in music."

He waited for her to say she was kidding, but she didn't. "What does one do with a degree like that?"

Her face reddened. "They teach at a university, do research, and write essays, books, any number of things." With her hand over her mouth, she moaned and bolted for the door. "My violin! What if it's destroyed?"

Joe caught her before she reached the door. "Hold on, I'll go check on it."

She nodded and wrung her hands. "I'm also a substitute violinist for the Houston Symphony. A colleague is filling in for me while I'm gone.

Lonan was impressed. She must be very talented to play for such a large orchestra.

Joe returned a minute later. "Miss, it's not damaged, but is being dusted for prints. You'll get it back in the morning."

With a sigh, she sagged to sit on the bed. "Okay. Thank you."

Joe cleared his throat. "Now, just a few more questions."

Madison returned her attention to Joe. Lonan watched her body language as she answered his questions—home town, family, any enemies, etc. At the mention of home and family, she smiled. Eyes wide, she shook her head when he asked about enemies. "Do you have any other reason for being in New Mexico other than a trip?" Joe asked.

She appeared stunned at his question. *Oh boy, here it comes,* thought Lonan.

"Why do you ask? Do I look like a suspicious character or like someone breaking the law?"

"No, Ma'am," said Joe. "We're trying to decide if you are a random target or this is someone you knew."

"Look, I've said I don't have anything of value, nor do I have any enemies. It has to be random."

Lonan watched as Joe studied her, his thoughts hidden behind his stoical façade. "Anything is possible. They may have seen your new car and figured you'd be carrying something they could hock." His gaze never leaving Madison, Joe used his pen to push his hat back on his head. "How can you can afford a car like yours on a student's salary?"

Her face sobered. "My Saturn is not that expensive, but my mother passed away and left me some money. That's how I can afford this vacation, the car."

Okay, Lonan would buy that, but he wanted to know one more thing. "What made you decide to come to New Mexico, to Chaco Canyon in particular?"

Her eyes brightened. "I thought I told you. I'm doing some research on turquoise, in particular a piece of jewelry passed down by an ancestor from the 1880s."

Joe sat up straighter in his chair. Lonan thought, *Now we're getting somewhere.*

"Oh, no..." Mouth covered with her hand, her eyebrows shot up, her baby blues rounded.

She jumped up, searched through her saddlebag, and came out with her car keys. "Thank God, I didn't leave my family papers in the room. If they were destroyed, I'd be devastated."

Lonan took the keys. "Here, let me get them for you. Where—"

"In the trunk."

He returned with a wooden box and set it on the small table. From inside, she removed a journal, ran her hand over the surface, and sighed. "This is the most valuable thing I own. It's my heritage."

She pulled a pendant from the neck of her blouse. "The papers and this locket. They've been passed down to the oldest female of each generation."

24

"May we see the necklace?" Lonan asked.

She lifted it over her head and passed it to him.

"Is turquoise all you're researching?"

She nodded.

The stone was a beautiful piece, carefully embedded in the gold of the locket for protection. An excellent color, most likely old, it was almost triangular in shape, but with curved bottom edges, probably from one-fourth to one-eighth of an inch thick.

He handed it to Joe, who whistled. "Very nice." Eyeing Madison, he asked, "Can you prove the provenance on this piece? A lot of old pieces of turquoise have been stolen in the last twenty years."

Her flared nostrils and pinched mouth convinced Lonan she told the truth. "Of course." She knocked on the book held to her chest. "Everything is recorded right here in this diary." Turning to a page, she twisted the book around, pointing to a passage describing the locket and the stone. The date was 1880. "Before it was made into a locket, the stone was passed down for many generations, but how the turquoise came into the family is a mystery."

Joe shot him a look before asking, "Can we take your journal in to study, try to determine if there's a link to this break-in?"

The expression on her face brooked no argument. "No, this stays with me."

Joe held up his hands. "Okay, okay, we understand. But, may we come here or meet you at the coffee shop to read it?"

"I suppose so."

Something wasn't right, but Lonan couldn't figure just what was bugging him. "Has someone in your family tried to take this from you?"

She cocked her head. "Odd that you should ask. My sister wanted the necklace, but she calmed down when she learned she got Mama's pearls."

"Would she have tried to steal from you?" Lonan knew some families had very little loyalty to each other.

She chuckled. "Goodness, no." Madison's smile dissolved into a scowl. She thought for a second. "But, you know, a gemologist in Albuquerque wanted to keep the locket to study for a few weeks. I wouldn't leave it with him. He and his son made me uncomfortable."

****

She lunged, trying to get the necklace from the old woman, but as she attacked, kicking and screaming, the warrior grabbed her by the waist and lifted her off her feet. The hag cackled at her success. The man's arm tightened around her middle, and she stopped kicking. He said something to the old crone. She shouted in outrage, but followed as he dragged Madison along with him.

They stopped in front of a ladder, and her captor motioned for her to climb. Fearing what he'd do if she didn't, she complied. He and the old woman followed. Grasping her arm, he pushed her to an opening in the roof.

This was getting worse by the minute. She looked at the warrior, and when he nodded, her heart dropped. He held her arm to steady her balance on the ladder. When she reached the bottom, a woman in richly decorated clothes sat on a mat, watching. For some reason, when the man reached the floor and stepped to her side, she felt safer.

The only light in the room was from a window and the hole in the roof. Trembling, Madison stood there as the woman, most likely an elder, studied her. Oddly enough, the hag kept her mouth shut. The woman must have been powerful and respected. She could have been a priestess or shaman. Rising to her feet, she spoke to the man glued to Madison's side, and he responded. Madison had about decided he must be the head warrior when he shoved her forward.

She stumbled, barely righting herself. The woman walked around her slowly, then stopped in front of her. She didn't stink like the hag. Actually, the room smelled of spices of some kind. Her hair, though gray, was neatly braided. The hand that reached up to touch Madison's curls was clean. Rubbing a strand between her fingers, she said something to her captor. His reply was clipped, but he nodded in respect, took Madison's arm, and urged her toward the steps. She didn't have to be told twice to move.

Once on the roof, she noticed the ladder they'd climbed up on was now on the ground below. The Indian took her arm and directed her to another part of the pueblo, to another hole, where they climbed down again. Here she saw rawhide shields, a bow and arrows, and animal skins. A mat lay against the wall, covered by a woven blanket of some kind.

He laid a hand on her shoulder and motioned toward the pallet. She shook her head. No way was she getting on his bed. This time he growled and raised his fist. Not sure if he'd use it or not, she decided not to try his patience, and sat. He considered her for a moment, filling her with confusion. His amber eyes glowed with kindness as well as something else. Was the emotion attraction? Her heart lurched at the thought. He nodded in approval. Before she could move, he was up the ladder, taking with him the only way out of her prison.

Madison jerked awake, sitting straight up, gasping for air, a silent scream on her lips. She shoved her wild hair out of her face and dropped her head to her raised knees. These dreams were driving her crazy. And the warrior with the yellow eyes, just like those of Lonan Stone, stirred her soul. He bore such a resemblance to the ranger, but for the difference in height, they could be twins. She was five-foot-eight, but Lonan towered over her. The warrior didn't have to look down at her.

She slipped her hand under her pillow, her fingers closed around cool stone and metal. The necklace was where she'd placed it last night before going to sleep.

Surprisingly, she'd slept well, until the dream.

At eight a.m., housekeeping knocked on the door and brought in her clothes. A quick search told her nothing was missing.

Showered and dressed in jeans, T-shirt, and sandals, she locked the box of papers, with the exception of the journal, in the trunk of the Saturn, and walked next door to the coffee shop.

Lonan Stone waved to her as she entered. She joined him at a booth. She couldn't deny he looked good in his parks' uniform, sans the ugly hat. His spicy aftershave reached her nostrils, taking precedence over the smell of bacon frying.

As she slid across the seat, his serious expression lightened as he smiled. It did wonders for softening the ruggedness of his face. And wow, there were those amber eyes. How could he look so much like the man in her dream?

"Good morning. Looks like you rested last night. Was afraid you might lay awake, worrying."

"No, it's not in my nature. If I can't do anything about the situation, why worry?" That wasn't true about all things, but Madison didn't think the culprit would try again so soon, if at all. The offender was probably some teenager hopped up on drugs, or wanting beer money.

He studied her face. "Good." He nodded. "Joe's got men in Albuquerque getting fingerprints of Rico and Luis Santiago."

"Did you find any other than mine and

28

housekeeping's?"

"We found a couple, which makes us believe it was an amateur, a kid looking for money. Most pros wear gloves."

The waitress appeared at her side. Madison ordered toast and coffee. Her stomach didn't feel too steady. "Aren't you eating?"

"Did already. I've been here a while. Now, what did Rico Santiago tell you about your turquoise?"

She swallowed a sip of joe. "He said the piece was most likely mined from the Cerrillos Mines, during the time of the Anasazi." Her heart thumped again at the possibility of the stone being an antiquity. "I never dreamed it might be that old."

A plate appeared in front of her, butter not completely melted on the toasted bread. The waitress poured them both more coffee.

"Can I look over the journal while you eat?"

"Sure." She passed it over. He wiped the table with his napkin before setting it down.

She watched him as he read, his expression changing from humor to skepticism, and then to incredulity. Eyebrow raised, he shot her a questioning glance.

Ah, ha, he'd gotten to the section about time travel. "I know, the possibility is hard to believe, but it makes more sense after you read the entire journal."

He shook his head and went back to reading.

The waitress returned to take her plate and refill their coffee. Finally, Lonan closed the book and handed it to her. "Do you have family pictures in that box of yours?"

"Yes, I do. Would you like to see them?" Sharing them was a pleasure. "I've already put them in the car, but we can take them back inside."

He stood and picked up the check.

"I can pay for my own."

"No need." He tossed a twenty dollar bill on the table, took her arm, and propelled her to the front of the restaurant. He was definitely a take-charge man—just like the warrior in her dream. She was tempted to jerk free of his hand and walk at her own pace. They bypassed his SUV and the motel office as they walked toward the carport, where her Saturn was parked.

He took her keys, removed the wooden chest from her trunk and carried it inside. He set the box on the rough-hewn dresser that matched the other furniture in the room, removed the pictures, and spread them out on the table. When he ran out of room there, he moved the rest to the bed. She watched as he studied each one, more closely if the subject wore the locket. Occasionally, he would hold a picture, look across at her, and then back down at the photograph.

"It's amazing how the women in your family resemble each other. Were they all redheads?"

She shook her head. "No, not really. Texanna's tresses were strawberry blonde. Her daughter Rosie, my great-grandmother, was a brunette like her daddy. My grandmother Dorthea had auburn hair. Mama and Daddy were both dark-headed, so we can't figure where my red locks came from."

He sat in one of the chairs and held the portrait of Texanna and Royce, the one where they held the locket.

She leaned across the table to see better and said, "Texanna was a beautiful woman, as fair as the man was dark. If I'm not mistaken, Royce had Indian blood somewhere in his gene pool."

He nodded. "You favor her a lot."

I wish! She shrugged. "I don't see it myself, and have asked myself why I couldn't have her hair instead of this wild mane." Her entire life, she'd hated the unruly mop.

His expression sobered. "There's nothing wrong with being a redhead."

"That's easy for you to say. You're not wearing it on your head."

He glanced back at the picture and laughed, the sound shaking his large frame. "That really is a tennis shoe under her skirt."

She glanced over his shoulder at Texanna's mischievous smile. "Yes, I don't think anyone can deny that shoe is a twenty-first-century item.

He shook his head. "You really believe she traveled back and forth in time?"

Chapter Three

Madison shrugged. "I don't know what to believe. Our parents didn't share the journal and pictures with my sister and me. We knew nothing about them until Mama's death." Realizing she hadn't given an answer, she added, "If I accepted as true the data in these artifacts, the answer would be yes. But the part of me that's analytical says time travel isn't doable."

From Lonan's expression, Madison couldn't tell what he was thinking. He didn't laugh, which was encouraging. "What about you? Do you think it's possible?"

"May I see the locket again?"

She removed the necklace from around her neck and handed it over. Eyes closed, his thumb stroked the stone as if receiving an extrasensory message.

His face serious, he fixed her with his amber eyes. "Native Americans have many superstitions about turquoise. Some warriors attached it to the ends of their bows to make sure their aim was true. It was also used by medicine men to aid in healing."

A shiver ran up her spine and once again, she marveled at his resemblance to the warrior in her dreams. "Do you believe they're true?"

He grinned. "I'm part Zuni and Laguna, so my grandmothers would disown me if I thought otherwise." He clasped her hand and held it between them, palm up, and dropped the locket into it. The warmth of his touch caused her nerve endings to tingle. His skin looked so brown against her paleness. Her gaze jerked to his face to find him watching her. She pulled from his grasp. He finally spoke. "Yes, I believe the stone has some mystical powers, but to believe it could facilitate time travel..." He shook his head. "I'd have to see proof to believe."

"Other factors have to be present, you know." She'd read and reread the journal, and knew that for a fact.

"Yes, I've studied and am familiar with ley lines, their intersection, and power. The ancient pueblos in Chaco Canyon were built with solar, lunar, and cardinal orientations in mind. These are all factors attributed to ley lines, energy and spin torsion fields. If these attributes contribute to time travel, the canyon is the ideal spot."

His face free of expression, she couldn't tell if he were serious or not.

"So, you're saying it could happen?" Her heart thumped in excitement. "My ancestors always said the turquoise was the trigger that made time travel possible."

He stood. "I'm not saying anything, other than stating beliefs. What are your plans for the day?"

"I intend to visit the Cultural Center and possibly tour several of the houses."

"Take plenty of water and a hat." His gaze moved across her bare arms and neck. She felt heat rise in her face. "Wear lots of sunscreen. You'll burn to a crisp within an hour."

He turned and walked to the door, then stopped to glance back. "I really think the break-in was a random act, but until we know for sure, be careful."

"I will."

****

Madison neatly stacked the photos and album and returned them to the wooden chest someone had made for their safekeeping. She suspected the artisan had been Texanna's husband, Royce.

Roughly engraved on the lid were the initials TKD—Texanna Keith Dyson—and the year 1880. Below was a rough carving of a locket. The box had been sanded to a smooth finish and stained dark, as was the practice during the Victorian Era. Personally, she didn't particularly like the deep color, but this was an exception. Wear marks lightened the finish in places. It had been handled often by loving hands.

She locked the chest in the trunk of her car, and slid behind the wheel. The drive to Chaco Canyon would take close to forty-five minutes.

The park road was well-maintained, with panoramic views on both sides. In the distance, the walls of the canyon rose from the floor of the desert—and before her was Fajada Butte, the canyon's entrance. She felt small, like a dot on the landscape, approaching the massive natural wonder.

At the Visitor's Center, she pulled into a vacant slot, cut the engine, and got out. Excitement revved through her. The history of this area, which included the turquoise trade, called to her. Would the ruins the Anasazi left engraved in stone mirror those of her dreams?

After viewing the exhibits, Madison watched the movie describing early life in Chaco Canyon. Her head swam with historical facts, legends, and lore. She'd left Sotol without having lunch, and her toast was long gone. The only food she could find was in the gift shop, and it was junk—chips, candy, etc. She did find granola bars, bought a couple, and a bottle of water.

Remembering Lonan's words about a hat, she picked through a display, trying to find one that would fit. She tried several on and examined herself in the mirror. They were either too big, sat on her ears, or too small for her thick hair. She'd have to do without today. It was late, almost seven, so the sun would be down before long.

A ranger announced the last walking tour to Una Vida, ruins of a Chacoan public building just a short walk from the center. She quickly finished her snack, disposed of the trash, and joined the group.

The park ranger led them through several of the pueblo rooms, describing their construction. "Of all the great houses, Una Vida shows the longest span of building, as indicated by the tree-ring dates on the timbers." The lady definitely knew her business and held her audience captive. "The Navajos call Una Vida the 'witchcraft woman's house.' According to legend, a local witch took human captives and held them atop Fajada Butte without food or water."

The hair on the back of Madison's neck stood on end. *The Witch Woman?* Could she possibly be the old hag from her dream? She took a deep breath to dispel the jitters in her stomach. Her nightmare was exactly that—a figment of her subconscious mind. But, usually she dreamed the same thing over and over. Never had one continued like a television series.

She tried to shake the sense of unease and focused her attention on the large mesa that stood at the entrance of the canyon. It was tall enough to keep someone captive, but how did they get people to the top, especially if they didn't want to go? Of course, being a witch, she probably just conjured a spell that zapped them up there.

Their escort continued to talk, and Madison started the climb toward the cliff behind the house. The face contained rock art depicting geometric forms and animal shapes. She hadn't gone far along the trail when the ranger shouted, "Hey, lady. Come down. It's too late in the day to go up there. The sun will be setting soon." All eyes from below were on her. She felt conspicuous.

Madison squinted at the cliff, then back to the group and waved. "I won't be long. I'll be back before sunset." The distance wasn't extreme. She had plenty of time.

The path was smooth from regular wear, but it took her thirty minutes to reach the top. Sunlight was quickly fading. She should have listened to the ranger and stayed below. Just able to make out the petroglyphs on the rock face, she ran her hand over them in wonder. Pictures of four-legged animals and what appeared to be a total solar eclipse.

She turned and peered below on Una Vida and imagined she'd stepped back over a thousand years. But for the cars in the lot and the modern building, the canyon appeared as primitive as it must have during the time of the Anasazi.

The ranger said the last construction on the house had been around A.D. 1093. Without thinking, she touched the locket and rubbed the stone with her thumb, an action that was quickly becoming a habit since she'd started wearing the necklace. With the fingers of her other hand, she traced the drawing of the solar eclipse. She'd always appreciated history. It had been tough to choose between it and literature. Being able to observe something so old and sacred caused her heart to swell with awe.

A shout from below startled her. As she whipped around, a bright flash of light hit her in the face, a jolt of energy knocked her to the ground. She screamed and waited for her flesh to hit sharp rock and her body to skid down the path. But, she never hit earth, just kept falling.

****

Lonan got the call that a member of the Una Vida tour had disappeared and crews were meeting there to search. He pulled his truck to a screeching halt next to Chief Johnson's vehicle, got out, and walked toward him where he stood talking to a young ranger. He'd met her before, last name of Hardy, Diane Hardy.

Cars and trucks were filling the parking lot, men and women piling out dressed and ready with lights, a few with dogs, to search. He joined the chief and Hardy. "What've we got, Chief?"

"Twenty-something female, red hair, wearing jeans, T-shirt, and thank God, a jacket." He nodded toward the parking lot. "That's her car over there."

Heart sinking, Lonan turned to look, knowing he'd see Madison's tan Saturn. "Shit!"

"You know who she is?" Johnson barked.

"Yeah, it's Madison Evans. She's the lady whose room was ransacked out at the motel." He turned to Diane. "What was she doing separated from the group?"

Diane bristled. "I turned around and she was halfway up the trail to the cliff face. The sun was beginning to set, so I told her to come down." She shook her head. "The fool woman waved and said she'd be along before dark."

"And you let her go?" Lonan roared. Dammit, his anger wasn't with Diane. Madison should have stayed with the group. He'd specifically told her to be careful today.

"Well, what was I supposed to do, go haul her down physically? She had a few minutes, and I thought she'd be right along. Thirty or so minutes later, she was standing at the first set of petroglyphs. I turned and yelled for her to come on. She waved and said, 'I'm coming.'" Next thing I know is she's falling. Diane's face was pinched with worry. She hunched her shoulders and bit back a sob. "Me and one of the members took off at a run. When we got to the spot where she'd fallen, she was gone." She covered her face. "Oh God, she'd just disappeared."

Lonan put his arm around her shoulders and squeezed. "It's not your fault, I'm sorry I yelled. Don't worry, we'll find her." He cast a glance at

Johnson. "Why don't you go home and rest? You've done all you can for now, and we've got plenty of volunteers."

"That's a good idea." The chief patted Hardy on the back, awkwardly. "We'll let you know as soon as we find her."

They both watched her walk toward her Jeep, struggling to keep herself together. Johnson turned to him. "What do you think? Weirdest story I've ever heard."

Lonan knew it was odd, but feared the chief would send him home if he voiced his honest opinion. He wasn't sure he even believed it himself. Time travel. He felt stupid just considering the possibility. But what else could have happened? "I don't know what to think, but I'm ready to start looking."

Johnson whistled, and the volunteers gathered around. "We'll do this by the book. Go in pairs, check in every 30 minutes. Take flares, blankets, first aid kits, and water for when you find her."

He broke the group into two teams and assigned Lonan to head one. It was nine-thirty p.m. when they started toward their assigned search area. At ten, Lonan found Madison's purse and handed it to Lisa, one of the EMTs and his search partner. Madison's footprints were all around the cliff face with the petroglyphs. That she'd been here was obvious, but there were no tracks leading away. They covered each piece of ground, inch by inch, for any sign of what had happened or which direction she might have taken.

By midnight, the teams had covered a five-mile radius around the large rock formation, at least a mile across itself. They called the search off until morning. Lonan sent Lisa home with the others, but decided to spend the night. He'd brought a bedroll, energy bars, and plenty of water, so he'd be fine.

He found a niche in the rocks to block the wind

and unfolded his sleeping bag. With the blanket rolled up for a pillow, he settled in for the wait. What must Madison be going through? If she'd traveled back, he prayed she'd be treated kindly and given shelter. Hell, he hoped she wouldn't be murdered or die from exposure. It could grow cold in the desert at night, even during the summer.

****

Madison was still screaming when she hit the ground, but it ended on impact, to be replaced by a wheezing sound. As she struggled to get air into her lungs, her body continued to roll until stopped by a prickly bush. She lay still and gazed up at the sky, now dark and filled with stars. *Oh, drat.* She was going to be in trouble. That ranger had good reason to be angry.

Groaning, she pushed herself up on an elbow and peered down the path to see if the ranger was coming to help her. Though moonlight lit the trail, she saw no one. She wasn't really hurt, maybe a bit scratched and bruised, but a little concern would be nice.

Below, the area was full of activity. Several fires were lit and people worked around them. The smell of something cooking filled the air. Smoke rose from some of the apartments. Wait a minute, the park service wouldn't allow fires inside the ruins. She shook her head...no, no way...she'd hit her head...this couldn't be happening. She blinked to focus better. The parking lot and visitor's center were gone, replaced with barren red dirt. A scream rose in her throat as she stared at the well-maintained house and its occupants. She choked the sound down to a groan before it left her mouth. She dropped her upper body back to the ground and closed her eyes. *This is a dream. You'll wake up in a minute and someone will be bending over you, chewing your ear off about not following the rules.* Fumbling with her jacket, she removed her small binoculars from the pocket and, lying on her back, worked to adjust them.

Madison jerked to a sitting position as a shrill shriek pierced the air. Her hands shook as she tried to focus on the scene below. She expected to see someone being murdered, but instead, an old woman began to chant and yell around one of the fires. Her graying hair hung to her waist in matted disarray. As she continued to harangue, mothers grabbed their children and ushered them inside while the men formed into groups, talking but keeping their eyes on the old woman. Madison gaped at the Skystone hanging from around her neck.

"Oh my God, it's the crazy witch woman from the legend." Madison slapped her hand over her mouth to stifle her squeaks of terror. She curled into a ball and prayed the shrub hid her from sight. At the sound of feet on the path above her, she rolled to a crouch, prepared to run. Three children stood frozen, looking down at her. Her screech elicited yelps from them. They scattered and ran the remainder of the way down the hill.

The witch woman watched their descent, as they yelled at the top of their lungs. Her head turned from side to side as she scanned the path, looking for whatever had scared the children. Then she cackled and went back to her chant.

Please God, don't let the children tell anyone I'm here.

It seemed like the woman ranted for hours. Finally, she tired and stood still, shoulders drooped. For good measure, she shook her stick at the men and yelled one last time. Then she turned and walked into the darkness. Within minutes of her departure, the women came out with their children and the outdoor area buzzed with their socializing.

Madison crawled back up toward the face of the

bluff, as far away as she could get. On hands and knees, she searched the crevices for a place to hide. An indention in the rock face was big enough for her to scoot inside and be hidden from view. She shivered at the thought of scorpions and snakes, but right now they were preferable to the witch woman.

The moon rose high in the night sky, allowing her to see a little. The temperature had dropped considerably, felt like forty degrees, and she was cold. But the rock had stored the sun's heat, so she squeezed closer. She was hungry, thirsty, and scared. She wanted to get back to the twenty-first century. She'd even welcome a chewing out by Lonan, or from anyone, for that matter. Tears rolled down her cheeks as she clutched her jacket close to her body.

Her eyes drooped and she blinked in an effort to stay awake. Surely it wouldn't hurt if she slept for just a minute. Just for a minute…

The sound of scurrying and giggles jerked her awake. Backed into a corner, she was defenseless in her hole. Muscles tense, she waited for the attack, but one didn't come. Slowly, she relaxed and smelled something good. Food. Her stomach rumbled in appreciation. Had the children taken pity on her and brought her something to eat?

She inched toward the opening in the rock and could just make out a bowl. It felt like pottery and was warm to the touch. Looking left and right, she searched the shadows for a threat. This could be a trick to get her to come out.

Then she heard the voices of children, softly talking between themselves about half-way down the trail. They said something in their language; she didn't have a clue what it was. But, they'd been kind to her.

"Thank you." She spoke softly, but they heard. With excited giggles, they ran back down the path to their home.

Madison didn't expect the children would try to poison her, so she took the bowl and lifted a chunk of food with her fingers. It was tough, but tasty and warm. She wasn't about to complain. Within minutes, she'd eaten it all and noticed another bowl a short distance away. She scooted further out to reach it. She dipped a finger into the liquid and raised it to her lips. It was water.

Her thirst and hunger quenched, she moved back into her hole and fell asleep.

The rising sun woke her. She looked out at Chaco Canyon, her situation reassurance she hadn't had a bad dream. She was back in the time of the Anasazi. Grasping the locket, she sobbed at her dire situation. How could she get back to her time? What had she been doing yesterday when she was zapped to the past? The catalyst had to be the petroglyphs and the locket.

If she went outside, she'd be seen. The children had been kind, but if the adults saw her, how would they react? She had to take a chance.

She crawled out of her hiding space and dropped to her belly to observe the activity below through her binoculars. Awesome, absolutely incredible. She was seeing life as it had once been, history in the making right before her eyes. The people seemed healthy, happy, and well-fed, so she must have arrived before the beginning of the drought.

The children who'd fed her sat at the base of the path. She peeked up over a rock and waved. They signaled back and chattered among themselves. Suddenly, the witch woman rushed up behind the children, shrieked, and pointed at her. Her little friends cried out as they were shaken and slapped.

Madison wanted to go down and protect them, but knew she had to make a run for her life. Surely their parents would intervene, but just in case, she stood and yelled, "Get your hands off them, you old bat." At the sound of her voice, the witch stumbled back a step and the kids broke free. Within the next second, she began chanting and pointing.

Madison started running, trying to reach the petroglyphs, but tripped and fell. Warriors sprinted up the path toward her, led by...*oh, my, God*...her warrior, the one from her dreams.

Their eyes locked and she froze. *He's real.* He raised his arms, shouted an order, and the others held their ground, but he continued up the path. *Oh, God, please help me.* She struggled to get to her feet, but fear held her immobilized. Too tired to fight or run, she leaned against the mountain of rock, and waited for him.

He stopped before her, reached down and lifted her to her feet. Tears rolled down her cheeks, but she held her sobs inside. He released her, and bringing both hands to her head, his thumbs wiped the tears from under her eyes. His touch sent a jolt through her. He must have felt the shock too, because he smiled.

For a minute, she thought he would kiss her, but instead he dropped his arms and took a step back. He uttered one word, she didn't have a clue what was said, but he gestured toward the cliff drawings. He was letting her go. Unable to speak, she nodded, then turned and ran. When she reached them, she grasped the locket, fell against the rock, and cried, "Lonan."

Chapter Four

Lonan woke before sunrise and stood alert, waiting as the sun peeked over the horizon. The already red sandstone looked on fire when hit by the rising sun. Below, at the Visitor's Center, crews arrived to continue the search.

Wind whistled through the canyon stirring the dirt, tossing dust about. This morning the breeze talked, sending chills up his spine. "Lo...nan." He'd heard voices in the wind as a boy. His grandfather explained many lost souls, those who had angered the gods, cried out for a resting place. He whipped around, listening, straining to hear. Today's cry unnerved him like no other before.

"He...lp!" There it was again. He turned in all three directions, searching. He heard her soft crying before he found her. She lay huddled in a ball a few yards from the rock art.

Relief washed through him as he knelt beside her and grasped her shoulders. *Thank you, God.*

She screamed and fought, trying to get away.

"Shhhh, Madison. It's me, Lonan. You're safe now." His words finally broke through her panic and she stopped struggling.

"Lonan?" She threw her arms around his neck, her grasp choking him. "Oh God, please tell me last night was a nightmare."

He leaned against the cliff face and hauled her across his lap. His fingers twined in the wild red hair and tried to push it back from her face, but got tangled. Dirty and bedraggled, she didn't show any injuries. He held her close, grateful she was unharmed. "What happened?"

She stiffened and pushed back to gape at him. Tears streaked her dirty face, and mascara smudges made her look like a raccoon. "What happened? I was zapped back in time and had to hide all night."

Could it be? Maybe she needed a while to collect herself before talking about her experience. She might be irrational after hours of darkness out here alone. "Don't think about it right now."

With a handful of his jacket twisted in her hands, she sputtered. "You've got to be kidding! I may never get the memory out of my mind." She shuddered. "The legend of the witch woman is true. I'm lucky to not be stuck on top of Fajada Butte, being toasted in the sun without food or water."

If the entire situation wasn't so serious, he'd have laughed at her comment. But, facts were facts. She'd been nowhere near this cliff last night or they'd have found her.

He awkwardly patted her back as she burrowed against his chest. "Put last night out of your mind for now. You can tell me all about it later." A sigh escaped her lips and she nestled closer.

Her shaking eased and he loosened his hold. "Here comes Chief Johnson and half the search crew. We've been scouring the canyon looking for you. They'll be full of questions."

She pulled back and glanced down the path. Her eyes rounded. "What are we going to tell them? They'll think I'm nuts."

"You let me do the talking. I'll come up with something."

Lonan moved Madison off his lap, stood, and helped her to her feet. Chief Johnson was running up the path, face growing red from the exertion. Not a good idea at his age and weight. Lisa jogged along behind him, carrying her emergency kit.

"Slow down, you guys. She's fine, just has a few

scrapes and bruises." He looked down at Madison.
"You are, aren't you?"

She nodded. "Being scared senseless pretty
much sums up my list of complaints."

"Okay then, let's walk down to meet them before
Tom has a heart attack trying to get up here." He
took her arm, and with his pack strapped to his
back, they started the descent. Under his breath, he
muttered, "Remember, I'm doing the talking."

"Fine. I hope you've got a good imagination."

About halfway down, the Chief stood, chest
heaving like a bellows. "Thank...God...you found
her."

****

Lonan insisted he drive her back to the motel.
While she showered and dressed in clean clothes, he
walked over to the coffee shop. When she emerged
from the bathroom, he had coffee and cinnamon rolls
spread out on the table. The caffeine hit her system
and gave her the jolt she needed. "Hmmm, this is
good."

As soon as they were finished, he ordered,
"Okay, start at the beginning."

He didn't interrupt, just sat, one booted foot
propped on the opposite knee, and watched her.
Occasionally he'd raise his coffee cup to his lips, then
realize it was empty. When she finished, his face
was expressionless and he didn't say a word. "You
don't believe me, do you?"

Elbows on the table, he dropped his head to his
hands and raked his fingers through his short, dark
hair. He looked up. "Yes, I do. I'm just having a hard
time accepting the fact."

She released the breath she'd been unaware she
was holding. It came out as a sigh of relief. "Yeah,
me too. The entire situation seems like a dream."

"I wish I'd been the one. I'd give anything to
observe the Anasazi culture." His expression of

disappointment reaffirmed his comment.

She felt sort of sad for him. After all, the canyon was part of his heritage. "How about next time I let you go in my place?"

"You've got a deal." He smiled and extended his hand for her to shake. It engulfed hers, and it felt so right enveloped in his. He turned hers over and ran his thumb across her palm. A streak of longing shot through her. She pulled away and prayed she didn't blush.

He cleared his throat. "Tell me, how could you tell the old woman was wearing the Skystone from so far away?"

"I can't say for certain, but I looked through the small binoculars I'd put in my pocket. The fire highlighted the stone, making it glow. The turquoise was big and a beautiful blue."

"I don't suppose you could tell if the stone was damaged or not."

"No, I really didn't think to look. But, if the legend is true, and a young man was the first owner, my visit must have occurred after his death."

He was staring at her. His amber eyes glowed, probing. Should she tell him about her dreams? Since she'd seen the Indian in the flesh, her nightmares were even more frightening, but she felt so foolish. She probably needed to talk to a psychiatrist. They'd have a good explanation for the nightmares.

"I do know the time must have been before the drought, or not far into it, because they were well fed and happy." She couldn't restrain her grin. "The children were full of energy. I'm sure they thought helping me a great adventure."

"Ah, kids and their quests are universal and timeless." His face turned serious. "And that's all that happened? You haven't forgotten to tell me anything?"

"No, what makes you ask that?"

"I don't know, just a feeling that you're holding something back."

Was he a mind reader? Had he sensed her worry? She struggled to keep from squirming in her seat. "No, that's all."

He pushed back his chair and stood with his hat in his hands. "I'll leave you to rest then."

She stood and walked with him to the door. Once outside, he turned and studied her. With bated breath, she waited for him to voice what was on his mind.

"What is it?"

"Do you have plans for this afternoon?"

Was he going to ask her out? Nah, just keeping tabs on her. "I'd like to attend the fireside talk tonight."

He nodded. "Don't go up to the cliff, stay around the visitor center area. If you want to do more sightseeing, I'd rather you didn't go alone."

"Okay. By the way, what did you tell Chief Johnson?"

"The truth. You'd hidden in a crevice of the rock face and didn't hear us calling."

"And he believed you?"

"Nope."

****

She spent the major part of the morning napping. The stress of her night on the cliff had left her exhausted. After a light lunch, she carried her papers and notes on Chaco Canyon into the motel office. The young man, who'd been on duty the evening her room had been ransacked, greeted her.

"Miss Evans. How are you? I heard about your adventure last night. The whole area was in an uproar, worried and looking for you."

She felt like a fool, but darn it, she hadn't planned on taking a trip back in time. "I'm so sorry

48

to have been so much trouble."

"Hey, don't worry, it's not like you got lost on purpose. By the way, was anything missing from your room the other night?"

"Nothing. The police recovered a couple fingerprints, but haven't been able to come up with a suspect yet."

"Odd, not much crime around here. Of that kind, anyway. On occasion, some idiot tries to deface park property. Even had a guy try to cut out some of the petroglyphs."

"You're kidding!"

"Nope, got caught red-handed."

She shook her head. The gall of some people was downright frightening. "Do you happen to have a computer I can use to get online?"

"Sure do. It's in the room next door here." He pointed to a doorway to his right.

"I'll probably need it a couple of hours. Will that be a problem?"

"Not at all. Take as long as you need."

Lost in her research of the Chacoan Anasazi, the time was almost four when Madison checked her watch. She'd printed out information from several sites and added them to her stack of papers to read more carefully later.

She went to her room and changed her sandals for tennis shoes. Her T-shirt was a deep blue, the perfect color for the funky dangle earrings and necklace Rosalie had given her. Made of three strands of silver and blue beads, she liked the way they danced as she moved. Though not at all her style, making her self-conscious wearing them, she wore them a time or two to please her sister. The pendant was made by threading beads on silver wire and shaping the long strand into a circle. The design was pleasing and she wore it often.

Madison left the motel and headed for the park

visitor's center. Hopefully, she'd arrive in time to get in on the tail end of the last tour through Una Vida. After seeing the house at its height of grandeur, she'd like to walk through again. She'd stay around after sunset to attend the campfire talk.

She pulled into an empty space at the Visitors' Center and got out, locking the car as she did so. Hooking her purse over her shoulder, she started for the trail.

By the time she reached the pueblo, the tourists had left for the area where the talk would take place. It was a stone circle a short distance away. Madison wanted just a few minutes alone among the ruins, to get the perspective of being a part of the people who once lived here.

As she stood in the middle of the ruins, the sun set, casting light on the reddish masonry, making the walls appear gold. Awestruck, she could almost hear the bustle of activity as children were called in for the night, and men and women went about their evening chores. Had she really spent the night on the ledge and seen and heard these things?

She shivered, then turned and walked toward the fire that had been built in the center of a stone ring. A group of older ladies chatted loudly, drawing attention. One of the women looked familiar, but Madison couldn't place from where. She found a spot far from the chatty group and got comfortable. As the sun dropped, so did the temperature. The jacket she'd brought along felt good on her arms.

Their speaker tonight wasn't a ranger, but an older Indian man of the Laguna people. His voice was deep, but soft. All chatter stopped to hear him.

"The Anasazi lived and thrived here during the time of the Dark Ages in Europe. Their 'apartment houses' were planned so that additions were sturdy and pleasing to the eye, the masonry work of excellent quality. Over four hundred miles of road traveled north to connect over seventy-five pueblos and farming villages."

He stood, raised his arms to the sky, and gestured to the north. "At the height of their prosperity, hundreds attended fairs and religious ceremonies held yearly at Pueblo Bonito. Farmers brought produce to exchange for turquoise, the most important commodity of the Chacoan Anasazi. The people were wealthy until turquoise was discovered elsewhere. Its value dropped. And then the fifty-year drought struck."

Madison sat mesmerized, as he explained the Anasazi struggle to survive. She stared into the flames of the fire, where images of parched land, failing crops, and hungry children danced before her eyes. "Contrary to popular belief, the Anasazi didn't just die out. Some authorities believe they left Chaco Canyon and moved to join other pueblo people and the Navajo for survival. Others believe they were destroyed by a rival troop, but the possibility has been raised, that their enemy was from within."

When the story ended, the audience clapped and started disbursing. Madison remained seated, basking in the serenity of the setting, the comfort of the campfire. As she stood to leave, the storyteller approached her.

"I see the history of our people touches your heart."

"Yes, it does." She extended her hand and he clasped it with his large, callused one. "My name is Madison Evans. I loved your presentation tonight."

Up close, his skin appeared like ancient tanned leather, lines of use and love creasing it for eternity. "You're the young woman who was lost last night."

She nodded.

"I'm Sam Spotted Elk. Sometime, I'd like to hear about your adventure. Come back in two days. My wife will be speaking, and perhaps she'll have information important to your quest."

"What do you mean?" What could his wife know about her search? Lonan and Joe Redhawk were the only two people here she'd told. "How—"

He raised his hand. "Have patience. Hurry now, the time grows late and the parking lot will empty quickly." With those words, he turned and walked back toward the Visitors' Center.

Madison watched him stride away, then headed up the trail. She wasn't the last to leave, as there were still several parked cars, and she chuckled as she watched the young couple across the lot usher their sleepy children into the back seat.

She unlocked the door of her Saturn and tossed her purse over into the passenger's seat. A sound like feet crunching on gravel caused her to turn. Before she could utter a sound, someone swung at her, hitting her on the right temple. She screamed in pain before all went black.

****

Madison woke to the sound of moans. She tried to locate the source when she realized they came from her. Her head throbbed as if her pumping heart had traded places with her brain. Park employees knelt on each side of her. One was Lisa, the EMT. She took her vital signs while the other peered into her eyes with a small flashlight. Twirling lights from an emergency vehicle threw colors across the faces of the bystanders and vehicles.

"What happened?" She tried to sit up. The world danced, she groaned, and lay still.

"Do you remember anything, Miss Evans?" Sam Spotted Elk squatted beside the EMT she didn't know.

She tried to think. "I heard a footstep behind me, and when I turned, something hit me." Gingerly, she reached up to feel her temple.

"Don't touch the wound. We've got you wrapped

and the bleeding stopped, but it's going to be mighty sore." Lisa patted her hand. "You're going to spend tonight in my cabin, so I can keep an eye on you."

"Oh no, that's not necessary. I want to go back to my motel room."

Sam spoke up. "You'll do like Lisa says or ride in the ambulance all the way to Farmington to the hospital."

Madison looked from Lisa to Sam, her vision blurred, and the motion made her queasy. She closed her eyes. "Do you really think this is necessary?"

Lisa nodded. "It's like Sam says, bunk with me or go to the hospital."

"What about my car?" She didn't want it sitting out here all night.

"Someone will drive your vehicle to my place. Don't worry, it'll be fine."

Two men approached with a gurney, and before she could complain too loudly, she was lifted onto a cot, and rolled toward the ambulance.

"I need to ask a few questions before you transport her, Lisa." Madison turned her head to see Chief Ranger Johnson approaching. "Young lady, it seems you can't stay out of trouble."

She tried to smile and groaned. "I'm sorry. I'm usually quiet and unobtrusive."

"Hmph, couldn't prove it by me. First your motel room, your, ah, night on the cliff face, and now this."

What could she say? It certainly wasn't planned.

"Can you tell me what your attacker looked like?"

"No, I just saw a shadow and, wham."

"We found your purse on the passenger seat of your car. Nothing seems to have been taken. Is there some reason why someone would want to attack you?"

"Not unless it has to do with my room at the motel being ransacked, but nothing was taken then,

53

either." None of this made any sense at all.

He nodded. "I'll check with Lonan and Joe to see if they've turned up anything. In the meantime, hopefully we'll find a fingerprint on your car, or someone in the parking lot witnessed the assault."

Her head ached. She wanted to sleep and wake up to find this to be a bad dream. Then she remembered her purse and tried to sit up only to fall back with her eyes squeezed tightly shut. "Can...I have my purse?"

"You can have your handbag tomorrow. We'll keep it and your keys until we finish dusting your car and satchel for prints." He turned and hollered for Lisa. "What's the verdict here? She going to the hospital?"

Lisa explained what they'd worked out. "I'll watch her close, Chief, wake her every few hours."

"Good, good." He fixed Madison with a stare. "You listen to Lisa. She knows her stuff."

"Okay." What else could she say? She certainly didn't want to go to the hospital. Before he could walk away, she grabbed his jacket sleeve. "Can I get something out of my purse?"

He scrutinized her for a minute, and then shrugged. "Don't see why not." He opened the large paper sack and gingerly lifted her bag out. "What is it, and where in this huge thing you call a purse?"

"It's my locket—inside the zipper pocket."

Carefully, he opened the bag, touching as little of the leather as possible, unzipped the pocket and lifted the locket out. He held the necklace up and whistled. "Lord have mercy! That's one fine piece of turquoise. Bet a dollar to a donut, that's what the thief was after."

Madison touched her neck, feeling for the necklace she'd worn tonight. The imitation piece was gone, and in its place a sore welt was forming along her flesh. "My other necklace is gone. They stole it!"

****

As if by an unseen force, Rita's body was thrown against the interior of the car. Her head bounced off the window, only to be forced forward to hit the steering wheel. The voice in her mind reverberated off the walls of her skull, making it pound. *You are a stupid, stupid woman. Can you not tell the piece of trash you hold is not what I seek? Next time you fail me, your punishment will be worse.*

Rita lurched from the car and just made it to the grass before falling to her knees and vomiting. When her stomach was empty, she stood and stumbled back to her vehicle. It was still running and the lights were on.

Behind the wheel, she let her head fall back and rested for a moment. What was wrong with her? She turned to look out the window. Where was she? Sobs ripped from her body as she struggled to remember what she'd done or where she'd been. Did she have a brain tumor? Maybe she was crazy, losing her mind. This was the second occasion she'd lost a block of time in her day.

Her hand on the seat touched cold metal. She lifted the piece and stared in shock and horror at the fake piece of turquoise set in sterling silver. *Oh, God, please help me.*

Chapter Five

Lonan had just handled a family disturbance at the campground when he got the call about the attack on a woman at Una Vida. Trepidation inched up his spine. He called in to dispatch and learned the victim's name. It was Madison.

"She's being taken to the hospital?"

Judy, their night dispatcher, was an avid gum chewer, and after several pops in his ear, she rattled off the facts. "The injured party has a head wound. Looks like someone hit her with a rock. She refused to go to the hospital, so Lisa's watching her tonight."

"Are they staying at Lisa's?"

"Yep. Chief's keeping the vic's car to dust for prints. They're interviewing witnesses, but it doesn't appear anyone saw the attack."

Madison had something of value that the perpetrator wanted, and Lonan felt in his gut it was the turquoise in her locket. It was obvious the story in Madison's journal was true—the locket was the key to time travel. How would someone else know this? Maybe they didn't, but wanted the stone for its monetary value, or because of its age and beauty.

He pulled up in front of Lisa's cabin and killed the motor. "Thanks, Judy."

"You bet, Lonan."

Lights were on in Lisa's cabin, and she answered on his first knock. "What are you doing here, Lonan?"

"I just had to see for myself that Madison is all right." Dependable in any situation, Lisa was sharp, cute, and well-liked. Her dark hair was cut short and curled around her face, making her look like a pixie. Right now, her dark eyes twinkled and her eyebrows rose an inch. He knew what that look meant, and intended to stop her speculation before she said a word.

"Now, don't start that. Joe Redhawk and I investigated the break-in at her motel room. I want to see her and ask her a few questions." Hell, he had to see for himself that she was doing okay. His stomach was twisted in a knot.

"She's asleep." Lisa didn't budge.

He wasn't going to take no for an answer. "I want to see her."

"Okay, already. Come on. I put her in my bed, as I won't be sleeping. Need to wake her often."

The side table lamp cast a glow across the bed. Madison looked so fragile, lying there with a wide bandage wrapped around her head.

"How bad is the wound?"

"She's going to have a big bruise and a headache for several days, but if she has a concussion, it's a mild one."

Lisa sat on the bed and spoke softly. "Madison, you've got company." When she didn't respond, Lisa shook her shoulder gently. "Wake up a minute. A good looking man's come calling." She turned back and winked at him. He returned the gesture with a scowl.

Madison stirred. "Hmmm? Whatcha want, Lisa? I'm fine." She batted her eyes at Lisa and tried to keep them open. "See."

Lonan couldn't restrain his chuckle.

"Yes, I see. Very good. Lonan is here to see you."

Madison turned toward him. "Lonan? Is that you?"

Lisa headed for the door. "Call if you need me."

Lonan took Lisa's spot on the bed. He lifted Madison's hand and stroked her soft skin. "What happened?"

"Somebody bopped me on the head, that's what. Hurts like the devil, too." A tear rolled down her cheek, and she batted the moisture away. "Why's somebody picking on me?"

Unable to resist, he stroked her cheek with his knuckles. She turned toward the caress and sighed. As she did so, the column of her neck was exposed. A red welt marred her lovely white skin.

Rage and the desire to protect this delicate woman washed over him. He tempered his anger and tried to speak calmly. "Where's your locket? Were you wearing it tonight?"

She thought for a minute. "No, I had it in my purse. It's laying over there on the chest."

He followed her gesture to the opposite wall. "Good, I'm glad it's safe." He stroked the red mark on her neck. "But something was ripped from your neck tonight."

Her hand moved to her chest, as if feeling for a piece of jewelry. "I wore a silver necklace with some kind of fake blue beads tonight."

"What on earth for?"

"It matched my earrings, of course."

He looked heavenward. Of course, as orderly as she was, she wouldn't go out unmatched. "Thank God you weren't wearing the locket, or it would be gone." No doubts now. Someone was after the turquoise in the locket. The culprit was dangerous, a rock today, maybe something worse later, if needed. He'd talk to the Chief, see if he could shadow Madison and maybe catch the thief. When he did, he'd be hard pressed to keep his hands off the perpetrator.

She was drifting off again. "Yeah...grateful."

"Go on back to sleep. I'll stop by tomorrow to see how you're doing." And, he intended to stick to her like glue.

"Bye, Lonan."

She breathed deeply, with her mouth quirked up into a smile. On impulse, he bent down and gently kissed her. Her full lips were soft and she responded to his touch even though asleep. His body responded. He jerked back in surprise. *Damn, the woman is asleep and you have no business touching her.* It didn't mean a thing. She was a hot woman and he'd done what any red-blooded man would do. Except for one little old thing—he was a cop and she a victim. The two were not to mix. He stood up, strode from the bedroom, and out of the house without saying 'bye to Lisa. He'd just given her one more thing to needle him about.

All the way to his truck, he cursed himself again. He had no business kissing the girl. Thank God she was asleep and didn't know what he'd done. What had he been thinking?

He hadn't, that was the problem. That morning on the cliff face, she'd felt so right pressed against his body, and it'd been a long time since he'd been so drawn to a woman. He usually went for riper women, ones with dark hair and eyes, but Madison was long and lean. With her wild red mane that resembled the russet cliffs of the Chacoan landscape, pale freckled skin, wide mouth, and intelligent blue eyes the color of the sky, he'd immediately been attracted. She was in a sense a mirror image of this land he loved so much.

It wasn't going to go any further. They had nothing in common. Madison would want the city life and all it had to offer. His job was here, on the sacred grounds of the Indian culture. No, Madison was not for him.

But, damn, she was hot and sexy. His body throbbed with a driving need to know and possess every inch of her.

God, he needed his head examined.

As soon as he arrived home, he called Chief Johnson and asked to be assigned to watch Madison full-time. She was a target and wasn't safe on her own.

"I agree, son. I'll call the district office in the morning and see if they can find someone to fill in for you until we find this culprit."

"Thanks, Chief. I'll report in periodically."

"You do that." He was quiet for a minute, and Lonan waited. "Do you think this is all about that piece of turquoise of hers, or something more?"

"It's the turquoise. No doubt about that."

"Hmmm. Well, seems to be, son, if she locked it up in a vault somewhere, our problem would be solved."

Lonan wished it was that easy. "Sir, I'm afraid there is more involved than meets the eye." He cleared his throat. "I'd like to keep on this and try to catch the perp."

The man on the other end was quiet. Lonan knew the Chief respected him enough to value his opinions.

Voice gruff, Chief Johnson said, "Let me know what you need and what all we can do to help."

****

Madison woke the next morning in pain. A little dizzy, she wove her way to the bathroom. When she emerged, Lisa waited at the door to help her back to bed. "Hey, you don't have to mother me, I'm doing fine." Her knees buckled, and Lisa grabbed her arm.

"Yeah, I can see you are." She tossed the covers back and propped several pillows near the headboard. "Get back in there, and I'll bring you some coffee, toast, and another pain pill."

As she left the room, Madison called out, "Don't you need to get some sleep and go to work?"

From the kitchen across the living area from the bedroom, she shouted, "My replacement will be here soon."

A few minutes later, she returned with a tray, two cups of coffee, and several slices of toast. She set it on a side table and handed her a pill and a glass of water.

"Do you really think I need this? I bet a good shot of caffeine will do just as well."

"Take the pill, you'll be glad you did in an hour or so. It's not as strong as what I gave you last night, so you'll be able to function."

"Okay, whatever you say, Doc." She took the pill and handed the glass back to Lisa in exchange for a cup of coffee.

"Do you need cream or sugar?"

Madison shook her head. "No, this is fine." She took a sip. "Ahhh, heavenly."

Lisa pulled up a chair, sat down with her coffee, and propped her feet on the bed. She had on some kind of fuzzy animal house shoes. "You remember Lonan being here last night?"

She froze. "No, I don't. Did I say something stupid while all drugged up?"

Lisa giggled. "Not that I know of, but when he left, he stormed out of here like a man on a mission."

She stroked her neck and vaguely recollected Lonan mentioning a welt on her neck. "Yeah, I do recall him commenting on this mark on my neck."

"I put some salve on it to speed the healing. Looks like the thief yanked a chain from around your neck."

"Yeah, and whoever it was had a shock coming when they saw it in full light. It was a silver necklace with fake blue beads formed into a circular medallion."

"Why on earth would they be disappointed? Were they expecting something else?" She took her cup. "Let me get you another cup of coffee. Munch on that toast while you're talking."

Madison raised her voice to be heard in the next room. "Because it's not the locket I usually wear. It's got a real old piece of turquoise embedded in the surface."

Lisa returned, their cups refilled. "Oh, man. Aren't you glad you didn't have it on last night?"

Mouth full, Madison nodded in agreement and swallowed. She motioned to the dresser. "Take a look. It's on your chest over there."

She finished her breakfast. Lisa strode over and picked up the locket. "Wow, it's beautiful. The turquoise is like no piece I've seen except in museums." She held the locket across her palm for closer inspection.

"I saw a gemologist in Albuquerque, and he believes the stone dates back to the Anasazi period." Madison was about to add more when someone knocked on the front door. Lisa handed the locket back and went to let them in.

She heard the rumble of Lonan's voice before she saw him. "How's our patient?"

"She's much better this morning. Want a cup of coffee?"

"Sure, if it's already made."

He filled the doorway to the bedroom, expression guarded and stern. Today he was dressed in jeans, a western shirt, and boots. On his head sat a straw cowboy hat. He wore the different duds as comfortably as he did his uniform.

Handsome as the devil, well, he really wasn't handsome, but her heart skipped a beat in response to his features—the strong jaw, prominent cheekbones, and perfectly shaped nose.

"What are you doing here this morning?"

He sat in the chair Lisa had vacated. "Didn't Lisa tell you? I'm her relief."

"You mean you're going to be poking pills down by throat and making me stay in bed?"

"That's about the size of it."

****

Lonan carried her to his pickup, gently set her on the seat, and buckled her seat belt. "You doing okay?" She'd insisted she could walk, but he didn't give her a choice. Before she could argue, he'd scooped her up in his arms.

"Yeah, fine." Lisa was right about the pill. She didn't feel as drugged, and she didn't hurt either.

In her motel room, Lonan waited for her to change into pajamas and get in bed before leaving. He programmed his cell phone number into hers. "Just call if you need anything."

All morning she'd been trying to decide if she should tell him about her dreams. Would he think she'd lost her mind? After all that had happened, she was beginning to think so.

He grabbed his hat off the table and started for the door.

"Lonan, wait."

He turned back and waited for her to speak.

She struggled to find the right words. "I've got...need to tell you something." The nightmares were so vivid, yet she felt foolish talking about them.

"What is it?" His brow furrowed, he moved back toward the bed and sat on the edge. He looked so strong and capable in his faded jeans and a blue shirt. His shoulders were wide, his arms muscled. She wanted to throw herself against his strong chest and feel his embrace as she had on the cliff. She tossed the thought to the back of her mind and took a breath.

"Ever since I got the locket and put it around my neck, I've been having dreams, scary ones."

She waited for him to laugh, but he didn't. Mouth pinched, he said, "Go on."

"I'm in Chaco Canyon, being chased by the Anasazi. I fall, and am taken captive. At first I

63

thought I was at Mesa Verde, but after my trip the other night, I know different." Head down, she fiddled with the bedcovers. "The witch woman is there, and she snatches the necklace from around my neck."

He took her hand and squeezed. The gesture bolstered her courage and she continued. "The head warrior takes me before a priestess, shaman, or," she shrugged, "a powerful individual. We have to climb up and down ladders to get inside. This woman takes a strand of my hair, rubs it between her fingers, and says something to the man. He nods, takes me to his apartment, and leaves me there without a way to get out."

She shivered, and he ran his hands up and down her arms. They were warm, and eased the chill. "Are the dreams always the same?"

"They begin alike, but each one goes a little further." Grasping his forearms, she choked out, "Lonan, the warrior looks just like you. Even his eyes are the same color."

Unable to stop herself, she flung herself against him. He held her and patted her back. She absorbed his warmth and tried to tamp down her fear.

"Do you believe me?"

"Yes." Moments later, he asked, "Is that everything?"

Easing back from his embrace, she studied his stern features—jaw clenched, brow furrowed, eyes piercing her soul. Voice shaky, she told him the last. "That morning on the cliff, as I ran to get back to the drawings, I tripped and fell. The warrior stopped the others from chasing me. He helped me up off the ground and motioned toward the petroglyphs." She'd never forget his expression—one of kindness. "The warrior saved my life. He let me go, as if he knew I wasn't supposed to be there."

Lonan left Madison asleep in her room. He sat

in his truck waiting for his replacement to arrive. Someone would watch Madison's room around the clock. Arms braced on the steering wheel, he leaned forward and rested his head. Tension knotted his shoulder and neck muscles, shooting pain up to his head.

Many years ago, his great-grandfather, Spotted Elk, amused him with many tales of their past history. One in particular was about an ancient prophecy. He'd been young, probably eight years old, and couldn't remember much, but little details tugged at his memory. Yes, time travel, he'd said something about people traveling through the spirit world to save a nation. At the time, he'd been mighty impressed by the tales. But, as he grew older, he'd believed the stories were just that—folklore to entertain children and teach them their native history.

Could Madison's dreams be related to some ancient prediction? God, he hoped not, but, just in case, he knew right where to find out.

Chapter Six

This morning, she'd get out of here or commit murder trying. Madison spent the past day in her motel room, only getting up to go to the bathroom or sit at the little table when Lonan brought her meals. Lisa arrived after dinner and took her vital signs. She pronounced her well enough to get up, but she wasn't to drive or do anything strenuous.

Her head still hurt, but not as bad as before. She took a couple of aspirin, showered, and dressed in fresh jeans and a white cotton shirt, tucked in. She added a pair of thick socks with her tennis shoes. The night on the ledge, her feet had grown cold, and she didn't want to tempt fate. On impulse, before walking out the door, she hooked Granny's amber earrings in her earlobes. Of course, the locket was inside the neckline of her blouse. She ate at the coffee shop and returned to her room to find Lonan standing out front, her car in the little carport.

"You brought my car!"

She reached for the keys, but he held them back. "I'm to be your chauffeur today. Remember, no driving."

She noticed a red pickup parked behind her Saturn and asked, "Is that yours?"

"Yes."

"I guess that means we're not taking my car." She should have known by the size of the truck's wheels that the vehicle was his.

"You'd be right. It's hard for me to get in and out of the thing, and impossible for me to wear a hat." She unlocked the door to her room, and he followed her inside. "How're you feeling?"

"My head hurts a little, but I took a couple aspirin and the pain is nearly gone. Let me get my purse and I'll be ready to go."

She could feel his gaze on her as she moved about the room. Her jeans were a little snug, not her usual baggy style, and she felt somewhat self-conscious. *Oh, get over it, Madison. He's not interested in what you look like.*

"Have you found my attacker?"

"Nope, but we know it's the same individual who ransacked your room. Whoever the culprit is, he isn't a hardened criminal, or at least he's not in the fingerprint bank yet."

She grabbed her purse, turned, and froze as his gaze raked her from head to toe. Heat crawled up her chest to her face.

"Don't forget your jacket, we may be out after dark. And if you have a sun-hat, bring it along."

And here she thought he was checking her out. Her face burned brighter at her mistake.

"I don't have anything. Can you imagine me with one on this hair of mine?"

"Yes, I can. We'll stop at the store and buy you one." He frowned. "You feeling all right? You're face is flushed."

Before she could answer, his palm was on her forehead while he held her head still with his other hand.

She tried to jerk away. "I am fine."

He released her. "No fever."

"I could've told you that." She didn't want a hat, but wearing one made sense. "Let me grab something to put my mane up with, then." All she could find was a large tortoise shell lobster clasp. She dropped it in her purse and met him at the door.

He took her arm and led her outside to the truck, not releasing her until she was settled in the passenger seat. Thank goodness, it had a running board and she could step up to reach the cab, or he'd have lifted her in like a baby.

"Well, be forewarned, my hair isn't the manageable type."

He chuckled as he buckled up. "Maybe you've been shopping in the wrong places." He started the motor and backed out of the parking lot. "Fasten your seat belt."

Bossy man. She did, and then twisted her hair up onto the back of her head. The clasp held it in place. Without the weight, the cool air felt good on her neck.

As they clipped down the highway, Madison studied the truck's interior. Neat as a pin, just like the man. Today he wore jeans with a blue and yellow plaid sport shirt. His dark hair, cut short, stood up a little on top like those spiky dos men were wearing these days. Clean-shaven, he smelled of a subtle aftershave and fresh air. Damn, he was one tempting male.

He glanced over and caught her studying him. She pretended to be interested in the scenery outside his window. "What kind of cactus are those with the white flowers?"

"Those are yucca plants."

Now she felt stupid. She knew what they were, they covered most of West Texas. Thankfully, they pulled up to a pioneer building sitting all alone on the side of the road. It had gas pumps though, so probably carried anything a camper would need.

She hopped out before Lonan could round the truck. He frowned and took her arm as they walked inside. With one purpose in mind, he led her to the back of the store, where a row of shelves held a variety of Stetsons. He picked one up, peered inside to see the size, and plopped the thing on her head. With the rawhide string tightened under her chin, the hat wasn't going anywhere.

"Does that hurt your wound?" He leaned in to inspect the smaller dressing Lisa had put on it, and ran his fingers from it down her cheek. She shivered. "Seems to miss your bandage okay." Their eyes met and held, the moment awkward. He cleared his throat and stepped back.

She stuttered, "N-no...feels fine."

"Perfect. Looks real good on you, too." He adjusted the angle, stood back to study her, and then nodded. "You should never go out in this heat without a hat, especially with your fair skin."

She peered in the mirror on the side wall and studied her reflection long and hard. Dang, he was right. It wasn't half bad on her. And she did sunburn easily.

Before she could agree, he was leading her up to the register. He wouldn't let her pay, just took out his pocketknife, cut off the tag, and handed it to the clerk.

"Put the amount on my tab, will you, Joe?"

The old man grinned. "I'll do that, Lonan. Mighty pretty girl you're dragging around by the arm."

Lonan stopped, looked down at her, and loosened his grip. "Uh, sorry, didn't mean to rush you. Do you need anything else?"

"No, but thank you." She turned and waved to Joe.

Before they were out the door, Joe hollered. "Hey, she the girl got stuck out on the mountain?"

Lonan ignored the question and kept going, the screen door slapping behind them.

"Hee, hee, hee, she is, she's the one. I knowed it."

Lonan disregarded the comment and continued walking. "Sorry, Madison. You're a celebrity around here. The gossip line is staying hot and folks are competing to figure out what really happened."

He opened the door for her to climb in. She looked back at Joe staring out the window. "It's not your fault. Guess if it hadn't happened to me, I'd be wondering too."

Back in the truck, instead of turning back toward the park, they continued on in the opposite direction. "Where are we going?"

"You met Sam Spotted Elk the other night at the campfire."

"Yes, he said the oddest thing, something like his wife had information that might help me in my search."

Lonan didn't respond. Finally he looked over at her. "Lilly Spotted Elk is a mystic with strong powers. She can talk to the spirits."

He watched her reactions as they drove through the reservation, her gaze jumping from one place to another, trying to see everything. She smiled and returned the waves of the children they passed. He pulled into Sam's yard and killed the engine.

She twirled the strap on her purse. "I have to admit, I'm a little afraid."

"What on earth for?" Sam and Lilly were harmless, loved everyone they met.

"I'm not sure." She shrugged. "She might give me information I don't want to hear."

"Lilly's magic is good, not the kind to hurt you." He hopped out and slammed the door. She had hers open when he rounded the truck. "Let me do that for you. You need to be careful getting down, and not jar your head. What if you stumbled and bumped it?"

She nodded and he helped her from the truck. With his hand on her back, they started toward the door.

"Relax."

The house was stucco, with a big porch across the front. The yard had one large tree, no grass, but beautiful flowering cactus and other natural desert grasses. It was well cared for and fit perfectly with the terrain.

Sam stood on the porch. "Welcome." He held the door open so Madison could enter. Lonan followed, shutting the door behind them. "How're you feeling, young woman?"

"Much better, thank you."

"Good." He turned to Lonan. "And, it's about time you visited your grandmother, young man."

Madison appeared surprised. "The Spotted Elks are your grandparents?"

"Didn't I tell you? Guess I just thought I had. They're my mother's folks."

Sam ushered them into the living area. "Come on in. Lilly can't wait to meet you."

Lonan watched Madison's eyes scan the area. The room held comfortable furniture, beautiful woven rugs, and Indian artifacts covered the mantle and every other available surface. Everything was useful and portrayed with pride the heritage of the inhabitants.

"Oh, this is a wonderful room." She walked to the mantle to inspect the objects.

His pleasure evident in his smile, Sam replied, "Thank you. We like it."

He motioned to the arched doorway. "Come on into the kitchen. Lilly has lunch ready."

Madison stopped and looked at him in panic. "We didn't mean to come right at meal time."

Lonan couldn't restrain a grin. "Yes, we did. I forgot to tell you we had a lunch invitation."

Lilly rushed toward them, looking lovely as always, thought Lonan. Slim and graceful, her smile radiated happiness. She cupped both his cheeks and pulled him down for a quick kiss on the forehead before releasing him. "Lonan, my boy, so glad you could come."

He wrapped her in his arms for a tight squeeze and kissed her cheek. "I'd be a fool to miss your home cooking." He released her, and with a gentle nudge, urged Madison forward. "Grandmother, this is the young woman you've been hearing so much about."

Lilly took Madison's hand and steered her toward the table. "I'm so glad you've come." She motioned to a chair. "Have a seat between me and Sam."

Everyone jumped to do as she asked. Lonan seated Madison, and then moved to the chair directly across from her.

Madison was stunned at the beauty of the Indian woman. She had to be at least sixty, but her skin was as smooth as a forty-year old's. Her hair was almost completely silver, streaked with threads of black, held back from her face with two turquoise combs.

Around the table, they chatted as they ate. Sam told Madison how Lonan had gone into the Army and then on to college. It was evident both grandparents were proud of Lonan's decision to become a park ranger and stay in the region.

When lunch was over, they moved into the living room. Lilly patted the cushion beside her. "Sit here by me. Now, tell me what happened on the cliff face."

She retold the tale as she remembered it. Lilly clapped her hands. "The children actually fed you?"

"Yes. They were well cared for, happy, full of laughter."

Lilly sighed deeply. "How I wish I could make the journey. But, it was not meant to be." She shook her head. "And, the old woman, do you really think she was crazy?"

She thought for a minute. "If she wasn't, she sure put on a good act. I was terrified of her. And the people seemed afraid also. The women took all the children inside while the men stood around and listened to her ranting."

"Did the stone she wore around her neck look intact? Could you see it that well?"

Fingering her locket, Madison shook her head. "No, even with binoculars, I couldn't see it clearly."

Lilly took a deep breath and turned her intelligent eyes on Lonan, and then her. "Lonan and Madison, it is time for you to learn the part you will play in history. You are special to the people. A prophecy decreed one thousand years ago told of your meeting, but no one knew exactly when. The gods chose you both for an extraordinary quest." Lonan stared at her as if she'd sprouted an extra head, and then looked to Sam. Sam nodded.

"You're not kidding?"

Lilly's smile was sad. "No, I am speaking the truth. The minute Madison drove onto Indian land, I felt her presence and knew the time had come for the prophecy to be fulfilled. You're both being called to halt the evil that would destroy all we hold dear."

"The time for what?" Madison quipped.

"May I see the Skystone?"

"You mean my turquoise locket?"

"Yes, dear, it is part of the Skystone, and you are the stone's guardian."

Madison removed it from around her neck and handed it to the older woman. She glanced at Lonan, but he sat immobile, face taut as if in shock. "How can you know that?"

Lilly smiled. "I know, child, trust me. For many years, legend foretold it would surface in the hands of a worthy maiden, one with hair that shoots flames."

She handled the locket with reverence. "Oh, the turquoise is lovely. Whoever mounted it must have recognized its value. They took care not to damage the stone." Eyes closed, she rubbed the turquoise with her thumb and chanted softly. "This stone has never been used for evil."

She opened her eyes and regarded Lonan. "However, if ever reunited with its twin and the mother stone, the three could be the ruination of all our people hold dear."

Lonan's mouth was pinched in a flat line, brow furrowed. "What do you mean, the ruination?"

"Being both Laguna and Zuni, you know how revered Chaco Canyon and its dwellings are to all the area Indian people. We have a great enemy, a thousand-year-old decaying soul, whose essence will not find rest until he extracts revenge and the Anasazi ruins are wiped from the face of the Earth."

Lonan turned to Sam, but the older man's expression was grim. "I've never known Lilly's predictions to be wrong, son. This evil one has infected the heart and soul of a substitute—the person who attacked Madison. The malevolent spirit will find the third piece, take Madison's stone, and find a way to take possession of the mother stone."

"Yes," said Lilly. "In the hands of evil, the power is wicked, but, if reunited by good, its influence will be benevolent and its power will be safe."

"But..." squeaked Madison. "At the museum, the legend said—"

"I know what the exhibit says, child, but very few know the entire prophesy. You see, the man whose spirit is evil wasn't given a proper burial and led to the after life. He probably did something to shame his people. His body was burned, the ashes stored and sealed so his essence couldn't escape. So, as punishment, he's been locked away without closure."

Madison felt as if she'd traveled to the Twilight Zone. Lilly's claims were preposterous, but, she couldn't deny what she'd seen on the cliff face or the dreams.

"Yes, you need to tell me about the dreams. They started at the time you received the necklace, right?"

Madison nodded. "How did you know?"

"I assumed the ancient Elders would haunt you, but when Lonan called yesterday, I knew so for a fact." Her smile was sympathetic. "Tell me about them."

Lilly's eyes lit with excitement as Madison talked. When she finished, the older woman leaned back and closed her eyes.

Lonan's brow was furrowed, his mouth pinched. "What did you mean when you said, 'You are the one'?"

She pierced him with an intent look. "Did not Madison say you were the very image of the warrior in her dream? The prophecy requires that someone from the past, which is you, son, be chosen to be Madison's protector." Lilly turned to Madison.

Oh, no. I don't think I want to hear this. She held up her hands and shook her head. "No—"

"Yes, Madison, with hair of fire, whether you like it or not, the gods chose *you,* someone from the future, to find the third stone and reunite the twins with the mother stone. Together, you two will find a way to consign the evil one to the pit below Mother Earth, where he belongs."

Chapter Seven

Lonan had been withdrawn since they'd left Spotted Elk's home—which was fine with her, as she kept replaying Lilly's prophesy, or whatever she wanted to call it, in her mind.

When she'd finished explaining the prediction, Lilly said, "Lonan, you must now take Madison to see Leotie. She will conclude your preparation."

Face sober, he'd merely nodded, and with body taut, bid his grandparents goodbye.

When in his truck, he was quiet as he backed out of the drive and drove down the street. Madison asked, "Who is Leotie?"

"She's my fraternal grandmother, the one who raised me." Glancing over at her, he asked, "Do you mind if we go there now while we're so close?"

"No, not at all. How far are we from the park, anyway?"

"About eighty miles. It'll be another forty if we keep going. Actually, it might be so late we'd need to spend the night there, so if that's a problem, say so now."

"That's what Lilly told us to do, right? I'm surprised you're giving me a choice."

"I won't force you. You'll either help or you won't. The decision is yours."

"If we're going, now's the time." Might as well hear what she had to say and get this all over with.

A smile transformed his face. "Thank you. She probably knows what Lilly told us, but we need to know what Grandmother Leotie has to say to add to the mix."

"Please don't tell me she's a shaman too." This was getting to be too much for her. Spiritualists knowing the future...

His grin made her breath catch in her throat. It wasn't that he was so good-looking, because he wasn't. Dark, thick lashes outlined his amber eyes and complimented prominent cheekbones and a strong, stubborn chin. He might not be handsome, but he was sexy as hell. Just a tilt upwards of his lips, and her heart thumped overtime.

"Yes, as a matter of fact, she is, though shaman is a very old term that's not used anymore."

Oh, Lord, this whole affair was becoming overwhelming. "Do you actually believe what Lilly said? That I'm to find the third piece? I mean, really, how am I supposed to go about doing something like that? It'll be like looking for a needle in a haystack."

He didn't hesitate. "Yes, I believe Lilly. I don't understand her power, nor can I explain it, but her talents are real and have been proven many times."

Her heart sped up and she gasped for air. "But, I'm just an average girl. I don't know anything about Native Americans, their culture, or their legends. I've never done anything more adventurous than toilet paper one of my professor's houses." She paused for breath.

"All my life I've been meek and mild-mannered Madison, working and studying hard to get through school." She trembled and wrung her hands. And here she was riding along toward another Indian pueblo to visit another shaman and prepare to go on a freakin' quest for which she was unequipped.

Lonan clasped her knotted hands. "Relax. I know how you're feeling. I'm dumbfounded myself, but we'll be guided through this, shown the path to take."

"You really believe in all this hocus-pocus?"

Jaw clenched, he released her hand. "Your

comment is insulting."

"Well, I'm sorry, but I'm scared out of my mind."

She tried to concentrate on the scenery. The atmosphere inside the truck turned icy, not with air but with attitude. Mostly hers, she guessed. Lonan's face remained stony as he watched the road, his grip on the steering wheel tense, the knuckles white.

Oh, hell. "I didn't mean to be rude. It's just so foreign to what I'm used to, how I grew up." She didn't want to say more. To her, faith in healing stones and magic was almost offensive, but she knew that could be due to her ignorance. "I just don't understand how we're going to do this."

His face relaxed and his expression was almost sympathetic. "It's okay. I can see how you'd be spooked."

Spooked was putting it lightly. "Does your grandmother live on the Zuni Reservation?"

"Yes. It's where I grew up and lived until I went off to college."

"What was it like, growing up here?"

"Hot, dry, and hard. My father drank himself to death and left my mother with two children, me and my younger sister. We moved in with Grandmother. Two years later, Mother died of cancer."

She covered his clenched hand with hers. Finally, he loosened it, enfolded hers in his, and laid them on the seat between them. "Grandmother raised us. Lord, I don't know how she did it. Of course, she had Grandfather's help and if needed, Sam and Lilly were close by. I was a wild teenager, angry with the world.

"Grandmother never lectured me when I came home in the wee hours of the morning drunk. She'd wake me when the sun came up, and shove a plate of sunny-side-up eggs under my nose. After I puked my guts out, I spent the day working in the yard. If the lawn was in perfect condition, she had me transplant something, dig another flower bed, haul in rocks for decoration, but she kept me out all day."

He laughed. "Do you have any idea what it's like to have a hangover and do physical labor in the heat?"

"Afraid not. Luckily, I was never caught." Of course, her mother was the type to rant, rave, and make her feel guilty. His grandmother was smart. "So, did that happen very often?"

"After the third time, I learned my lesson." He winked at her. "I may be hard-headed, but I'm not stupid."

His teasing gesture almost left her speechless. She choked down the urge to giggle. "You're a lucky man, Lonan Stone, to have such a wise woman raise you."

Lonan felt a tug at his heart. "Yes, I am."

"So, are your grandmothers close?"

"They know each other well, but because they're not of the same clan, they don't get together frequently." She nodded. "Lilly is Laguna. Leotie is Zuni. Both are Pueblo tribes descended from the Anasazi, but very different in their beliefs."

"Wow, that's some heritage."

"Yes, it is. I'm as proud of my birthright as you are of yours." He respected the care with which she preserved her ancestor's papers, photos, and the locket for future generations. "There are many other tribes in this area that are direct descendants and hold the ruins and landmarks at Chaco Canyon sacred. The canyon is more than a place where the people lived, it's where they came from miles around to worship."

She stared out the front window. "A fact that makes the success of the quest even more crucial."

His chest swelled with appreciation at her understanding. "Yes, religion to the people is as much a part of their heritage as the landmarks."

They rode along in silence for a while. He watched Madison read the casino signs with interest. Out of the blue, she said, "You know, I've always wanted to go to a casino. Do you think while I'm here, you could take me to one?"

"Sure." *Honey, if we make it through this predicament, I'll take you anywhere you want to go.* He turned on the road leading onto Zuni land. When he neared town, he slowed, due to the foot traffic of so many tourists. The Zuni were an artistic people and well known for their beautiful pottery and fetishes. The artists' shops stayed busy.

Madison's eyes lit with interest as they passed the market area. She didn't ask to stop, so he continued on, and just outside of town pulled into a housing area constructed during the early 1970s.

The house he stopped in front of wasn't as nice as Sam and Lilly's, but the adobe structure was home. It was modest, but well cared for. Since his grandfather's death, while he was in the Army, Tusa, his sister Nina's husband, took over the maintenance. After he was discharged and entered college in Albuquerque, he came home often to help out.

For once, Madison waited for him to help her out of the truck. Before they made it to the porch, the front door flew open and Nina came out with his nephew on her hip.

"Lonan! What a surprise."

He caught her and the baby in a hug. "Hello, little sister." With his other arm, he drew Madison forward. "Nina, this is Madison Evans, a visitor to New Mexico. Madison, my sister, Nina, and this little guy is Tito."

"Welcome, Madison. I hope you're enjoying your time here."

Tito leaned toward Madison with his arms outstretched. She laughed and took him, nuzzling his neck. "Hey, little man. What's your mama been feeding you?" He reached for her red hair, knocking her hat back in the process, tangled his chubby fists in a wayward strand, and brought the tress to his mouth.

"Whoa, Tito. You're going to hurt her." He scooped him out of her arms while Nina, eyebrow arched in question at the bandage, worked at disentangling his hands. "Madison was attacked at the park the other night. Someone hit her on the head with a rock."

"Oh, dear, how terrible. I hope you are not in pain."

"No, not really." She raised her hand to the bandage. "It's just a bit sore." Chuckling, she turned to Tito and tickled his bare belly. He squealed with pleasure.

Nina backhanded Lonan on the abdomen. "And have you found this attacker yet?"

"Ouch!" He rubbed his stomach muscles. "No, but we're working on the situation."

"Good." Nina put her arm around Madison's waist and walked her inside. "Grandmother is going to be mad if we monopolize our guest's time." She looked back at him and winked. "And you know who she'll blame."

"Yeah, me as usual." It had always been a standing joke between them. Since he was the oldest, he bore the brunt of the responsibility when they got in trouble.

Madison immediately liked Nina, who led her into the kitchen where an older woman worked at the stove. Short and petite like Nina, her hair was completely gray and in a long braid down her back.

"Grandmother, Lonan has brought us a visitor."

The older woman turned and gave her a quick glance before turning on Lonan. She knew now where Lonan got his eyes, as they were the same color as hers, intense in their intelligence. "Oh, you bad boy. You should've called so I could look presentable." To Madison, she looked very nice. She pulled his head down and kissed him on both cheeks. He wrapped her in his arms, whispered something Madison didn't understand, and then released her. "Now, who is this beautiful young lady with hair that shoots flames?"

"Grandmother, this is Madison. She's staying at the motel outside the park, and I'm keeping an eye on her because of a couple of things that have happened."

The older woman's gaze held her still while studying her features intently. Then, she smiled. "Ah, Madison, you have finally come." She took her hands and looked into her face again for what seemed like a minute, and then stepped back, freeing her. Before she could respond to her comment, the older woman spoke. "Please, call me Leotie. Now, come to the living room. Sit, sit, both of you. Nina, will you bring us some iced tea?"

"Yes, Grandmother, coming up."

Lonan bounced Tito on his lap. "Where's Tusa?"

Nina handed glasses around. "He's at a conference out of town, so I'm staying here until he gets back."

"Nina is a teacher at the pueblo school, and her husband is the assistant principal," Lonan explained. He turned back to Nina. "Who's keeping peace while he's gone?"

"Your good friend, Manny. It's hard to imagine him in a disciplinary role. You two caused so much havoc at school. Your exploits are still whispered about."

He cleared his throat and looked sheepish. "I'm not proud of some of the things we did. Just hormone-driven kids letting off steam."

"We have much to talk about." Leotie glanced at

Nina. The young woman stood and retrieved the empty glasses.

"I'll be checking on dinner."

From where she sat on the couch, Madison watched Lonan cuddle the sleepy child. He must do so often, as Tito molded his body to Lonan's and his eyes drifted up and down.

Leotie was quiet for a moment. She seemed to be collecting her thoughts. Madison wondered what they would hear now. The scary thing was, in her heart she could feel the truth of Lilly's words. Like some inner part of her knew the woman's knowledge was factual. Now she dreaded what Leotie would add to the mix.

"First, may I see the Skystone?"

She removed the locket and placed it in Leotie's hand.

"Ah, it is as beautiful as the mother stone." Her eyes lifted to Madison's, and she felt the woman could see clear to her soul. Her heart thumped in apprehension.

"We of the spirit talkers have known for centuries you would come with one of the twins." She looked at Lonan. "And I have known for a long time, my boy, that you were the one chosen to protect the hunter with hair that spits fire."

"But Grandmother—"

She held up a hand. "Let me finish." Head bowed, she seemed to collect herself. When she looked up, there were tears in her eyes. "Do you remember how your life changed when you were seven years old?"

His jaw clenched and he stared out the window, unwilling to look at his grandmother. "My worthless father drank himself to death, and cancer started eating away at my mother." Madison's heart lurched at his obvious pain.

"Yes. And what was it that helped you through

those difficult days, my son?"

He turned to her, one corner of his mouth quirked into a smile. "You sent me to stay with Lilly and Sam during school break, so I could learn the Keresan dialect common to seven pueblos of our people."

"I can't tell you how hard those summer months were for me, but there was a purpose. While you were with me, I also spent hours teaching you Zuni and Hopi."

He nodded. "I've always wondered why learning the languages were so important to you and Lilly. I guess now I'll find out."

"Yes, it was all in preparation for this quest. We hope that between the three dialects you'll be able to communicate with those in the past."

She took a deep breath and sat up straighter. "Lonan Stone. Lonan, meaning 'cloud,' can be interpreted to signify 'sky.' Your name translated would be Skystone."

Madison watched as shock froze his features.

"Many centuries before you were born, the spirits chose you to protect Madison, woman with the flaming hair, huntress for the missing twin. Your destinies have been intertwined yet secret for hundreds of years, but no more. Together you will find a way to defeat the evil one and reunite the twins. Only then will the mother stone and her babies be out of danger from the rotting spirit."

Lonan looked at her, apparently to see how she was taking this news. She sat, hands folded tightly in her lap, but met his gaze and remained silent. Hopefully he knew she wasn't about to run screaming from the house—yet. She'd hear the rest of what the woman had to say first.

Leotie continued. "My son, do you still have your bear fetish?"

"Yes, I always wear it."

"Good, it will keep you in good health and give you strength throughout this endeavor." She turned to Madison. From her pocket, she removed another rawhide band with a tiny badger. "For you, my dear. He is a brave, persistent animal, and can be fierce when in battle."

Hands shaking slightly, Madison took the necklace and studied the small turquoise figure. "It's beautiful. Thank you."

"No need of thanks. It will provide you with a way to use your inner resources when they are needed. Do not take it off."

Madison cleared her throat. "This may be a dumb question, but do you guys have some kind of plan as to how we're supposed to go about finding the other twin?"

"There is no plan, only a cycle of events that have already begun—your dreams, you coming to Chaco Canyon, the ransacking of your room, your journey back in time to see the witch woman, and the attack on you at the park. The spirits will guide you."

"But, how...?" She struggled for the words.

Leotie held up her hand. "There is more. I could scalp Lilly for letting me be the one to have to tell you this."

Madison shuddered at what the more could be. Nothing good, that was for sure.

"For the prophesy to be fulfilled, you two must be joined."

Lonan paled.

Nervous, she giggled. "You mean like attached at the hip?"

"No dear."

"Oh, God." Lonan dropped his head into his hands and massaged his scalp. "Grandmother, please."

"Have faith, my boy. You and Madison are

destined to be together, to share a great love. The prophecy just speeds things up."

A great love? She and Lonan? The idea wasn't totally without appeal, but they'd never shared so much as a passionate kiss. It was too soon to talk about love. She thought she'd had a great love with Walter and look how that turned out. He dumped her when he learned she was pregnant.

"The people are asking a lot of us, Grandmother. Madison may not be prepared to give that much for a heritage that is not her own."

Madison sat with bated breath as Leotie drilled her with her eyes and smiled. "Oh yes, she's willing. The small amount of Indian blood in her DNA will call her to do the right thing."

"What makes you think I have Indian ancestors?" She knew Royce appeared to be part Indian, but the fact wasn't recorded in the Dyson family Bible.

"Your ancestor, the one who had the locket made for his wife?"

Madison bobbed her head.

"His grandfather was full Laguna For close to eight-hundred-fifty years, his family guarded the stone. It was given into his keeping because the stone spoke to him. He'd been chosen to help fulfill the prophecy. As were you."

Her head buzzed, and for a minute Madison thought she'd faint for the first time in her life. She glanced at Lonan for reassurance. His jaw rigid, his amber eyes glowed with resolve and regret.

"Just what exactly does this joining entail?"

Leotie got up and took the sleeping Tito from Lonan's arms. "I'll leave you to explain, Lonan. Call me if you need me."

Lonan took Madison's hand and tugged until she scooted closer to him on the sofa.

"Lonan, please, I'm drowning here."

"It means that for the prophecy to be fulfilled, you and I must become one."

She gasped. "You mean like get married?"

"Yes, and not in name only. The marriage must be consummated. We must become one flesh."

Chapter Eight

"You...you mean we have to have sex?" The look of shock on her face was almost comical, but he didn't dare laugh. There was nothing funny about their situation.

"Yes, we would. For the prophecy to be fulfilled, for our quest to be successful." He put his arm around her shoulders and drew her over until they were hip to hip, enjoying the heat of her softness against him.

She pulled back. "You're actually considering this idea?"

"Look, we have very little in common and Lord knows, I didn't intend to marry for a while, but it's an honor and my duty to do whatever it takes to fulfill the prophecy." He'd been attracted to her immediately, which was unusual for him. His brow furrowed. "Do you find me repugnant? Would having sex with me be a chore?"

Blood rushed to her face. "No, I think I could manage."

Manage? He didn't consider himself a Romeo, but plenty of women had let him know they'd welcome his advances. Perhaps the feeling wasn't reciprocated. No, he didn't think so. He'd seen her examine him from under her dark, thick lashes. He'd have no difficulty giving this woman pleasure and taking it in return. She might look like an up-tight librarian, but he suspected it was a cover.

He took a deep breath, then let it out. Why was he accepting this responsibility without arguments? In truth, neither he nor Madison had a choice if the prophecy was to be satisfied. He had an obligation to his people. He'd learned obedience and loyalty at an early age, and the importance of sacrificing his own personal happiness for the security of their future generations. Madison didn't have that motivation. Her willingness to help would be out of the goodness of her heart. If she agreed.

Madison had to admit, he wasn't hard to look at, smelled scrumptious, and had a hot body. But, it all seemed too sterile. Not that the idea of sex with him was repulsive, but jeepers, she'd prefer to be in love before getting married. And being involved in some kind of relationship would be nice.

Maybe they could get married, let folks think they'd had sex, and then get a divorce. That way, neither would be hurt, especially her. Lonan was a man she could fall for, and she didn't want her heart broken again. She was a skinny, freckled woman with an unruly mane of hair. There wasn't a thing glamorous or pretty about her, and they had nothing in common. He could do much better, and most likely wouldn't want to be tied to her permanently.

"So, will you marry me?"

Her heart thumped in her chest. Why couldn't this happen to her under different circumstances? In all honesty, she couldn't say no and see their heritage destroyed. She had no choice.

"How about we get married, just pretend to consummate the marriage, and then after the quest is over, get a divorce?"

He frowned. "Or we could enjoy the benefits of marriage, have sex, and after the quest is over, if it suits us, go our separate ways."

She chewed her bottom lip, thinking. The idea wasn't without some merit. He was a hunk and probably a good lover. Good? Cripes, she bet he'd be excellent with a capital E. But could she keep the sex and her heart separate?

"Look, an entire nation of people is counting on us. Can you turn your back on them?"

No, she couldn't. If she didn't help, she'd hate herself for the remainder of her life. "I'll marry you. The sex part, we'll work out later."

The lines in his forehead smoothed, and he released his breath in a whoosh. "Thank God." He turned and drew her closer. His eyes never left hers as he slowly lowered his head and took her lips in a kiss that jolted her mind and body. Took was the only way she could describe it, because he left no doubt who was in control. A whirlwind of warmth started in her stomach and branched out to her extremities, setting her survival instincts on alert. She was putty in this man's hands.

Gasping for air, she pulled back and dropped her head to his shoulder. His arms surrounded her in a comforting embrace. Voice husky, he said, "Thank you."

Lord, help me. It would be so easy to fall in love with this man.

****

Dressed in a dark suit, Lonan stood with his arm around her waist. She'd learned it was a great honor among his people to stand before the assembly to say their vows. The Elders of each tribe in the Four Corners area were present to watch the next step in the prophecy take place. Most dressed in their best tribal clothes, in honor of the occasion. The room abounded with color. The atmosphere was reverent, rather than jovial.

She loved the long, creamy white dress that hugged her body to the hips and then gently flared. Somehow, Nina and her grandmother had found it at a small shop in town. They'd piled her hair on top of her head and wisps of curls danced around her face. Her amber earrings dangled from the lobes of her ears. The turquoise locket fit just between her breasts where the neckline dipped to a low vee. They'd tried to cover, with little success, her bruise.

She shivered, and Lonan squeezed her waist reassuringly. Chin quivering, she looked up and tried to smile. He bent and dropped a soft kiss on her lips.

Madison was grateful a minister would perform the rite. On each side of the preacher, a Zuni and Laguna Elder stood dressed in full regalia, a solemn expression on their faces in respect for the sacred occasion. The service would be a traditional one, but blessed by Lonan's forefathers. When the preacher began the ceremony, the assembly hall rang with his clear voice, not another word heard in the silence around them.

When Lonan removed two gold wedding bands from his pocket, Madison gasped in surprise. She hadn't dreamed they'd have rings. Water pooled in her eyes as he slipped the ring on her finger and recited his vows. Her lips trembled as she lifted the other ring from his open palm. When she slid the larger one on his finger and pledged her love, something cracked in her heart, leaving a gap that needed to be filled.

****

By six o'clock, the party was over. Lonan ushered Madison out of the large room before another group of well-wishers converged on them. They left by a side exit and ran around the building to where his truck was parked. He lifted Madison into the cab, slammed the door, and rushed to his side. "Buckle up and let's get out of here before someone else stops to offer congratulations."

She giggled. "My face is about to crack from this pasted on smile."

Just as they pulled away, two of his cousins ran into the road and hollered for him to stop. He waved and kept going, and then took her hand. She'd dropped her head back against the seat, with her eyes closed. "I hope you weren't disappointed by the ceremony."

She straightened. "Why would I be? It was beautiful."

"It wasn't your traditional religious ritual. And all the native dances after..." He shrugged. "I know it's not what you're used to."

"I thought the dances were beautiful, very moving."

Yes, he'd seen the sheen of tears in her eyes. Maybe Grandmother was right, and her native DNA called to her during the performance.

"Are you hungry? I don't remember seeing you eat much."

"You've got to be kidding. Every woman there stuffed something down me. Why, are you?"

"No, they made sure I ate, too." He glanced in her direction and tried to stifle the laugh that threatened to erupt from his mouth. "They all wanted to make sure we had enough energy to make it through the night."

She blushed scarlet, but giggled. "You're kidding, right?"

"Nope." Thank the stars, his people didn't believe in being around to make sure the consummation took place. He glanced over, awed at how beautiful she looked in the dress and with her hair swept up to show off her lovely neck. The past few days had been stressful and tiring. "How are you feeling? Tired?"

"I'm definitely worn out, but mostly feel lost, like I've been thrust into another realm." Though dark inside his truck, her big blue eyes relayed the unease she felt.

He took her hand. "We'll be all right, Madison. I promise." She squeezed his hand and returned her attention to the darkness outside the window.

They would stay at his place tonight and then tomorrow, get her things from the motel. It was late when they arrived, the only light one that came on automatically when he drove in the drive. "Let me carry you inside. I don't want you to get your skirt dirty on this filthy cement."

"No need for that. I can hold it up out of the way."

"What? Do you think I don't have enough strength to carry you? Are you insulting my manhood?" He wanted to laugh at her pretty mouth, wide open, shock written on her face. "Why do you always have to argue?"

She blinked and pinched her mouth shut.

"Ah, look. You're lovely in that dress and I don't want it to get messed up. Okay?"

"Okay."

He lifted her and shoved the truck door closed with his hip. At the door, he fumbled with getting the key in the lock. Her skirt was in the way. She giggled and lifted it so he could unlock the door.

"Thank you." Inside the living area, he set her on her feet. "Welcome to our home, Mrs. Stone."

"This is nice." And it was. A large stone fireplace covered one wall, the floor of clay tile. It was a small room, so the brown leather sofa sat against the opposite wall. Above it hung a beautiful rug or blanket. "This is beautiful. Is it Navajo?"

"Yes."

"Why is it hanging instead of on the floor?"

He reached out and ran his hand over the woven cloth. "It's too valuable." He jerked his hand back. His brow furrowed, he appeared to be in pain, but quickly erased the expression. "It was made for me in memory of a good friend."

She was curious to know the story, but from his response, she decided it best not to ask. The coffee table was littered with *American Geographic* and archeology magazines. An acoustical guitar stood in the corner by the patio door that looked out onto a wooden deck extending out from the small cemented area. The overhead light cast a glare on the glass so she couldn't see what lay beyond.

"Is there a gorgeous view out there?"

"Yes. It faces east so the sunrises are beautiful, and we don't get the heat from the west in the evening."

Lonan put his hands on her shoulders and turned her to face him. "I realize this isn't the ideal marriage, but I do believe we should abide by certain customs."

She cocked her head. "Such as?"

"You go by the name Madison Stone and sleep in my bed. It will be your decision if we have sex. You know how I feel. I'm a man, and sex is important."

"But—"

He held up his hand. "Let me finish." This was uncomfortable for him, but he wanted to get his feelings out in the open. "To be honest, you stirred my blood from the first. You're not only pretty, but you're smart and care about others, qualities that make you desirable to me. I want you, but I can control my lust."

A blush appeared on her breasts and moved up her face. She was a lovely sight, and his body throbbed with need. He wanted to fulfill their marriage vows and make love to her. Not just for the quest, but also for him. He wanted her with a fire that seethed inside him, and he sought to quench the flames, but he didn't love her or want to hurt her.

Her lips were in that tense line again. "Mr. Stone, where I choose to sleep will be my decision."

Hot damn! At least she didn't say no.

****

Madison lay in Lonan's bed, staring at the ceiling. The very idea of him giving her orders. She mimicked, "You'll sleep in my bed and go by Mrs. Stone." It just so happened, she wanted to, or she wouldn't be here. Not that she'd made up her mind to have sex, as she hadn't. She was more than a little unnerved by everything that had happened in the past week, and he'd be good protection. *Hah! Keep telling yourself that, you fool. You've got the hots for him, and admit it, you're curious.*

He'd let her have the shower first, so she'd been stretched out here for a long time, but couldn't fall asleep. When he'd finished in the bathroom, she heard him leave through the living area and go out onto the deck. Maybe he was as nervous as she was, and letting her fall asleep before he came to bed. She snorted. Him, nervous? Not likely.

His words earlier stunned her. She stirred his blood and he thought she was pretty. The confession thrilled her and left her aching with longing for something more than sex. If she hadn't been so boggled by his words, she'd have flatly refused to sleep with him.

She'd been drawn to Lonan from the beginning, but was afraid part of the attraction was his resemblance to her dream warrior. Was he telling the truth about wanting her, or just playing along with the prophecy? Was she willing to take a chance he'd been honest with her? He was an honorable man, she didn't believe he'd lie, and he'd taken pains to consider her beliefs when arranging the wedding. Of course, wanting didn't mean love. She had to remember that.

She measured her options. She could stay here and molt, or go outside and enjoy the night sounds with Lonan, and see how things progressed. Dressed in her sleep shirt, she walked quietly into the den.

The blinds on the patio door were open, filling the room with moonlight. The sliding entry opened with ease. She stepped outside and closed the glass behind her. Lonan sat in one of the deck chairs, his bare feet propped up on a table. She froze at the sight of his bare chest and legs. A beautiful expanse of male flesh, but she dared not look too long.

Barefoot, she padded across the wood planks to stand at the rail and look out across the vastness below. There was just enough light to make out the canyon and some landmarks. It was nature's beauty in all its glory.

She missed her violin. If she had it now, she'd serenade the canyon. She could almost imagine an orchestra set up on the far mesa, and her playing for the ancient peoples in the chasm below. But, not quite. The presence of the healthy, testosterone-emitting male in the deck chair unnerved her.

She could sense Lonan's gaze on her and the air was charged with tension.

"Why are you up, Madison? Have you changed your mind, or did you come out here in that getup to tease me?"

Her heart thundered at his question. Why, the very idea. Couldn't a girl want some fresh air? And what was wrong with what she had on? The long T-shirt covered her to mid-thigh. She heard the chair give as he rose, and the boards of the deck vibrated slightly as he walked toward her.

She felt his heat against her back, the smell of his aftershave mixed with soap and the scent that was only Lonan's. It was a heady combination, and desire rushed through her. But it was something more powerful than just the need for sex, it was a longing from the pit of her soul to be validated—to be something more than the smart student, the talented musician. She wanted someone to think her pretty, desirable, and sexy.

His breath rustled the hair at her ear as he spoke. "Tell me." She gasped when he moved closer and she felt his hardness pressing against her.

Relief washed through her. He hadn't lied. He did desire her.

He bent and trailed kisses from the base of her neck to her ear. She shivered at the sensation his lips evoked, and thrilled at his words. "Tell me, Madison. Do you want me?"

"Lonan. We need to take things slowly." The words rushed from her in a hoarse plea.

He growled low in his throat, his lips against her hair. "You just want a sample of what sex might be like between us."

"No...I don't know what I want."

His arms encircled her and pulled her back against his arousal. He moved, letting her feel how much he desired her. One large hand on her rib cage, he held her flush with his body. His other traveled over her lower belly, causing the muscles to jump in anticipation. When he cupped her mound, she arched against him. She struggled to turn in his arms, but he kept her immobile while he caressed her breasts, making her ache to have his mouth there.

"Please, let me touch you."

He turned her in his arms and placed hers around his neck. His eyes searched hers in the darkness before he lowered his head. His kiss was hungry, yet tender as his lips moved on hers, eliciting a thrill only he'd been able to drag from her. She pressed her body closer to him, rubbing against his arousal.

He arched against her. "God, Madison, you're pushing your luck here." He lifted the hem of her nightshirt, his fingers teasing the softness of her upper thigh and then the skin above her bikini panties. He delved inside the skimpy briefs to touch the moistened flesh beneath.

A groan of longing tore from her throat as he stroked the throbbing flesh.

She pushed against him with her hands and made an effort to wiggle away. "Stop, it's...too much...too soon."

He bent her back over his arm and laved her nipples through her shirt while he slipped two fingers into her sheath and continued to rub the sensitive tissue with his thumb.

She jerked in his arms and keened softly.

His arms tightened around her as she rode the wave. Weak, her legs trembled as he lifted her and carried her inside.

They fell onto the bed. Arm still tightly around her, he reached down to pull up the sheet. Their heads on one pillow, nose to nose, he brushed the hair back from her face and then caressed her cheek. "Go to sleep."

She twined her fingers in the hair on his chest. He cuddled her close, bringing her head to his shoulder. Her body still felt weak from the mind-boggling orgasm he'd given her.

Chapter Nine

It was dark and she stood alone, wrapped in a blanket for warmth, in the center of the stone circle at Una Vida. The only light came from the large fire pit at her back. People sat on the rock wall that surrounded the area. All eyes were on her, waiting, wondering how tonight would end.

Her captor shoved her to stand in front of several older men dressed in capes covered with bright colored feathers. They had to be the Elders. Her heart sank. These men would determine her fate, and from the stern expressions on their faces, things didn't look promising. The warrior pushed on her shoulders, forcing her to sit before the men. They talked among themselves, and then the one in the middle stood to address the gathering.

From his richly decorated cape and headpiece, she assumed he was their leader or head Elder. His language was odd, guttural sounding. When he finished speaking, he fixed her with a stare and walked toward her. Her heart leapt into her throat, stifling the ability to scream. When he stopped before her, her body shook with tremors. Her teeth clattered. He drew a knife. She shrieked and tried to scoot away, but the warrior held her in place. Eyes closed, she waited to have her throat cut, but instead felt a tug on her hair. She looked up to see him holding one of her curls for the people to see. He pointed to the fire and then at her, while speaking in his dialect.

Suddenly, she was jerked to her feet. The old man started singing and the others joined him. To the chant, they shuffled around her in a dance of some type, while the warrior stood guard with a face devoid of expression.

The chief shouted, and everyone stopped and turned toward a gap in the circle. Standing as tall as her bent body would allow, the witch woman entered, wearing the turquoise locket along with the Skystone. She smirked at Madison as she passed on her way to the man.

They talked. Words of anger flew from the witch woman's mouth as she ranted and shouted. Two warriors appeared from the sidelines, to restrain her if needed, but she stilled and peered at the chief defiantly. When he reached for the locket, she pushed his hand away, removed the necklace, and handed it to him. Then she whirled and strode to stand in front of Madison. Her eyes were intense as she examined Madison from head to foot. Afraid, but determined not to show it, she stood her ground and returned the woman's glare. The old hag lifted both fists into the air and shrieked. Startled, Madison jumped, but the shriek turned into a chant and the others joined in with her.

The elder approached Madison. He held the necklace up for all to see, then slipped it over her head. Then he turned to his people, held up the lock of her hair, pointed to the fire, and then back to her necklace.

"Madison! Wake up. You're dreaming." Lonan gently shook her shoulder and then wiped the tears from her face.

Smiling, chin quivering, she said. "I got the locket back. In my dream, the chief took it from the witch woman and gave it to me." She described the scene from her dream.

"The leader made sure the people knew you were guardian of the turquoise. His reference to your hair was to alert them to prepare for Hair of Flame to return and fulfill the prophecy." She shivered and he cuddled her close, enjoying the silky texture of her soft skin. "Go back to sleep, sweetheart. We have a long day tomorrow."

She rubbed her cheek against his chest. "Okay."

They needed to sleep. Tomorrow, they had to develop a plan to bring the evil one into the open.

They'd just finished breakfast when the phone rang. She heard Lonan saying, "Good...appreciate it...makes me feel we're prepared. Yeah, I'll let you know." He must have lowered his voice, as she had difficulty hearing. Then Lonan laughed. "I'm not joking, Chief. Got the ring on to prove it."

She twisted the gold band on her finger. It all seemed so surreal, but she hadn't imagined the heat between her and Lonan last night. Her cheeks heated at her unrestrained behavior.

Lonan returned to the kitchen just as she dried the last dish. From behind her, he said, "The Chief has called in a replacement for me until we get this settled. Fella named Gene Collins will be here tomorrow. That way, I can be with you every minute."

She turned to face him. Madison liked the thought of him being with her, but she wasn't stupid enough not to worry. Both of them would be at risk until the person was arrested. Of course, knocking someone in the head might be as far as he'd be willing to go for the necklace. But, then again, he could be capable of murder. What was she thinking? A rock could kill, just as a bullet could. She didn't want either one of them to get hurt.

"Do you think this individual is dangerous, capable of murder?"

"I don't want to scare you, but if Lilly and Grandmother are accurate in their predictions, I'd say he could be deadly. Grandmother didn't explain this, but the spirit inside this person's body can't be touched, harmed by human hands. The human being whom he's infected can be destroyed, but the essence will find another shell in which to hide."

Dang! He was just feeding the flames of her already overactive imagination. "Doesn't this entire situation make you doubt your sanity?"

He was quiet for a minute. Voice soft, he asked, "Do you believe you traveled through time several days ago?"

She didn't want to say yes, but, "Yeah, I do."

"Then, if time travel is possible, why can't the power of a strong shaman or a mystic be real?"

She shrugged. "You're right, but I'd like to wake up and find this was a bad dream."

"It would be nice if we knew if this someone had the second twin." He lifted the locket to study the turquoise. "Do you know if this stone can transport more than one person at a time?"

She had the answer to that one. "Yes, if both are entwined in the chain." Her great-great Grandmother Texanna had been taken back to the future by her husband. "If you see, feel," she shrugged, "hell, I don't know what, about to happen, grab me with one arm and the necklace with your other hand."

"You're sure?"

"Yeah, pretty much."

"Good, because we need to go back to 1000 A.D. to visit with the witch woman."

Jeepers, they were going after an unseen force they couldn't harm? This was lovely, just dandy. "If we can't destroy it, why bother going?"

"For him to get your necklace, he'll have to follow us. If the witch woman is as powerful as legend portrays her, she'll have the power to force his soul into the afterlife. Only then will he be harmless."

"Without the locket, how will he be able to time travel?"

"We can only hope that he has the third piece."

That made sense. If he didn't, they'd just have to find another way to get him back there.

He cupped her cheek. "I know what you're thinking, but don't worry about it right now. If necessary, I'll come back with the locket to get him."

"And leave me there by myself?" Could she deal with being alone? She had once before, she guessed she could again.

Hands in her hair, he pulled her head to his chest. His other arm circled her waist and tucked her close. She breathed in his familiar scent. "You could handle it, woman with hair that shoots flame."

If it came to that, she wouldn't have a choice. Lonan's hand strayed to cup her butt. She could feel his arousal against her belly. She pulled back to see his face.

"Did you tell Chief Johnson about the wedding?"

He grinned. "Yeah, left the old man speechless for about ten seconds. Then the questions flew."

"What did you tell him?" Surely not the truth.

"That we'd fallen madly in love, and I couldn't wait to make an honest woman out of you."

Why, the man was enjoying her discomfort. "You did not."

"Did too." He grabbed her around the waist, sat her on the kitchen counter, and stepped between her legs. His face was inches away from hers. "I had to tell him something."

She supposed so, but could imagine the looks they'd receive from the park people. Oh well, they couldn't be much worse than the ones she'd received after spending the night on the cliff.

He nuzzled her neck and all thought vanished as his lips traveled up to kiss her. She curled her arms around his neck and her legs around his waist. As they made contact, Lonan groaned. That she could elicit such a response from him thrilled her almost as much as the feel of his lips on hers. She opened her mouth, allowing him inside to tease her tongue with his. Fire coiled in her belly and shot lower. His hands lifted her T-shirt and cupped her breasts. With a snarl, he pulled back and yanked her top down. "We better get on the road before I toss you in bed."

Madison tucked her head and smiled. No doubt about it. This man was intent on seducing her, and the more she learned about him, the more willing a participant she became.

****

Deep in thought as he drove, they neared the front gate and Lonan almost passed by without stopping. Two rangers were on duty and both walked out of the small building to talk to him.

"Hey, guys, did the Chief call you?"

"Yep, sure did. We've got a full alert for firearms." One nodded in the direction of Madison. "Aren't you going to introduce us?"

"Nope. My wife and I are in a big hurry. We'll stop by later."

Both men gaped, and Lonan couldn't resist a chuckle. "Thanks, fellas." He waved and moved through the gate.

Madison turned in the seat and looked back. "They're both standing in the road, scratching their heads."

Lonan didn't blame them. He'd not mentioned being serious about anyone, and had never brought a woman to any of the park social activities. He'd have some fancy explaining to do. "Talking about our marriage will give them something to ponder and help the time pass."

She laughed and resettled herself in the seat. "By the way, I meant to tell you, I like your family. They were all very nice."

Her comment warmed him. "I like them. But

you didn't get to meet the whole bunch. I've got aunts, uncles, and cousins scattered all over New Mexico and part of Arizona." Heck. Some he saw rarely, and didn't even know their names.

He wondered about her. She'd mentioned a sister, and that her mother had died, but no one else. "How about you, do you have a large family?"

"It's just my sister and me left of the immediate family, but we have oodles of relatives around the Texas area. We have lots of cousins, aunts and uncles. Most of them are Dysons. One of them is a Texas Ranger." Her lips quirked up in a smile. "So, mister, you better be on your best behavior."

"Hmm, is that so? I bet we could have some interesting conversations about law enforcement."

"Yeah, he'd like that."

They rode along in silence for a while, enjoying the cool morning air and scenery. It was nice to know she wasn't one of those people that had to keep a conversation going every minute. Chatty females got on his nerves.

He broke the quiet. "I've been thinking about how to draw this person out."

She turned toward him. Though she no longer wore a bandage, her head still carried a bruise. The skin was still tight and when she wrinkled her forehead, he saw her grimace and reach up to touch the area. "How?"

He hoped his trepidation didn't show in his eyes. "We must bring him out in the open by using you as bait."

She gasped. He took her hand and squeezed, trying to give comfort. He wanted to say everything would be fine, but, in truth, he knew they were entering dangerous territory. "I'll do everything within my power to keep you safe. To get to you, he'll have to go through me, first."

Her brow furrowed, she muttered, "Well, that's

reassuring. I don't want you to get hurt, either." Her grip on his hand tightened.

Lonan could accept a little hurt, but feared their situation could turn fatal if they didn't handle the evil spirit just right. They'd have to outsmart him, draw him out, and then pounce.

"We'll pose as a couple, a couple newly in love and wanting to spend time communing with nature, so to speak. I'll be near you at all times. Most likely the person will approach you in a public area, making it harder to spot him." She didn't interrupt, so he continued. "On the way back, we'll stop at home and get camping gear and set up a site in the tent area at the park. During the day, we'll spend time touring the pueblos, and the park in general."

"You mean watch and see if anyone looks suspicious?"

"Yes. If the perp doesn't take the bait, try to steal the locket while we're sightseeing, they may try at night while we're sleeping." He was a light sleeper and would hear any noise out of the ordinary.

"While we're sleeping? That's not too reassuring."

"Don't worry. I won't put you in danger, I promise." God, he hoped he wasn't. Hopefully, Joe would come through for him and provide them with the extra protection they needed.

"I'm not worried." The expression on her face said otherwise. "You'll be carrying your gun, right?"

"Yes, a pistol and a rifle. Firearms aren't allowed in the park, but just in case, everyone's vehicle and belongings will be checked as they come in the entrance."

"If you think it'll work, I'm game."

****

Rita pulled into the restaurant a mile or so down the road from the motel. Her head ached terribly, she was nauseous, and she needed to go home, but something inside her kept pushing, digging at her, putting ideas into her mind. Maybe the caffeine in a cup of coffee would ease her pain. She hadn't eaten since that morning, so food might help.

The sandwich was delicious and she finished it off, even emptied her plate of the pickle and chips. The food hit her bloodstream and she noticed a spurt of energy. The pounding lessened to a steady thump.

As she paid her ticket and left, she bumped a park ranger on his way inside. He steadied her and removed his hat. "Pardon me, Ma'am. I hope I didn't hurt you."

She shook her head and noticed the name on his uniform—Collins. "I'm fine. Thank you."

He held the door as she walked out. The hammering against her skull increased in tempo and strength. She made it to her car and collapsed against the bumper as the voice pounded in a steady rhythm. *Do it. Do it or you'll pray for death. Do it now!*

****

By nine-thirty, they'd reached the motel. He killed the motor in front of her room and turned toward her. "I'll help you collect your things."

He got out and rounded the vehicle to open her door.

As she slid off the seat, he caught her around the waist and helped her down. She smiled her thanks "It won't take me long to pack." Inside, she tossed her things into a suitcase and soft carry-on bag. He carried them out to the truck. She followed with her violin.

"Where's your box of family papers? In your trunk?"

"No, I asked the manager if I could put it in his safe. He was agreeable."

"We could take it in to one of the towns and put

107

it in a bank vault, but it's probably just as secure here."

"When I check out, I'll ask if it's okay to leave it for a while longer."

"I doubt they'll care."

The man behind the counter assured them it would be out of harm's way and waiting for them when they returned to pick it up.

"We enjoyed having you with us, Miss Evans, and hope you'll return."

Lonan put his arm around her and tucked her to his side. "It's Mrs. Stone. We got married yesterday."

Madison wanted to laugh at the shocked expression on the young man's face, but fighting off her blush cancelled the urge.

He stuttered. "Well now...what a surprise...how nice... congratulations...." He shook Lonan's hand.

Lonan kissed her, taking too long in her opinion, then winked at the clerk. "Thank you."

On their way out the door, the clerk called out, "Wait a minute, Miss Evans...I mean Mrs. Stone. I have a message for you."

He rounded the counter and handed her a piece of paper. She scanned it quickly. "It's from my sister. She's not heard from me since I arrived, so I need to check in with her."

"You can call her at home."

The manager tapped his temple. "Oh, I need to tell you something else. There were two people in here asking about you yesterday. Wanted to know when you'd be back."

Lonan tensed. "Did they give their names?"

"No. I asked if they wanted to leave their name and a message, but both said no."

Lonan's eyes searched hers and she shrugged her shoulders in confusion.

He asked, "Did they come together?"

"No. One stopped by in the morning, the other

late in the afternoon."

"Can you tell me what they looked like, age, height, how they were dressed, etc.?"

"The man was tall, dark, and wore slacks and one of those polo type shirts. He was a real classy dresser. Had on loafers with tassels."

Lonan was curious. "That's a pretty detailed description. Why'd you noticed so much about his clothes?"

He shrugged. "Don't get many folks around here dressed like that. He wasn't like our usual clientele. Now, the woman fit right in. She wore jeans, tennis shoes, and a T-shirt with a big straw hat. Her hair was gray. Figure she's probably around fifty-five to sixty years old."

"Thank you. You've been a big help."

"You're mighty welcome. Glad to be of assistance." He raised one finger. "Oh, one more thing. That old woman, she wore red framed glasses."

Chapter Ten

Hand on her back, Lonan escorted Madison to her car. With her door open, he captured her waist and turned her to face him. "Do those two people sound familiar to you?"

She stumbled and grasped his forearms for balance. "Yes, the man sounds like Luis Santiago. The woman..." She shook her head. "The only person I can think of is the woman at the museum who sent me to Mr. Santiago's shop. I don't know her name, but now that I think about it...she may have been the woman at the campfire who seemed familiar. I don't know if I mentioned that to you or not, but I just couldn't place her."

"No, you didn't. Why the hell not?"

She shrugged. "It didn't seem important at the time."

He cupped her cheek and tilted her face up to see her reaction. "From now on, you need to let me decide what's important."

"All right, I will."

It wouldn't help things to get angry, so he let it drop.

"And that day at the museum, she did wear red framed glasses. I noticed because they were such a contrast to her blue eyes."

"I'll call Joe and he can get someone in Albuquerque to find out who she is." He brushed the hair back from her forehead and studied her wound. "It's looking much better, but you need to keep some cream on it to keep your skin supple."

She reached up and touched it gingerly. "I have

some antibiotic salve in my cosmetic bag."

"That'll work." He pulled her in for a thorough kiss. When it ended, he was breathing hard. He was pleased to note she appeared a bit flustered herself.

"Don't you think that kiss a little overkill?"

"We want people to know we're lovers, and whether you agree or not, after last night we just about are." His voice thick, he added, "It'll take about forty-five minutes to get to my place." He tapped her on the nose. "Don't fall too far behind. I'll keep pretty much to the speed limit."

Hummph, bossy man. Madison watched as he strode to his truck without looking back. She slid behind the wheel, buckled up, and started the engine. Lonan waited for her to pull in behind him before getting onto the two-lane highway.

How long after they completed the mission would the relationship last? A day, a week, a month? They didn't have much in common. And she didn't see what a good-looking man could see in a skinny redhead like her. The idea of staying with Lonan, sharing a tent with him, made her a little nervous. Not that it was any smaller than his bed, but there were open spaces around his bed. They'd be enclosed in the tent, and it'd be hard to keep her attraction for him in check. It made her more vulnerable.

They were somehow connected in this quest thing, but that didn't promise happily ever after.

Lonan glanced in his rearview mirror to make sure Madison was keeping up. His body still throbbed from their kiss. He needed a cold shower. It would be hard to keep his attraction under control. He didn't want to ruin the progress he'd made last night. She hadn't tried to push him away this morning when he sat her on the counter. His erection had to be obvious to her, but she'd wrapped her legs around him and returned his kiss. He'd almost lost it right there.

111

Could they make a marriage work? The gods appeared to think so. In his opinion, she needed a professor, someone who shared the same interests, but maybe that wasn't for him to decide.

He pulled into the double carport and cut the engine. Madison pulled in beside him. They gathered her belongings and walked around to the front door.

"My, God. What on earth is that?" Her gaze was on the wooden statue at the corner of the house where he'd hoped it would go unnoticed. She walked straight to it and looked up and down the eight-foot figure with its teeth bared and big claws reaching out to grasp any unsuspecting passerby.

"Can't you tell what it is? It's a grizzly bear modeled using a chain saw. One of my cousins gave me the treasured piece."

She whipped around and stared at him. "Uh...yeah, it's very nice. Bet you're proud of it."

"Hell, it's a disgrace to nature. Ugliest thing I've ever seen. Keep hoping someone would steal it or it'd come a big freeze and I'd have to cut it up for firewood."

She giggled. "Shame on you. It would break your cousin's heart."

"Yeah, I know, that's why after five years it's still standing." He shook his head. "Come on. Let's go inside and get you settled."

In the bedroom, he made room for her hanging clothes in the closet and cleaned out several drawers in the rustic pine chest that matched the headboard and footboard of the bed. It felt odd sharing a room with her. He'd only had one live-in girlfriend, and that had been in college. Both had known it wasn't something permanent. This state of affairs was different. He'd married Madison, and though they didn't love each other, they'd made a commitment before God. Ending this relationship wouldn't be as cut and dried. Oh well, no need borrowing trouble right now.

Madison appeared to be deep in thought as she put clothes away. He leaned against the doorframe and watched expressions flit across her face. Was she thinking about them in that bed, or something else?

"I don't understand something." She turned to face him, her brow furrowed. "With Lilly and Leotie's powers, why can't they do this job?"

Well, so much for wishful thinking. "They aren't strong enough." He stepped close and caressed her cheek. "And, they weren't chosen."

She sighed deeply and nodded.

Lonan thought her last dream had been promising. The witch woman seemed to accept Madison's part in their destiny, but one could never be sure. If she didn't kill them on sight, hopefully she'd help with their quest. After all, the heritage of her people was at stake.

****

Rita stood on the side of the road, hurting so badly she feared she'd faint, but her plan worked perfectly. The ranger would be headed to the park, so she'd hidden her vehicle and pretended to have car trouble.

He eased off the pavement, stopped, and rolled down the window. "You need some help, ma'am?"

"Yes, thank you. A tire blew out and I need a way to the camp store." She saw him look up and down the road, probably wondering about the whereabouts of her car. "Oh, I pulled off the road into some shrubs to keep from causing a wreck."

He nodded. "Hop in and I'll have you there in no time."

When she got in, her head fell back against the seat, and she took deep breaths of the cool air. She knew she must look terrible, she felt like she was dying.

"Are you sick? How long have you been standing in the sun? You could have heatstroke." For a minute, she thought he'd reach for the mike and call for an ambulance.

"No, I'm fine now that I'm inside." She used her shirttail to wipe the sweat off her face. Suddenly, her pain eased and she sighed with relief.

"Okay, if you're sure." For the first few miles, he shot glances her way, but finally relaxed. He must have decided she'd told him the truth.

At the 'five mile to camp store' sign, she pulled the pistol she'd stolen from her husband's gun cabinet. She cocked it, a sound anyone with firearms knowledge would immediately recognize.

His body tensed and he glanced sideways at her. "What the hell are you doing?"

"I'm hijacking your SUV, Ranger. So, just do as I say and you won't get hurt."

"Are you crazy? I'm an officer of the law and you'll rot in jail when you're apprehended."

She snorted. "Makes me no difference—rot here, rot there."

The vehicle swerved and the passenger side tires hit the gravel. "Shut up and drive. Keep your eyes on the road."

Ten minutes later, they were far into a thicket of brush. "Look, tell me what you need. I don't have much cash, but I've got a butt load of credit cards."

"Lock your hands behind your head and get out over here on the passenger's side. One sudden move, and I'll shoot."

Later, after she'd finished puking, she looked back at the terrible thing she'd done. The ranger lay on the ground, blood pooling around his shattered skull. The throbbing in her head was back, accompanied by a maniacal laugh. She fell against the side panel of the SUV and sobbed, fists beating against her head. If God would strike her dead, she'd die gratefully. The pistol lay on the ground. She picked the weapon up, cocked it, and pointed it at the side of her head. The gun was knocked from her hand, and her head slammed against the glass.

Stop it, you stupid woman. You'll die when I get ready to kill you, when you're no longer useful to me.

Terrified, moaning in agony, she screamed, "Who are you? Why can't you leave me alone?"

Look into the glass and see your reflection, you brainless female. My name is Nukpana.

Her head was shoved close to the window. Staring back at her was an Indian man, gaunt face looking like death, eyes crazed, and a leer of teeth stretched back over black gums. The stench of rotting flesh slammed into her face, gagging her.

Screaming, she stumbled back, and then turned to run. She was tripped, fell, and knew no more.

****

Lonan spent all afternoon packing camping supplies in his truck. He'd left Madison with a Coleman icebox and instructions to plan for four days out. Fortunately, he'd been to Farmington a few weeks ago and laid in plenty of food. He hoped she had some idea of what could and couldn't be cooked out on a camp stove or over a fire.

Just before they left, he called Joe Redhawk and told him about Luis Santiago and the older woman's visit to the motel.

"Lonan, we've identified the woman. Her name is Rita Santiago. Her husband is the owner of that jewelry shop Madison visited."

The campsite he'd selected was east of Una Vida, so it didn't take long to get there. It was a pretty spot and backed up to a large butte. It was isolated, but relatively close to the restrooms. He wanted to be able to see Madison as she came and went without being too obvious about it.

Due to the heat, the park wasn't usually

crowded and today was no exception. Lonan saw only three other tents. Of course, other tourists might come in later.

As he pulled the truck to a stop, he turned to Madison. "Well, what do you think?" He watched as she looked around at the rocks, red soil, and what small amount of vegetation grew wherever it could take root.

"It's definitely primitive, but I bet it's gorgeous when the sun sets and rises on those cliffs in the distance."

It was. He got out of the truck, slammed the door, and went around to help her out.

"Yes, and when it's dark, you'll feel you can reach up and touch the stars." He couldn't imagine living in the city and not being able to see them for the smog and bright lights. "Let's get to work. I'll start the fire if you'll get the potatoes ready to bake in the hot coals."

He'd brought plenty of wood to burn in the rock fire pit, and within a few minutes had a nice blaze going. Before long, the sun would set and the temperature drop. The heat would be welcome.

Madison had the potatoes oiled, salted, and wrapped in foil. She sat them on one of the rocks and started unpacking their gear. Each campsite was equipped with a tent pad, so their sleeping bags would be relatively comfortable. When the tent was up, he noticed how much smaller it seemed than before. It was a three-man tent, but at the thought of sharing it with Madison and not being able to make love to her, it shrank. Having her close could become a bad habit if he wasn't careful. He rolled out their bedrolls inside and returned to help Madison with their meal.

An hour later, they'd eaten and cleaned up the dishes.

The sun inched closer to the ground and cast a

golden glow over the land. Lonan took her hand. "Let's sit down and enjoy the sunset." He scooted his camp chair closer to Madison's and slipped his arm around her shoulders. Dang, the chairs wouldn't cooperate. "Come sit in my lap."

"Boy, you're playing this relationship up to the hilt."

"We do have to keep up appearances. Remember, we're newly married and in love. That means we can't keep our hands off each other." Which wasn't a lie on his part, and he didn't think she was immune to him either. She'd certainly participated in their foreplay the night before.

She cuddled up in his lap and he prayed the chair would hold them both. It sagged, but held. "In that case..." Her fingers inched between the buttons of his shirt, slipping a couple undone, fanning them out across his skin. His belly jerked in response.

He grabbed her hand. "You're playing with fire, Red." He nodded toward the tent. "You know sound carries out here in the desert, so, unless you're prepared to have an audience, you better behave."

She glanced around, figuring out the distance between the campsites. "I see what you mean."

He pulled her head to his shoulder. "Share this with me. This is nature in all its glory."

She relaxed in his arms and they were quiet as the sun highlighted the cliffs, making them glow like gold. Then slowly, it slipped behind the rock face, leaving a strip of turquoise sky. Inch by inch, the blue-green disappeared as the weight of darkness pressed it down.

"It's beautiful out here. Can you imagine enjoying this every evening, and the reverse each morning of your life?"

Yeah, he could, and that was why he loved this country so. This site had been left pretty much as it was back a thousand years ago—raw and primitive.

Madison shivered. He rubbed her arms to warm them, then stood and set her on her feet. "Let me grab a blanket and our jackets. Move closer to the fire."

When he exited the tent, she had both chairs pulled closer to the rock ring. He sat down and propped his feet on a boulder.

"Can I get in the truck?"

"Sure." He tossed her the keys. She returned with a book and sat in the chair beside him.

"You'll go blind if you try to read by this firelight."

"I pretty much know it by heart, so I won't need much light."

The book that she held appeared to be leather-bound, old and well-used. He watched as she opened it and read several pages. She paused and leaned her head back against the chair, eyes closed. "What are you reading?"

She turned her head and smiled. "*As You Like It.* It's one of my favorites."

As a matter of fact, it was one of his favorites too. Or maybe he should say, one of just a few of Shakespeare's works that he liked. He quoted one of the phrases he remembered.

"All the world's a stage,
And all the men and women merely players.
They have their exits and their entrances,
And one man in his time plays many parts,
His acts being seven ages."

"I'm impressed, Ranger." She grinned. "Hey, are you trying to woo me by spouting poetry?"

"Not unless those words turned you on. That's the limit of my repertoire."

She giggled and he enjoyed the lilting sound. Her hair and eyes glowed in the firelight. Her vibrant coloring, as well as her turquoise necklace and amber earrings, were indicative of the earth and the sky. Madison had no idea how attractive she was or why she'd been chosen for this mission.

"Did you know that Shakespeare had a quest of his own?"

"No, I didn't. Tell me what he longed for."

"He sought immortality through his works." She closed the book and held it against her chest. "I think he succeeded, don't you?"

"Yes, he did. Let's hope we're as successful in ours."

Eyes big and rounded, she nodded and went into the tent. When she came out, she carried a towel and her toiletries bag. "I'm going to head for the restrooms."

He caught her arm. "Not without me. It's too dangerous. Let me grab my stuff."

As they walked the short distance, she said, "You know, I just can't believe this is happening to me—the dreams, the break-in, and the attack, but most of all, the prophecy."

He slung his arm around her shoulders and shook her gently. "I understand your confusion. Hopefully it will all be over soon." He stopped at the women's side and pulled her close. "Don't try going back without me."

She nodded and went inside. He went into the men's restroom and cleaned up as best he could with lukewarm water. Not the greatest for a shave, but better than no water at all. Towel hanging around his neck, shave kit under his arm, he stepped out to wait for her. She came out with her face scrubbed clean of what little makeup she wore, and smelling like flowery talcum powder. "Feel better?"

"Oh yes, much."

They walked back to their tent. "You go on in and get settled. I'll follow in a minute."

He checked their area to make sure their supplies and equipment were properly stored, the

119

fire completely out. Lights from a vehicle made their way around the circular drive to their campsite. Joe Redhawk pulled his pickup in beside Lonan's and got out.

"Hey, Joe. What's going on?"

His expression grim, Joe leaned against his truck. Hans, his German shepherd, stuck his nose out the window and woofed at Lonan. "I've brought your back-up. He's been fed but will need some water. I'll pick him up in the morning."

"Thanks, Joe. I appreciate you loaning him out."

"No problem." He opened the door and Hans hopped out and nuzzled Lonan's hand.

Lonan dropped the tailgate of his truck and snapped his fingers. The dog hopped into the back and made himself comfortable on the quilt Joe tossed in the bed. Then, he scratched the dog's ears and leaned in close to talk to him. His words were barely discernable. "Guard this tent tonight, boy. No hunting."

The dog yipped, and Joe turned back to Lonan. "Have some more news about Mrs. Santiago. She's been a trusted employee at the museum for years."

"Whoa. Isn't it odd that she and Luis both appeared at the motel looking for Madison, but didn't come together?"

He nodded. "Yep. Luis came in late this afternoon. Said he's concerned about his mother. She's been behaving strangely and won't answer her cell phone, and he's afraid she's developed some type of dementia."

Joe looked tired. He removed his hat and tossed it through the window onto the seat. "We've been asking around the area about her. The chief has the staff on alert to call in if she's spotted. People have been known to get lost if they wander off on their own."

"Did Luis say why he was asking about Madison

yesterday?"

"No, he danced around the issue, something about wanting to see if she'd been able to find out anything about her piece of turquoise."

"What about his mother? Why would she be looking for Madison?"

"He didn't have a clue. As far as he knew, his mother had never met Madison. All sounds fishy to me." He opened his truck door. "Keep your eyes open. An all points bulletin has been put out on her. You know what can happen if someone goes missing in this remote area."

Yeah, he did know. It was easy to get lost, the outlook wasn't good.

"You know what you're doing, what you're getting into—searching for this spirit, Lonan?"

"Yeah, I do. I'm not crazy about the idea, but don't have a choice, do I?"

"Doesn't look like it, friend. It's a great honor to be chosen so. I'll pray for your safety and Madison's, and for a successful mission."

He watched as Joe drove away, thinking about his words. It was good to know his people had faith in this quest. He looked up at the star-studded sky and wondered where Mrs. Santiago could be.

He walked to the tent opening. "Can I come in now?"

"Yes."

It was dark as pitch, so he stripped down to his boxers and crawled into their bag. He'd zipped their bags together, and so far she hadn't complained. "Are you comfortable?"

"Yeah. How about you?"

"Great." He turned and drew her close, inhaling her sweet scent mixed with the powder.

"Was that Joe Redhawk you were talking to?"

"Yeah." He explained what he'd learned about Mrs. Santiago, and about their watch dog.

121

"Aaaa, a dog? Where's he sleeping?"

"In the truck bed on a comfortable pile of blankets. He's on alert and will hear if anyone gets close." But, the dog was trained to wait until they were close enough to apprehend.

"So, she could be wandering around in the wilderness, hurt, thirsty, hungry?"

Lonan could feel her worry in the tenseness of her body. He tucked her head under his chin and let his fingers comb through her hair. "They'll find her." Unable to resist her closeness, he let his hand wander over her back and down to the swell of her buttocks. She didn't complain, so he left it there.

"I hope you're right." She rubbed her cheek against his shoulder. His body throbbed with the tempo of his heart. "Lonan?"

"Hmmm?"

"You're a nice man. You smell good, too."

The throb of before was now a full pounding. "So do you, sweetheart." *Oh boy, and honey, you feel even better.* He hoped he'd survive this wooing period. "Go to sleep."

Chapter Eleven

Her body throbbed as tension built in her lower belly. Her breasts ached for more touching, but she couldn't turn around and press them against his naked chest, feel the crisp hair tease her nipples. He had her open to him, her calf thrown over his bent leg as he stroked and teased the sensitive folds between her legs. Her buttocks rode the length of his erection, the friction and his hand bringing her to the brink and fully awake.

She wasn't dreaming. For just a moment she struggled to break free of his embrace, but then shuddered and moaned, the sound growing in volume until his mouth covered hers to swallow her soft cries as the ripples subsided. Drained, completely sated, and now fully awake, she wanted to burrow into the sleeping bag and become invisible. Cripes, all he had to do was touch her and she fell apart. It was a nice shattering, but still...how embarrassing.

He trailed kisses along her neck and shoulder. Goosebumps followed in their wake. "Lonan."

His hands and mouth continued to caress her. Weighed down by his leg, she couldn't move. His body was spooned behind hers. "Mmmm?" He kissed the side of her neck. "I'm sorry I took advantage, but you're so damn sweet and touchable, I couldn't resist."

"Let me up."

With a heavy sigh, he moved his leg.

She turned toward him, flattened her breasts against his chest, and reached up to bring his head down to hers. He didn't react until she stretched up to place her lips against his. Instantly his arm locked around her like a band of steel pressing her closer. Their kiss was hot, wet, and desperately seeking, as if they couldn't taste enough. With her one free hand, she explored his bare back, the skin smooth and warm, muscles rippling beneath her touch. His buttocks jerked when she cupped them and urged him closer.

When her hand moved between them to his erection, he groaned. Gasping for breath, voice raspy, he caught her hand. "Madison, don't tease me."

She kissed a path down his chest to his belly. "I want you, Lonan."

In one swift movement, she was on her back and he knelt between her knees. He lifted her nightshirt over her head and tossed it aside. He pushed her knees up to her chest and slipped her panties off, then shimmied out of his boxers. They joined the pile of the other discarded items.

Lonan reached over and turned on a low-beam battery-operated lantern.

She reached for the cover. "What are you doing?"

"I want to see you." She tried to relax as he stared at her face, his eyes and hands making her jump and gasp as they trailed down and up her hips and outstretched legs. He cupped her breasts, kissed her belly making the muscles contract, and explored each leg and foot finding spots that made her shiver. "You are lovely, Madison—like an alabaster goddess."

Me? Lovely? She shook her head. "No, I'm not. I'm too skinny."

"Trust me, you're perfect, just like you are."

Was he being honest, or was this part of a line? No, one thing she knew without a doubt, Lonan was an honest man. He meant it now in the heat of the moment.

He loomed above her, his wide shoulders tapering to a trim but muscled waist, with hips of the same width. Her eyes traveled to his sex, thick and ready. Unable to resist, she reached out to touch the silken length of him.

Head thrown back, he groaned and trembled. With a growl, he took both her hands and held them beside her head. "I didn't bring any protection."

She marveled at the intensity of his need. Could he truly desire her that much? "I'm on the pill."

He stilled and studied her. "Are you sure you want this?"

She lifted her hips in invitation. "Oh yes. I want you." And she did. Her body yearned for him to take her. If he didn't enter her, she'd die right here and now.

He leaned down to take a nipple between his lips. She almost howled as pleasure shot through her. Carefully, he drew it into his mouth and sucked, and then laved it with his tongue. He turned his attention to the other breast teasing and tasting until she was gasping and squirming beneath him.

Lowering himself to his forearms, he took her lips in a sweet kiss, positioned himself at her opening, and in one swift movement filled her. Her body shuddered and gradually relaxed to accommodate him. When she felt the tensing, seeking of her muscles, she pushed against him trying to get closer, wanting more. Her body craved this man's touch and she feared once would never be enough.

He dropped his forehead to hers. "I'm sorry, sweetheart, I can't go slow."

Her body had a mind of its own. She pushed against him, already feeling the tension spiral inside her. "It's okay. I can't either."

He drove into her again and again, his strokes

rough and uncontrollable. His wild response increased her pleasure. With her legs around his waist, she held on tight, meeting him thrust for thrust. She sobbed for completion, each plunge making her vaginal walls quake as she strove for the climax she longed for. Lips on her neck, whispered words of passion teased her nerve endings sending her over the edge, her muscles clenching around him in spasm after spasm. He growled low in his throat as he came.

When he collapsed on top of her, Madison was grateful for his weight, clutched his back, and ran her hands up and down the muscled expanse. He rolled over taking her with him. Head on his chest, she listened to the rapid thump of his heart. She propped her chin on her crossed arms. "Wow, that was awesome."

He chuckled. "Hot damn, sweetheart." He caught her under the arms and lifted her until they were nose to nose. His lips covered hers tenderly, and then broke the kiss. "It blew my mind." With his teeth, he nipped a trail from her neck to her shoulder. "And my body."

With a sigh, she relaxed against him, reveling in the touch of his flesh against hers. They kissed, talked, touched, and then made love again. Curled against Lonan's side, Madison gave in as contented sleep washed over her mind and body.

Lonan lay awake, listening to the night sounds, and Madison's soft breathing. She was a passionate woman, open and honest in her responses to his touch. That she didn't have a clue how beautiful she was confounded and intrigued him. She was unpretentious, and he liked that about her. He knew they played with fire, and both could easily get burned.

But, without a doubt, the gods were pleased with their joining. The haunting sounds of music on the wind weren't his imagination. The lilting melody of the six finger hole flute, accompanied by the rhythmic foot drumbeats and chants of the ancient people, echoed throughout the canyon.

****

Madison heard Lonan rustling around and allowed her eyes to creep open to just a slit. In the dawning light, she couldn't see much but a shadow of his large form. He cursed and thrashed about as he struggled to pull on his jeans in the confining space. She released a giggle.

He froze and turned to her with a growl. "Think that's funny, hey?"

"A little." She could just make out the breadth of his bare shoulders. *My, he's a fine specimen of manhood.*

With his jeans unzipped, he crawled toward her, a look of mischief on his face. "Let's see how funny you think this is." He yanked the sleeping bag back, grabbed her legs, and tickled that sensitive spot above her knees.

She howled and he covered her mouth with his hand. "Shit! Be quiet. Sound echoes around here."

"Okay, already." She sat up and started searching for her discarded clothes from last night. *What kind of love nest is this, anyway?* He didn't even kiss her good morning. When she looked back toward Lonan, he was staring at her.

"Madison, you are a beautiful woman. I don't know who made you think you weren't, but they were a fool."

Heat filled her face. She knew it must be as red as her hair, but his words were worth 1,000 morning kisses and soothed many hurt feelings. Her voice squeaky, she said, "Thank you."

"One of these days, I want you to tell me about this person who hurt you."

That he cared dumbfounded her. That he'd

recognized her insecurity only added to her amazement. Afraid to speak, she nodded.

"Better get dressed. We have a long day ahead of us." He crawled out of the tent, taking his shoes with him.

As she shimmied into her jeans, she better understood Lonan's dilemma. She stuffed her feet in her tennis shoes, stood, and bent over to walk through the flap. The air was fresh and clean, the sun just beginning to peek over the far cliff. Hands locked behind her head, she leaned back and stretched. "Oh, God, that feels good."

"Nothing like fresh, unpolluted air." He put one hand on her shoulder and cupped her cheek with the other. "Did I wish you a good morning?"

"No, sir, you did not."

"How uncouth of me." He lowered his lips to a breath away from hers. "Good morning, Madison."

Her eyes met his. They were pure yellow with the rising sun hitting them. "Good morning, Lonan." She grinned. "I think it would be very remiss of you if you didn't kiss me."

"Hmmm, well, I do aim to please." His kiss was sweet and tender and a feeling of panic struck her. *Don't fall in love with this man.*

"Grab your toiletries and let's head to the restroom." He whistled, and a large German shepherd dog jumped out of the truck bed. The dog was a beautiful animal. "Madison, this is Hans. Joe loaned him to us for a few days. Best guard dog in four states. One of these days, I'm going to get one of his pups."

She held out her hand and Hans sniffed it and then her feet.

"He likes you." He popped her on the butt. "Hurry up, the coffee will be ready to remove from the burner by the time we get back."

What was with men—always doing this butt-smacking thing? Even on the football field and the basketball court. She rubbed the sore spot.

She re-entered the tent and exited with her make-up bag. He turned the burner on the butane cook stove to low, snatched his shave kit from the bed of his truck, and they set off for the restrooms, Hans on their heels. What she wouldn't give for a shower.

Inside the men's restroom, Lonan quickly took care of his morning ablutions and went to wait for Madison.

She didn't dawdle, he had to give her that. No sooner had he turned the corner than she appeared, looking fresh and younger than her twenty-six years, the big dog at her side. At his truck, they draped their towels over the edge to dry and stowed their toiletries.

The coffee was perking steadily, so he removed it from the burner to allow the grounds to settle. While he fried bacon and eggs, Madison made sandwiches for their lunch. By the time the sun was above the butte, they were ready to go.

"Is it all right to leave our stuff here?" She glanced back toward the tent.

He followed her gaze. "I doubt anyone will bother things. You do have your locket on, right?"

Hand protectively on the necklace beneath her T-shirt, she nodded.

His backpack held their jackets, water, a first aid kit, and sunscreen. Madison had a long sleeve shirt tied around her waist, and her hat hung by the rawhide tie between her shoulder blades.

Joe was right on time. Lonan saw his truck stirring up dust as it approached and stopped. Grinning, Joe tipped his hat at Madison. "Morning, Mrs. Stone."

Lonan noticed the blush on her cheeks, but she returned his greeting. He opened the door for Hans, and the shepherd joined Joe on the front seat. "Thanks for letting him stay. Didn't hear a thing last night." Except for some of the ancient people celebrating, but he didn't dare voice his thought. Joe would understand, but he wasn't sure about Madison.

"No problem. I'll have him back tonight." He cocked his head. "We've got a litter of pups that'll be ready to wean in six weeks. You still want one?"

"You bet. I'll be over as soon as possible to pick mine out."

Joe nodded and drove off.

They settled into the truck and he eased out onto the narrow camp road. It circled around to where it joined a paved road leading to the visitors' center.

The morning was cool, the air fresh. While he drove, Madison flipped through her notebook, reviewing her research notes and drawings. She looked up. "Do you think, if we have time, we could go see the ancient staircase?"

"Sure, I don't see why not." It was the only way to reach Pueblo Alto, believed to be the 'house of the great chief' because of its location atop a tall mesa. "You know we can't climb the stairs. They're too fragile."

She tilted her head and queried. "But, there are pictures of the pueblo, right?"

"Yes, there are plenty. The bookstore sells postcards of every pueblo and several books with great photos of all the sites in the park, with documented facts about each. One of them would be more complete than what you'd be able to get with your own camera."

She smiled. "And since I'm a book hound..."

"I figured you appreciated them. I'm rather fond of them myself."

"What do you like to read?"

"History, some of the classics, and I love a good western."

"I can see you reading a western. I have to admit, I like a steamy romance on occasion."

They pulled into the parking lot of the visitors' center and as soon as he killed the motor, she unbuckled, and reached for her door. He caught her hand. "Wait for me to come around."

He put his arm around her shoulders and bent down to kiss her forehead. "Remember now, we're newly in love. Act the part." He studied her fading bruise. "It's almost healed."

She touched it gingerly, and then nodded in agreement.

They reached the door and Lonan knocked to catch the attention of one of the guards, an older gentleman in freshly pressed park uniform. "Morning, folks. Come on in. Lonan, Joe Redhawk called just a minute ago. Wants you to call him as soon as you arrive."

He turned to her. She waved. "Go ahead, I'll be fine here."

"I won't be long," he said as he entered the office.

While Madison waited, she surveyed the books on display in the window of the gift shop. She noticed several titles she'd like to have. One, a complete history of Chaco Canyon and the other, a book on gemstones found in the area.

Lonan appeared at her side. She pointed to the two volumes on the area. "I want to buy those before we leave here today."

"Good choices, both of them."

"What did Joe have to say?"

"They still haven't found Mrs. Santiago, but her little red car was found wedged in some thick brush about a mile from Sotol." He shook his head. "Her son identified the car. Found some blood on the steering wheel. It doesn't look good."

****

They spent several hours in the Chacoan Cultural Center, going through old documents, studying copies of cliff drawings, reading anything that made reference to the Skystone. Madison was amazed at how much research material they'd accumulated.

The big library table was strewn with papers. Her nose was in a book written in the late 1800s, with sketches and descriptions of picture graphs and petroglyphs discovered in the area. She'd made copies of as many as she could in her spiral notebook, with notes in the columns.

When she closed it, Lonan reached over and gently massaged her sore muscles.

She purred. "Oh, man, that feels good." She dropped her head to her crossed arms as he worked the kinks out of the tendons in her neck. He stood up and moved directly behind her and used both hands. She would melt and slide out of the chair any minute.

He stopped and leaned over to look at her drawings. "If you've made copies of everything you need, let's get out of here."

"I'm ready, but don't forget, I want to buy those books."

Lonan waited while she browsed the gift shop. She saw him talking to several people as they came in. Apparently he was well-liked by the men and women. He did cut a fine figure, standing there in his jeans and blue T-shirt. He looked up and their eyes met. She held up one finger and turned to pay the cashier.

On the way out, they stopped and put her books in Lonan's truck. Then he turned to her and studied her from head to toe, spending more time on her feet. She wore tennis shoes with socks, nothing like the hiking boots he wore. "You up for about a four-mile trek in this heat?"

Dang, that was a long way and if it wasn't 100 degrees already, it soon would be. Being a Texas girl, she should be able to withstand the heat, but she wasn't stupid. At 6,400 feet above sea level, the air was much thinner at this altitude and she'd tire faster.

"Of course I am."

"I thought we'd go to Fajada Butte this morning and save the stairs for this afternoon."

"What's to see at the butte?" She looked to the south, where the mount stood alone against the landscape.

"The primitive calenderical site is there. We can climb partway up and see some of the drawings."

Cool. She nodded. "I'd like that."

He tossed her a tube of sunscreen. "Put two coats of this on. Let it dry before reapplying."

"Yes, sir, Ranger. I know how to apply it." He must think she didn't know how to do anything. Either that or just plain bossy, or maybe he cared just a little for her welfare.

He directed his attention to finding something behind the front seat. He surfaced with two empty plastic bottles, each probably two liters in size. "I'll go fill these."

She was stunned. "You think we'll need that much water?"

He called over his shoulder, "I believe in always being prepared."

Well, made sense, but if she drank that much water... Surely they'd have restrooms along the way. She was not peeing behind a bush, if she could keep from it, that is.

When he returned, he slid both containers into his rucksack and put his arms through the straps. He adjusted them on his shoulders, removed his pistol, checked the rounds, and returned it to the small holster on his belt. "Let's go."

Fortunately, the ground was flat, so the two miles to get there wasn't bad. Climbing up the side was. She was gasping for air as they reached the drawings Lonan wanted her to see.

They were spiral in shape. She looked at him in question. "What is it?"

"It's a vortex, a whirling mass of energy. They're considered to be portals to other dimensions."

"You're kidding, right?" She'd never heard of ley lines, vortexes, and spin torsion fields until she'd read Texanna's diary. Of course, she wasn't part of the scientific community, but...she thought she'd at least have seen something about them on the Discovery or Learning channels she enjoyed watching.

With his head, he motioned to the crest. "There is a tree on top that is twisted due to these forces. And, believe it or not, vortexes are very common in Arizona." It was an interesting concept—gateways to other realms—and creepy.

The trip back to the visitors' center didn't seem to take as long. Madison was grateful to see the restrooms near the parking area.

After they'd washed up, Lonan lowered the tailgate of the truck and took their lunches from the ice chest. She hoisted her rear up to the truck bed and sat crosslegged while they ate. He hopped in and leaned against the fender weld, and devoured two sandwiches in the time it took her to finish off one.

The parking lot teemed with people. Madison found it interesting to watch and took note of their differences. Old men in Hawaiian shirts accompanied ladies dressed in polyester pant suits. Young couples with tattoos, body piercing, and purple hair mingled with families with chattering children. They were all here for one thing—to experience history firsthand.

Lonan said something. She looked up. "What? I'm sorry, my mind was elsewhere."

"I asked if you found anything interesting in your research."

"Yes, I did." She reached for her notebook and flipped through to the last page. "Look at this."

He lifted the pad and studied the drawing. "This appears to be a man with a lightning bolt striking his chest." His eyes met hers. "Do you think he's the one who first owned the Skystone?"

"I don't know, but turn back a page. See the woman, hair sticking out around her head?"

He nodded. "The witch woman."

"Yeah. Do you see what she has around her neck?"

He studied the drawing carefully. "You think it's the Skystone?"

She shrugged. "No one can know for sure, but it could be. And, if that's the case, she had the stone after the man."

Lonan scratched his chin. "I found several legends about the hag. One story showed up several times. Of course the telling was different with each." He handed her notebook back to her. "What it boiled down to is that some believed the man struck by lightning was the witch woman's son. He'd gotten the stone from his father, but used it for evil.

"And that she called on the sky god to send lightning to strike him down as punishment."

"Criminey. She killed her own son? That'd make anyone crazy."

He continued. "His mother was so angry and bitter, she wouldn't allow his spirit to be led to the afterlife...she wanted him to suffer for eternity.

"Guilt drove her crazy."

Chapter Twelve

Lonan picked up their trash and tossed it into the lidded receptacle just outside the parking lot. Madison hopped off the truck and dusted the seat of her jeans. She watched as he closed the tailgate and leaned against it, arms crossed over his chest. "Do you feel up to hiking to the stairway? Roundtrip, it's probably another four miles."

"I'm game." Hopefully her body was, too.

"Good. I'll get us more water."

"Lonan! Hey Stone, I need to talk to you." They turned to see a park employee jogging toward them.

"What's up, Jason?"

The young man was perhaps her age and his skin almost as fair. His nose was blistered and peeling.

"Need to talk to you." He glanced toward her and tipped his hat. "Sorry ma'am, but I need to speak to him in private."

Lonan excused himself and they moved out of her hearing range.

"What's going on?" Lonan was afraid it wasn't something good, or Madison would have been able to listen in.

Breathless, Jason said, "Joe Redhawk called a few minutes ago. It seems some kids stumbled on a body in that small thicket before you enter the Laguna Reservation."

Oh hell, not the old lady. "Male or female?" he asked, fearing the answer.

"A man, approximately thirty-five years old, about five feet, ten inches tall, and one-hundred-ninety pounds." He pushed his hat forward and rubbed his neck. "Odd, whoever killed him took all his clothes and identification. Then they left him laying there in his boxers and socks." He shook his head. "Poor man, I wouldn't want to be found like that.

"Lordy, but those kids are upset. All of 'em between the ages of ten or twelve. Ran home hollering at the top of their lungs. From what I hear, it took Joe thirty minutes to get the story out of them. He finally got the oldest one to show him the way."

Lonan nodded, thinking. They rarely had a crime like this. Usually, if someone was killed, everyone knew who did it because they'd been in a fight. "How was he killed?"

"Bullet right between the eyes, a clean shot. Won't know what type of weapon until the coroner digs the slug out."

"Does the chief want me back on duty?" He glanced toward Madison. He hoped not, as he didn't want her out on her own.

"Naw, he just wanted you to be in the loop, on the lookout, in case someone got in the park with a weapon. Not that they think that'll happen. He's taking extra precautions and brought in a firearms canine team to examine every car coming on the premises."

He patted Lonan on the shoulder. "Now, don't you worry about a thing. They've got a squad over there taking tire impressions and such right now."

"Do they have any idea when he was killed?"

"Most likely last night sometime." Jason scratched his chin and glanced toward Madison. "Is it true you and that pretty lady got married?"

"Yep, sure is."

Jason stuck out his hand. "Well, congratulations, Lonan. Heard it was one of those 'love at first sight' experiences. Is that true?"

Lonan grinned while shaking his hand, his gaze on Madison. "Yeah, that's about the size of it." He didn't believe in love at first sight any more than he did the man in the moon. But, if it explained their sudden marriage, he'd go along with the idea.

"Thanks for bringing me the chief's message, Jason. I'll be on the alert." He waved and walked back toward Madison.

What the hell was going on around here? They'd never had any crime to speak of at the park. Oh, on occasion they had illegal hunting or damage to park property, but no suspicious deaths. And now, it was all around them. He didn't think it had anything to do with the attack on Madison, but you never knew. That it happened outside the park and that far away was a good sign.

Brow furrowed, she watched as he approached. "Everything all right?"

"Group of kids found a body over by the Laguna Reservation. A man shot through the head." He hesitated to tell her they'd taken his clothes, not that it really mattered.

Hand over her mouth, she gasped. "Oh, my God. That's terrible." She reached for his arm, and squeezed. "Do they know who did it?"

"No, they don't even know the victim's name. Nothing of his to identify him and no vehicle nearby, but they'll know more in a few days."

"Oh, no. Do you think the murder might somehow be connected to Mrs. Santiago too, that the same person murdered them both? Or, if alive, she could be wandering around in the wilderness, unable to find her way to help."

"Let's don't speculate. She may be just fine, holed up somewhere safe and sound. The two situations most likely aren't related." He thought they could be, but saw no reason to worry her.

Hopefully, Mrs. Santiago would turn up with a minor injury of some kind. But, from Jason's description, someone had attempted to conceal the car. Had she hidden it, or had her son, Luis? Could one of them be the person they were trying to find? Worse yet, did they have a killer loose in the canyon area?

"Now, don't let this spoil your enjoyment of this afternoon."

"I'll try."

As they walked, Madison tried to put Mrs. Santiago from her mind, but it wasn't easy. She kept thinking about that little old lady out in the heat somewhere or worse, laying wounded or dead, miles from help. She'd seemed so sweet in the museum shop, and so helpful.

About a quarter mile down, the trail split in two directions. They took the one that ran along Chaco Wash at the base of the north mesa. The canyon was wide, and down the center small trees and thickets followed the line of water. Due to the dry summer, very little water was visible. In the time of the Anasazi, it was never a major source of water for their crops. They'd had an intricate irrigation system that caught rainwater that ran off the rocks in the summer, and moisture from melting snow in the winter. Dams would be used to control the direction of the water flow.

Lonan stopped every thirty minutes or so and made her drink water. On the last stop, he took her arm and examined her skin. "You're getting a little sunburnt." He took the tube out of his pack and squeezed a good portion into his hands. Slathering some on each arm, he rubbed it in and then added some to the exposed flesh around her neck. He even put some on her face. "Why don't you put on your long sleeve shirt?"

"Do I need it with all that sunscreen?"

"It's possible to burn through light cloth, so yes, I'd say you do."

Rather than argue, she pulled it on over her T-shirt. Perspiration trickled down between her breasts, but the shirt did help hold moisture next to her body, allowing the slight breeze to cool her. As they continued walking, her legs grew heavy and she stopped to stretch them. "How much further?"

He pointed and she followed the direction of his hand. "Five more minutes and we'll be there."

It didn't take them that long. Anxious to see the artwork, Madison gathered her strength and forged ahead. At the bottom, she covered her eyes and squinted, amazed at the twisting path leading to the top of the mesa. In places, there were gaps where the stone steps had broken away and rolled to the basin floor.

"I can't imagine having to go up that path very often." There was nothing to hold onto, making it dangerous to navigate. She shivered. "Guess they weren't afraid of heights."

"The cliffs were a way of life for them. Children learned at an early age to traverse their environment."

"What about the elderly?"

"Most likely, they didn't make the trip. For one thing, they wouldn't have the strength, and a broken bone back then could easily spell death."

He pointed to what appeared to be ruins. "This path leads to Pueblo Alto, supposedly the 'great chief's house.'"

She could see how it would be safe from people in the canyon, and the chief would have an excellent view in both directions. But if someone from the north attacked, he'd be extremely vulnerable.

"It's amazing to think that this stairway dates back to prehistoric times." She slipped her hand in his. "Thank you for bringing me."

"You're welcome." He removed his hat and wiped his brow. "Now, let's retrace our steps and climb up a little way to see the cliff art."

To reach the pictographs, they followed a well-worn trail to a large crevice in the mesa wall. There was enough sun for them to see clearly. Some were easily identifiable, others weren't. She had no clue as to what they represented. Madison continued to search, trying to find ones that she'd made copies of in her notebook. She'd about given up when she spotted what looked like a bolt of lightning.

Excitement took her breath. "Lonan, I think I've found something."

The drawing was low to the ground requiring her to bend over to see. Lonan directed his flashlight to the area, making the artwork show up better.

"Yes, I think you have." Squatting, his fingers traced what appeared to be a man, hand on his chest. Flashes radiated out from him indicating he'd been hit. They moved deeper into the crevice and found what they needed. Standing over a body, a woman, with her dark hair in braids, had something dark spewing from her mouth. "The curse," said Lonan.

A little ways further in, they found another depiction. This woman's appearance was similar to the one cursing, but she'd changed drastically. Her hair hung wild about her face, her dress was tattered and torn, and she clutched at what looked like a stone hanging from around her neck. Still, dark material flew from her mouth and formed a cloud above her. Madison felt goosebumps rise on her skin. "That is creepy."

"Yes, it is." He removed his backpack to get to her notebook. They both compared the witch woman on paper, to the one on the rock. "Can you make a copy of both of these while we're here?"

"Sure." It didn't take long, maybe fifteen

minutes for her to make the crude sketches. She glanced around. "Anything else you want a copy of?"

"I don't believe so. Let's sit down and rest for a minute, drink some water." They left the crevice and sat in the shade of a boulder that had probably rolled into the canyon centuries ago. The water was good, and she poured some on her shirt to cool her.

"Don't waste too much. You may want it before we return to camp."

He stood and repacked his knapsack. As he slipped his arms into the straps, she asked, "What all have you got in there anyway?"

They started down the incline, his hand gripping her upper arm to steady her. Loose gravel poured down the trail as they walked. "I've got enough food for two days, a first aid and snake bite kit, a thermal blanket, and matches. Even have some spare water."

"Do you have a lot of snakes out here?"

"We've got our share of rattlers. They try to stay away from the visitors, though. Main thing, don't go poking your hand in any holes in the rocks without checking it out first."

"I'll remember that." They reached the main path and started back toward the visitors' center. Her legs ached. No doubt they'd hurt even more tomorrow.

Lonan stopped her. "You've done real well. You're a regular trooper when it comes to hiking."

She liked the admiration she saw in his eyes, the sincerity of his smile. "Thank you, sir."

He pulled her into his arms. "You're welcome, ma'am." He cuddled her closer, kissed her temple, then her ear, and whispered. "My warrior woman with hair that shoots flames, I feel the need for the privacy of our tent." His words warmed her, heat like lava shot through her body. His lips traveled down her neck and with his teeth, he nipped her collarbone.

She jumped and giggled. "Stop it."

"Play along, Red. We're being watched." He lifted her off her feet, and arms around her like bands of steel, kissed her. His tongue dipped inside her mouth before she knew what he was doing.

She broke the kiss and hissed, "Put me down. We're making a public spectacle." Her face heated as a couple split and walked around them to grab hands again on the path.

His grin was wicked as he stroked her cheek. "I didn't mean to embarrass you."

She snorted. "Yeah, I bet."

Lord, she didn't know what to think about the man. One minute he was clowning, and the next as unbending as a nail. She left him smirking and took off down the trail.

He jogged to catch up with her. "Oh, now, don't be mad. I had to make it look good."

"I'm not mad."

"Good, 'cause there's nothing worse than a pouting woman."

"I do not sulk." Ugh, the man was infuriating.

He caught her by the pocket of her jeans. "Whoa, now. Slow down." She slapped his hand away.

"Just suppose I was able to arrange for you to get a bath—one complete with running water, soap, shampoo—the works?" He stood, hands on his hips, head cocked. "Would that make you happy?"

She stopped, her gaze calculating, trying to decide if this was a joke. Arms folded across her chest, she raised a brow and asked, "And how would you be able to do that? You said there weren't any shower facilities in the park."

"That's right, but there are at my house. It's just a twenty-minute drive from here." Her face lit up, but then she frowned. He held up both hands. "I'm not teasing." He seemed sincere. If he wasn't he'd sorely regret it. Finally, she decided he was telling the truth.

"Oh, I'd love a bath, a shower, a dip in the river. I'd even settle for a water hose—anything to cool off and get clean."

A flash of light flickered on Chacra Mesa at the south end of the canyon. Instinctively, Lonan dove for Madison, taking her with him to the ground as the report of a rifle echoed through the ravine. She shrieked, but he rolled and had them on their feet, running toward the line of trees near the water before she could make another sound. Two more gunshots echoed across the canyon. One hit a sandstone rock behind them, the other whizzed over their heads.

As soon as they hit the trees, he took Madison to the ground and dove for cover until they were completely under the foliage. Rocks bit into his back and he did his best to protect her by wrapping his arms and legs around her.

Madison hadn't made another sound. Terrified she was hurt, his heart stopped as he ran his hands over her body. "Are you hit, are you hit?"

Chapter Thirteen

She gasped. "I'm okay, not hurt."

"Thank God." Relief crashed over him like a wave. He couldn't go through this again. Iraq had taken his best friend and several good buddies. He held her close for a moment, then loosened his grip to remove the two-way radio at his belt.

"Dispatch, Stone here. Shots fired from Chacra Mesa into the canyon. They barely missed us, but we're okay."

"Lonan, Judy here. Chief Johnson and several others are on it. You are to stay put until you hear from us."

"Got it, Judy."

He pulled Madison along with him to a large boulder, propped himself against it, and wrapped his arms around her. Tremors shook her body. "I've got you, sweetheart, you're safe now." He kissed her forehead and stroked her hair. "Chief and several other rangers are at the site. Whoever it was is probably fleeing for their lives right now."

What the hell had he been thinking, bringing her out in the open like this? The whole situation didn't make a lick of sense. If the shooter had gotten them, how on earth did he expect to get down to the wash and take the necklace before help arrived? Obviously this person wasn't rational, and more dangerous than he'd first thought. If someone tried to jump Madison on the way to or from the restrooms, or in the visitors' center, it would have been more logical. He'd expected another attack like the one in the parking lot. Someone close, not from a distance.

She clutched his shirtfront. "Are you hurt?"

He grabbed her hand and held it still. "I'm fine." As long as she wasn't hurt...

"How'd you learn to haul ass like that?"

He chuckled. "Did I mention I was an Army Ranger for three years before college?" They were the worst years of his life. First Desert Storm, and then the time he spent in Somalia.

"Nope, guess we didn't get that far in our conversation." She shivered. "Thank you, Lonan. You saved my life. If you hadn't been here, I'd be bulletridden and dead by now."

The thought made the blood freeze in his veins. He hugged her to knock the chill from his heart. "Aw, now, don't sell yourself short. Remember, that badger fetish around your neck indicates you're a warrior. I bet you'd have done fine."

His radio squawked and he answered, "I'm here, Chief."

"You guys all right down there?" Tom's voice vibrated from the rattling of his SUV as it bounced over ruts. Lonan had been in one often enough to know.

"We're fine, just dirty and rattled."

"I'm coming down to pick you up."

"We'll be listening for you."

It wasn't more than ten minutes when they heard the roar of the vehicle and a horn honk. Lonan helped Madison to stand and they walked out of the brushy area to meet Chief Tom Johnson. Tom stood outside the truck, silent, and watched them approach. Lonan escorted Madison around to the front passenger door and held it open while she slid across the seat. When both he and the Chief got in, she was wedged in tightly between them. He put his arm around her shoulders so she could lean against him.

146

Chief eyed them both carefully, then his gaze settled on Madison. "Young woman, it looks like we're going to have to lock you up somewhere to keep you safe."

Her expression frantic, she shook her head. "No, that's really not necessary." She turned to him. "Is it, Lonan?"

The idea had merit, but it wouldn't be the answer to keeping her safe. They needed to know who in the area had an evil spirit residing in them. Then, they had to find a way to drive it out without harming its host body. He shook his head and squeezed her shoulder in reassurance.

"Chief, drop us at the campsite. I'll load our equipment and take Madison home with me."

"And then what? You plan to keep her under lock and key 'til this is over?"

"No, I thought this would draw the person out, but after today, we'll need to re-evaluate our plan." He couldn't tell the man he and Madison had to travel back in time to 1000 A.D. and talk to the famous witch woman to get this settled. The senior ranger would suspend him from duty and take Madison in for Joe Redhawk to watch. "Did you find anything of interest up there on Chacra Mesa? Some hint of who this might be?"

"Found tire tracks and a couple of .270 shell casings." Tom scratched his neck. "Odd thing is, the tire tracks appear to be the same as the tires on our vehicles."

Lonan couldn't help but stare. "You think one of our people could be involved in this?"

Tom shook his head. "Not likely, but whoever fired those shots might have been driving a park SUV. They've all got the jumbo tires with treads for this rough country. We're checking the whereabouts of all our trucks at that time."

Chief Johnson pulled to a stop in front of their

campsite. "I'll help you pack up so you can get her indoors."

"Appreciate it."

"No problem."

"She should be safe at my place. It's isolated and you can only get in one way—the front road."

They'd tossed the last of the gear in the truck bed. Chief Johnson stood on the driver's side, leaning against the door. "Just in case, I'll send someone to watch the road leading up to your house."

Ten minutes later, his pickup was loaded and they waved good-bye to the Chief. He hollered, "We'll keep you posted. You do the same."

****

Lordy, what a day. Madison stared at her grime-streaked face in the bathroom mirror. She'd never been this dirty in her entire life. Though her mother had allowed her and her sister to play outside and traipse through the field behind their house, she'd always managed to stay clean. It was her tomboy sister, Rosalie, who came home dust-caked. The girl never failed to fall in the creek or rip her jeans climbing a tree.

She smiled at the thought. And that rough girl grew up to be a fashion designer. Who'd have thought it? Of the two, Rosalie was the pretty one. Boys flocked to her like bees to honey, but not around Madison. They saw her as a friend, a confidant, someone to advise them and help them with their homework.

She jumped at the knock on the bathroom door. "You about through in there?"

Shoot, she'd not started. "Ten more minutes," she said, as she bent to turn on the water in the shower.

His mumble of "women," could be heard as he walked down the hall. He shouted, "If you're not out by then, I'm joining you."

"Oooh, promises, promises."

After washing and putting a cream rinse on her hair, she noticed her legs needed shaving. She was almost finished when the bathroom door opened and closed. The curtain was yanked aside and Lonan joined her in all his naked splendor. Oh, man, he was the picture of manhood. "Oh, did you come to get your legs shaved?"

He snorted. "Not hardly." He wiggled his eyebrows. "I came to taste your delicious flesh." He snarled and nibbled on the soft tissue of her shoulder.

She pushed him back and shook her finger. "No you don't. You joined me, so you have to suffer the consequences." Taking the soap, she worked the bar into a thick lather. "Turn around."

He complied without argument and she ran her hands over his muscled back and tight butt, marveling at how nicely he was formed. She soaped her hands again and knelt to wash his legs and feet. That done, she stood, took his shoulders, and turned him to face her.

"My, oh my." He was fully erect and magnificent. "We're going to have to take care of that, but let me wash you first."

She watched his face as she soaped his shoulders, arms, and chest. It was taut, jaw fixed. When she knelt to wash his abdomen, he growled and yanked her to her feet.

"You better be ready, woman." He lifted her to ride his hips, positioned himself and entered her.

Oh yeah, she was ready. She stayed ready for this man.

Twenty minutes later, they walked from the bathroom, she in her short robe, with wet hair curling around her head, Lonan with a towel wrapped around his middle.

By the time she was dressed and her hair tamed, Lonan was already in the kitchen, taking food from the refrigerator. "Do you like enchiladas?"

"Well, yeah. What respectable Texan doesn't?"

He grinned and tossed her a chunk of cheese. She caught it before it hit the floor. "Good. The grater is in the drawer by the refrigerator." She located the utensil while he spread waxed paper on the counter for her to use. "Use the whole thing. I like lots of cheese."

"Me too."

He arched a dark brow. "How about onion and jalapenos?"

"Of course."

"Green sauce or red?"

"Doesn't matter. I like both, so you decide."

She fixed a salad while he assembled the enchiladas and placed them in a lightly greased casserole dish. They worked quietly, moving around each other from time to time. Being busy was nice. It kept her from thinking and worrying about their situation.

They ate on the patio and washed their food down with ice cold bottles of beer. As the sun set, she curled up in his lap and enjoyed the view. The smell of enchiladas mingled with the pine scent of the pinon trees and junipers scattered down the cliff's edge. Sounds of nature filtered from the tree tops, the only part visible from where they sat. Madison often attended plays, and on occasion could afford a ticket to the opera. Tonight, nature's orchestra and panoramic show entertained her.

Lonan stood, set her on her feet, and started clearing the table. She helped him. "How come you don't have a dog? This seems like the perfect place for one to run and explore."

"It's too dangerous for the average dog. They love to chase and would end up getting crosswise with a mountain lion or other wild animal."

"Oh."

"One day soon, I plan to train one that'll hang close to the house. Joe has a litter that will be ready in about six weeks. I need to get over there and pick one out."

She pictured Lonan sitting outside, watching the sunset with a dog at his side, and a beer in his hand. Her imagination wandered into dangerous territory—sitting out here with him in the mornings, drinking coffee, watching the sunrise. Hmm, she'd like to—

"Madison."

"What?" Startled, she tried to cover the blush rising on her cheeks. "Sorry, I was daydreaming."

"I asked if you'd rather wash or dry."

"Wash, of course. I hate to dry. It's a pain waiting for someone who's a slow poke at washing."

When the kitchen was clean, she hung the dishrag across the sink divider. Lonan had been quiet since they'd come inside, and she felt awkward. "Is something bothering you?"

Expression serious, brow furrowed, he studied her face. His fingers traced the shape of the locket where it nestled between her breasts under her shirt. Need spiraled through her, again, and she struggled to brush it aside. "Tomorrow, we must go to Una Vida and try to travel back in time to confront the witch woman."

Unable to speak, she nodded.

He watched her eyes as his fingers continued to stroke. "This is a serious undertaking and I want you to be fully aware of the dangers involved." His hand moved to her cheek. "We could be hurt badly, killed, or be unable to get back to our time. Are you willing to risk that?"

Throat dry, she tried to swallow her fear and managed to squeak out a "yes."

"Are you sure? You have no idea what life would be like back then."

No, she didn't. But, if she didn't try, and a rogue spirit wiped the Anasazi history from the face of the Earth, she'd never be able to live with herself. "We don't have a choice."

He drew her into his arms and stroked her back. Head against his pounding heart, she reveled in the strength of his embrace and sucked in the scent of his body mixed with his aftershave. "You know I'll do everything in my power to protect you."

As I will you. "Yes, I do."

They made love and then lay spooned in the bed. Madison snuggled in the safety of Lonan's arms, one of his heavy legs thrown over hers in possession. Her hand was captured, fingers twined with his.

She sighed as he pulled her closer. She and Walter had never lain together like this and just enjoyed the closeness. Lord, sex with Walter had been nothing like what she'd experienced with Lonan. She'd always thought he was a good lover, but...

Lonan's lips nuzzled her neck, kissing that sensitive spot just under her ear. "Madison, I've not seen you taking any pills and I sure haven't found a patch anywhere, though Lord knows I've tried to learn every inch of you."

She giggled. "I get the shot every three months. It's easier that way."

"Do you have a boyfriend waiting for you back in Texas?"

Breath caught in her lungs, she slowly exhaled. "No, why do you ask?"

"You don't appear to be the type of woman to have numerous sexual partners, so why the pill?"

Should she tell him about Walter? What could it hurt? "I had an unplanned pregnancy while in graduate school."

She could feel the muscles in his body tense. "You have a child? Where is it now?"

"No. My boyfriend, actually the professor I had moved in with, didn't want a child. I think his words were 'I don't want a houseful of redheaded brats.'" She swallowed the lump in her throat. His words still hurt, though she despised Walter now. He was a weak, self-centered man who thought only about himself and his career.

"You had an abortion?" She could hear the condemnation in his voice.

"No, I'd never kill my child. Walter gave me five thousand dollars to get one. I took the money and figured to use it to help with expenses. Several weeks later, I miscarried."

He turned her in his arms and drew her closer. "Oh baby, I'm so sorry."

"A month or so afterward, I ran into Walter on campus. He stopped and said, 'I'm glad you took my advice and got rid of the baby.'" Her voice cracked, feelings still raw. "I went crazy and screamed out what had happened. He tried to quiet me as we were attracting attention, but I didn't care. He was embarrassed. People looked at him like the worm he was. I heard sometime later, that he'd been asked to resign. It was bad enough to be in a personal relationship with a student, but to have the situation aired on campus was the final straw."

"Oh, honey." Her tears dropped onto his chest and she wiped them away with her hand. He massaged her back while kissing her forehead. "The man was a fool for not recognizing the jewel he had in you. I'm sorry you lost the baby, but glad you've seen the last of the jerk. I'd like to get my hands on the wimpy bastard for just five minutes. It'd be a long time before he considered having sex again."

She giggled. "Would you really do that?"

"You bet, I would. In a heartbeat." He took the

corner of the sheet and dried her tears. "Is he the reason you think you're unattractive?"

"But I am. I'm pale as a ghost, skinny, have small boobs, and this hair."

He growled in her ear. "Let me tell you something, sweetheart. You are lovely inside and out. Yes, you're thin, but after a few children, you'll fill out. Your breasts are perfect, not all men like big ones. Your legs are long and exquisite, and your butt is the best looking one west of the Mississippi." He flipped her over and popped her lightly on the rear. "And I'm here to tell you, I'm an expert on posteriors. I'm an ass man."

Chapter Fourteen

They'd left his house shortly after breakfast, their quest heavy on Lonan's mind. He considered their options. If they made it back to the witch woman, she might not believe their tale—even if she took the time to listen. But, the evil one had to be present to be destroyed. How would they make that happen? It might require two trips, or possibly bringing the hag to the future.

Madison was quiet. Her elbow propped on the door frame, her head supported by her hand, she stared at the road through the front window. Today she'd put her hair up on top of her head, under her hat. Her grandmother's amber earrings swayed with the movement of the truck.

He liked them, they highlighted the sheen of her hair, and folklore credited amber, the fossilized resin of trees, as having healing powers, because when rubbed with a cloth, it developed static electricity. When worn with turquoise, it represented the sun in the sky. The color was beautiful with Madison's red hair, blue eyes, and fair skin.

They pulled into the visitors' center parking lot. It didn't open until nine a.m., so few cars were there. Madison opened the door and slid out of the vehicle. They would be traveling light with only water, jackets, energy bars, and their hats. Lonan had decided to carry a pocket revolver and had a knife inside his boot.

Lonan asked, "Do you have your binoculars?"

She patted her jacket pocket and nodded. He handed her one canteen and carried three looped over his neck and shoulder. "Okay, looks like we're ready to go."

"I can carry two. Don't baby me."

"All right." He removed one and fit it over her head and below her arm.

Behind him, she could see a park SUV pulling into the lot. She pointed. "Do you think it's someone who needs to see you?"

"Could be. Let's wait a minute."

The SUV pulled in beside them and an older woman in uniform got out. "Hi, folks. Where you headed so early in the morning?"

"We're hiking up to see the petroglyphs before it gets hot." He stuck out his hand. "I'm Lonan Stone. You must be my replacement." Madison hung back.

She smiled. "That I am. Gene Collins. Good to meet you." She turned to Madison. "And who is this?"

Confused, Madison stepped forward and offered her hand. "Hello, I'm Madison Evans...I mean Madison Stone." Lonan's replacement was a man.

As they shook hands, Madison took stock of the ill-fitting uniform. Then she looked into the beautiful blue eyes and noticed the red frames of her glasses. "Lonan..."

Before the word left her mouth, Rita Santiago had her pistol drawn and stuffed in her belly. She spoke to Lonan. "I'd suggest you not move a muscle, or I'll shoot her."

He lifted his hands. "I'm not moving. What is it you want? Take it and leave us alone."

She laughed, the sound low and evil. "Move around here beside the redhead." He did as she asked. Madison watched as his body tensed, waiting for a chance to jump the woman. "Now, dearie, take off the locket and hand it to me."

Careful not to reach for the locket, Madison asked, "Why do you want it? It's a family heirloom.

What value would it have for you?" As if she didn't know, but maybe if she could stall her, Lonan could get the gun.

Rita transformed before their eyes. Madison had never seen such evil. Her face looked like that of a skeleton, her mouth stretched completely across her face, exposing every rotten tooth in her head. The eyes turned from blue to black and scared the bejeebers out of her.

Her laugh was a high shriek that ended with an animalistic growl. Madison shivered and goosebumps popped out on her skin. "You know why, don't you?" She turned to Lonan. "You do, don't you now, Ranger?"

Voice calm, a monotone, he said, "You want the power it holds."

She cackled in delight. "Hooray! Right answer." She snickered. "And when combined with the mother stone and the third piece, I can destroy, take revenge on those who killed me and hid my ashes away for eternity." Rita, or whoever possessed her body, poked Madison again with the gun. "Now, hand it over."

Madison stood her ground. "I'm not wearing it today. It's back at Lonan's place."

The woman growled and slapped her. Madison stumbled back a step. Lonan started forward, but at Rita's snarl, stayed put. "Don't lie to me. It's under your shirt. Give it to me before I shoot you both and take if off your corpse."

Hand protecting the locket, she yelled, "No! It's mine."

"Madison!" His voice was low, commanding, cautious. "Give it to her. It's not worth your life."

"I'd listen to him if I were you." The eyes Madison once thought beautiful gleamed with madness. Hands trembling with anger, she lifted the locket from around her neck.

"Ah, lovely. Just as I remember it. Hand it over."

Rather than drop it in Rita's outstretched hand, Madison threw it toward Una Vida as far as she could.

Rita screamed. "You little bitch!" She shoved Madison in the direction of the pueblo and spat out, "Go get it."

It was just the opening Lonan needed. Within seconds, he'd wrestled the gun from Rita's hand and popped her on the jaw. She fell to the ground in a heap. Madison ran for the necklace. Just as she picked it up, Lonan grabbed her arm as he ran by and tugged her along with him. "Hurry, get to the petroglyphs before she wakes."

"Why couldn't you just cuff her...then we wouldn't have to...go through all this time-travel business?" She gasped for a breath of air as Lonan almost pulled her up the hill. "Joe could just throw her in the clinker." Lordy, the woman had killed a park ranger, shot him between the eyes. She was beyond dangerous.

"It wouldn't work, Madison. The spirit would find another body. This is the only way we can end it for good."

They were almost at the rock face. Lonan had barely broken a sweat, but she was huffing for air. When they reached the cliff drawings, the rising sun highlighted Una Vida below them. Rita was beginning to stir. He grabbed her hand. "If anything happens to me, if I get hurt, killed, or captured, you get back to this time. You hear me?"

Her throat clogged with emotion, but she managed to nod. His kiss surprised her. It was sweet, yet hungry and demanding. As suddenly as he'd embraced her, he released her. "You ready?"

"Yes."

He stood behind her and brought his right hand under her arm and up to clasp the locket. His forearm sealed her to his body. With his left arm around her waist, he positioned his hand to place on the drawings.

Madison struggled with panic. What if they got separated or worse, died?

"Come on, we've got to do this." He reached down and took her left hand and held it hovering over the petroglyphs. She covered his hand on the locket with hers and pressed her forearm against his.

A bullet whizzed between their heads, chipping the stone not two feet away. She flinched at the sound, and again as shards hit her in the face. Rita was coming up and there was no turning back.

Shaking, she managed to mumble, "Okay."

Hands side-by-side, they touched the cliff drawings when Lonan said, "Now!"

She felt a jolt. White light engulfed them, and they were knocked to the ground. Arms around each other, rocks biting them in the back and elsewhere, brush scratching exposed skin, they rolled down the cliff until a large rock halted their descent.

The air knocked from his lungs, Lonan took a deep breath. His lips were near Madison's ear. He whispered. "You okay, sweetheart?" He ached all over and most likely would have a collection of bruises by morning, but nothing serious. Her tender skin would be black and blue.

"Other than a few scrapes and a rock digging into my hip, I'm okay."

He adjusted their twined bodies. "That better?"

"Yeah. How on earth did we manage to keep our hats on during our descent down the hill?"

"Pure luck, I guess." He patted her on the butt. "Are you ready to peek over this rock and see what time period we're in?"

"Do I have a choice?"

"Not really." They sat up and peered over the

top. Yep, they were back in time, and the entire village stared up. Wide-eyed children stood within arms' reach of parents ready to hurry them off to safety if necessary. Madison had been right—they looked healthy and happy. He couldn't believe he was actually standing here over a thousand years in the past, looking down on Una Vida.

"We might as well stand up. We've been made." He helped her to her feet and dusted her off before shaking the dirt off his jeans and shirt.

A war whoop and cries filled the air as a group of warriors ran through the villagers and up the cliff side. Lonan thrust Madison behind him and stood ready to draw his knife if necessary. He'd only use the gun as a last resort. Twenty feet from them, the leader held up his hand and his party of braves stopped.

Lonan couldn't believe what he was seeing. Standing before him was his mirror image—hair, eyes, and face—all the same. The only difference was their height, which was no doubt the result of diet, modern medicine, and genetics. The warrior's hair was twisted into a bun at the base of his neck and held several feathers.

Madison hugged his back and hissed, "That's him, that's the warrior I dreamed about."

"Stay here. I'm going closer."

She clutched at his sleeve. "No, I'm going with you."

Through clenched jaws, he growled, "You will obey me in this. Do you understand me?"

Her answer was weak, but he caught the muted, "Yes."

His eyes never left the Indian as he walked down the cliff and stopped ten feet away. He slowly raised his hand and whipped the hat off his head.

The warrior cried out, stumbled back a step, and then held his ground. His braves muttered excitedly among themselves. He barked a warning and they shut up.

He looked Lonan up and down and asked in his language, "Who are you? Why do you invade our home?"

Lonan struggled with the dialect, but hoped his words said he needed to talk to the witch woman.

With his spear, the native gestured toward Madison and Lonan shook his head. Not turning his back, he ordered, "You are to stay where you are, Madison. If things don't go right, remember what you promised me."

"Lonan, please—"

"No. We are both safer with you up there where you can get to the petroglyphs if necessary."

He heard her muffled cry, but stiffened his back and walked down to meet his ancestors.

Madison stifled her sobs with her fist. *You don't have time to be hysterical. Get a grip and keep your eyes open. Lonan may need you.*

The warriors surrounded Lonan and, afraid for him, she started down the cliff.

Lonan shouted, "I said stay where you are."

She stopped in her tracks and tried to swallow her fear. No way would she go back without him. She'd stay as long as there was any chance of their quest being successful and Lonan was alive. *Stop buying trouble, Madison.* As yet, their situation was fine.

People made a path for them as they walked into the pit area. Voices were raised in what she assumed to be speculation and curiosity, and being superstitious, why he looked like their chief warrior.

Once in the circle, their fighters moved back to allow the Elders to approach. Madison could see they were talking, but couldn't hear and it sounded liked gibberish. Suddenly, she heard Lonan shout. There was a struggle and his arms were grabbed from behind and tied.

Panic inched up her spine. She had to do something. He wasn't supposed to face this task alone. It was hers and he was her protector. Lonan struggled and kicked out with his feet knocking several people down. The badger fetish at the pulse point of her neck grew warm, reminding her the figure represented fierceness.

Someone swung their war club, hitting Lonan on the head. He fell like a tree. Stunned, she stared down in horror. *Oh, God. What am I going to do? Please help me.*

Lonan's lookalike strode toward the path that led up the cliff. Rage consumed her, her scream of fury and panic echoed off the canyon walls. She knocked her hat off, removed the clip holding her hair up, and using her fingers scrubbed the mass into a wild bird's nest. The sun was behind her, so no doubt her head looked on fire.

At her scream, the warrior stopped. Hat hanging against her back, she started down the cliff, picking up speed until like an angry bull she met the man head-on, her momentum knocking him on his butt. She went down with him, but was on her feet, running before he could recover.

Yelling and chanting like the crazy witch woman she'd become, she snarled and snapped at people in her way. No one challenged her, but let her pass, mouths agape. She dropped beside Lonan, pulled the large knife from the scabbard in his boot and cut the bonds on his wrist. His head wound wasn't bad but bleeding profusely. She had nothing with which to staunch the blood. Afraid to turn her back on her audience for more than a second, she stood and strode around him, swinging the big knife warningly, growling at anyone rash enough to test her. If they did, she knew without a doubt she'd kill to protect Lonan.

Her heart beat so hard, she thought it would explode. *Keep your cool, Madison.* She heard Lonan moaning, but was afraid to look at him for fear someone would jump her.

"Lonan, wake up, please wake up." A few warriors stepped forward, but her scream stopped them. To keep them on their toes, she made jabbing movements with the knife, sending them staggering back.

"Good, Lord...Madison...is that you making that racket?"

Out of the corner of her eye, she saw him pushing himself to his feet. "They think I'm crazy. I couldn't let them tie me up, too."

He walked up behind her. "Let me have the knife now."

"No, not until they understand you're my man and I'll not let anyone hurt you." She lowered her voice. "I think they know who I am."

Lonan said something in their native tongue. The warrior scowled and shook his head.

"What'd you say?"

"I said you are my woman. Your sweetheart doesn't like the idea."

She snorted, grabbed his shirt front, and yanked several times shouting, "Mine, mine!" Then slapped herself on the chest and then him. "His, his!"

"Settle down, now. I think he got your message." His look-alike's scowl told her he didn't much like the idea.

All of a sudden, her legs felt weak. "I think I may faint." She handed the knife over.

"Don't you dare." He put his free arm around her waist. "Lean on me. Do a bit of that moaning and carrying on to distract yourself."

She started.

"Quietly, please."

She lowered her voice so he could talk over her.

One of the Elders said something and motioned for them to follow him into his apartment. Lonan's look-alike joined them.

The witch woman sat on a cushion inside, waiting for them. She pointed at Madison's wild hair with a bony finger and cackled like a loon.

Chapter Fifteen

The room was on the first level of the apartment. One window allowed light to brighten the area well enough to see. People arranged themselves in rows against the walls. The small space filled with racket. At the witch woman's mad laughter, Madison added her version of a lunatic's serenade.

Lonan grabbed her arm. "Stop it. You've made your point."

She snorted. "Tell her to shut up."

He didn't have to because one of the Elders barked an order and waved at the door. The hag closed her mouth, but continued to scowl at them.

More people filed into the room and the chief signaled for them to sit down. After the shuffling of feet as they settled, the room grew quiet. Everyone's gazes were on them, waiting. Finally the Elder in the scarlet feather robe spoke. Following his dialect was difficult, but Lonan managed to decipher enough to understand what he said.

"I am Red Bird, Chief Elder of our tribe." He motioned to the man on his right. "This is Deer Stalker, our Medicine Woman is Talking Bird.

Black eyes studied them, his attention more on Lonan than Madison. "Who are you? Why have you come?" He gestured to Madison. "We knew Hair of Flame would return, but did not expect her to arrive with a mate."

At this comment, the warrior yelled, "I do not believe this man. We will fight to determine who shall be her mate."

Lonan stood, removed his knife, and pointed it at his lookalike. "I will kill any man who touches my wife."

The Indian jumped into the circle, ready to meet his challenge. Madison screamed, but several braves stepped forward to restrain the warrior.

Red Bird placed himself between them. "Please forgive Gold Eagle. He cares for Hair of Flame and hoped she would return to become his woman." He nodded and waved them back to their places.

Across the circle, Lonan nodded at Gold Eagle. "The gods made that decision and chose me. I am Lonan Stone, also called Skystone."

Gasps and mutterings echoed around the room, but Lonan continued. "We are from the future, a time when the Anasazi are no more."

Wails and yells of anger accompanied Gold Eagle's shout. "You lie! The people will never leave the canyon."

The Elder held up his hand. Gradually, the outcries died down. He nodded to Lonan to continue.

"Many moons from now, water will be scarce. Your people will suffer from lack of food. To keep from starving, you will leave this canyon to join other pueblo tribes where you can grow food and find game to feed your children."

"We have been warned of this time by the Spirits."

"Even though you leave, your pueblos will linger. All the tribes in this area will revere this canyon, called Chaco Canyon in our time." Every eye in the room was on him. He marveled that he'd been given the honor to make this trip and speak to the Anasazi. He couldn't prevent the huskiness in his voice. "The gods have sent us here to fulfill a prophecy, to protect your cliff drawings, your apartment houses, roads, and the methods you use to grow crops. The children of our people in the future can come here to learn about their ancestors, to stare in wonder at the beautiful creation left for all eternity."

Murmurings rushed around the room. Their first reaction had been fear, but pride eased the sting from the bad news. Being remembered for all time was a great honor to their people.

"If we fail in our quest, the mark the Anasazi left upon the Earth for their future generations will be destroyed. Your descendants will not be able to look upon the remains of the apartment houses and listen for the sounds of the flute on the wind. Many will mourn the loss."

Gold Eagle snorted. "How can you know such a thing?"

Lonan shrugged. He'd like to toss this troublemaker from the room. Even now, Gold Eagle's gaze drifted to Madison. He tamped down his anger. "Listen to our story. Then you will have to decide for yourselves if we speak the truth and if you will help us." He turned to the witch woman. "The evil spirit of your son has escaped his prison. He seeks revenge on his mother and her people."

Talking Bird shrieked, "Nukpana." They had a name for the spirit at last. How appropriate—in the Hopi language it was the name for evil.

Madison couldn't understand a word Lonan or the Elders said, but when the witch woman keened and pounded her chest, Madison had a good idea Lonan had told her about her son. Other women of the clan gathered around, trying to comfort the wailing woman, but she shook them off.

Lonan's voice broke through her cries. The hag grew quiet and listened. Her eyes grew round, and she clutched the Skystone in her fist.

As Lonan talked, the Elders had many questions. When the sun rose in the sky, women brought in food and water. Madison wished she could understand their words, but it just sounded like gibberish to her. Occasionally Lonan would translate for her. Runners were being sent to the other pueblos to seek the aid of other Elders and shaman.

Finally, the Chief Elder stood to make a short speech. Lonan rose and helped Madison to stand. They followed a woman from the apartment, and she led them to an area where they could sleep.

Before they went inside, she turned to Lonan. "I need to go to the bathroom."

He spoke softly to the Anasazi woman. She nodded, smiled, and led Madison to what she assumed was the latrine area. At the irrigation trench close by, she washed her hands and face.

Madison had to climb up one ladder and down another to get inside the apartment they'd been assigned. Lonan waited for her. As soon as her feet touched the ground, the ladder was removed from the opening.

Her stomach knotted in panic. "We're prisoners in here."

He embraced her. "We'll be fine. They don't intend to harm us. It's probably for our own safety. I wouldn't be surprised if they hadn't posted a guard to protect me from Gold Eagle." He pulled back and grinned. "Your warrior is besotted with you."

She shoved him away. "Well, the feeling isn't mutual."

"Are you sure, Hair of Flame?" His brow furrowed as he waited for her answer.

"Of course I am." Surely he was teasing, but the serious expression on his face didn't look amused. She stepped into his arms and laid her head on his chest. "Do you think we're in for the night?" As he held her close, she marveled at how quickly she'd come to depend on this man, how his closeness was such a comfort. It was scary. Their relationship was nothing permanent. It would be hard to let him go.

Was she falling in love with Lonan? She had no idea how he felt about her. No, that wasn't true. That he cared was evident in his actions when around her. He was the only thing that kept her sane right now. Without his strength, she'd never have been able to even contemplate this quest. She snuggled against his shoulder, enjoying the sensations his hands on her hips evoked.

"No, we'll be called at sunset. Runners have been dispatched to the other pueblos to seek aid. The more magic they can garner, the greater their chances of harnessing the evil one."

He led her to the pallet. "Lie down and try to rest. Our night will be a long one." He stretched out beside her. In a quick, deft movement, he lifted her tee shirt over her head.

"What are you doing?" Rather than answer, he unzipped her jeans and started tugging them off. He caught her shoes to slip them off her feet.

Giggling, she shrieked, "Stop it!" She kicked out, trying to get loose. "Someone could see from that hole in the roof."

"It's too hot in here for all these clothes." He stood and quickly shucked out of his boots, jeans and shirt. Judging from the bulge in his jockey shorts, his mind wasn't on sleeping.

Looking directly at the evidence of his arousal, she shook her head. "Oh, no, it's not going to happen, mister." She tried to wiggle back into her top, but he jerked it from her grasp. It joined the pile of clothes tossed in a heap on the floor. Seconds later, his underwear topped the mound.

He kneeled in front of her in all his naked magnificence. Her heart beat double time. Already her skin tingled, anticipating his touch. "I want you, Madison." He covered her body with his, his weight on his forearms. His lips found the sensitive spot under her ear.

She moaned. "But, someone could see us," or even worse, "*Hear* us."

He chuckled. "I assure you, sweetheart, they couldn't care less what we're doing." Before she could protest further, her bra was tossed aside.

"Are you sure?" The hole in the ceiling made her very uncomfortable. She figured someone would need a ladder to peek in the window.

"Sex is as natural to these people as breathing. They show no embarrassment at their lack of clothing, do they? Why would lovemaking shock them?" He had a point. His lips covered one breast, his tongue swirling around the crest. "You do want me, don't you?"

She arched into his touch, moaning, "You know I do, you devil." The desire he evoked in her was a constant reminder their relationship wasn't permanent.

He raised his head, his lips tilted in a slight grin, but his eyes held tenderness. "Ah, my Hair of Flame, I'll never get enough of you." He reached down to tug on her panties. They both scrambled to get them down and off her feet.

Lonan lay between her thighs, his forearms bearing his weight. With his knuckles, he stroked her cheek. Her hands caressed his strong back, cupped his tight buttocks, amazed that the skin that covered those muscles was smooth to her touch. If only she could read his mind as he looked into her eyes, loved her skin, and touched her soul. *Oh Skystone, how will I bear leaving you?*

Remembering the hole in the ceiling, she tensed and glanced up. "We're alone, love," he whispered against her hair.

Love, he called her *love.* His lips moved down her neck, then back up to take her mouth in a scorching kiss. Joy? Oh yes, this heat they shared filled her not only with pleasure, but happiness and contentment. He'd learned her body so quickly, the places that made her tremble, her breath hitch.

Her body quivered with need. He kissed her, their tongues twining, tasting, loving. Breaking the kiss, their gazes locked and held, communicating his desire for her. Her throat tightened with emotion. It took all her willpower to keep the words, *I love you,* from tumbling from her mouth. Then he slowly entered her and stilled. Heels on his back, she lifted her pelvis to take him deeper.

They moved as one, giving and taking, striving to pleasure the other and obtain release. As the tension built, her mind registered nothing beyond the screaming of her nerves, the pulsing of her muscles, and the feel of this man inside her, touching not only her body, but also her heart.

She was there, her body shattered, jerking with the force of her orgasm. Lonan captured her mouth, muffling her cries. The aftershocks continued, rolling through her, the pleasure almost painful. Face buried in the side of her neck, he thrust once more, and joined her. She grasped his buttocks and held him closer as his climax shook his large frame. His body shuddered with pleasure as the contractions continued. When he raised his head, his lips found hers in a kiss so tender, Madison felt moisture gather in her eyes.

Rolling to his back, he took her with him, their bodies still joined. They were slick with perspiration, their breathing ragged. She lay with her head on his chest, listening to the loud thump of his heart. His fingers trailed over her back, thighs, and buttocks, stroking, making goosebumps rise on her flesh.

She giggled and shivered. "That tickles."

His palms replaced his fingers and warmed her now chilled body. He rolled to his side and threw one leg over both of hers, his arms pulling her as close as she could fit. It was a hold of possession, one Madison would never forget.

Lonan lay facing Madison deep in slumber. She lay on her side, her hand tucked under her cheek. Brown lashes, darker than what he figured was common on true redheads, brushed against her pale skin. Her eyebrows were the same color, full and well shaped. He smiled at the soft snore that escaped from her slightly open mouth.

Their lovemaking rocked his intention to keep her out of his heart. But their joining was more than mere sex, it was a deep connection that touched his soul.

Afterward, while holding her close, the satisfaction, the peace, the continued longing was beyond his experience. He'd had his share of women, some he'd cared deeply about. The sex was enjoyable, as was their friendship, but never had the thought of losing one of them filled him with panic.

He reached out and brushed his knuckles down Madison's soft cheek. She smiled, and without waking, turned and planted a quick kiss on his fingers. If Madison didn't want to make their marriage permanent, her leaving would hurt like hell.

Get it out of your head, Lonan. Now isn't the time to worry about your feelings.

Right now there were more important issues to ponder.

He eased from the pallet and sat cross-legged on the hard stone floor. He'd tried to sleep, but couldn't relax for thinking about what they faced tonight and his worry that Madison might be hurt. He didn't doubt her courage. This morning, she'd more than proved she deserved to wear the Badger Fetish. Leotie had been accurate in her assessment of Hair of Flame.

The sound of footsteps on the roof broke his

reverie. Grinning, he conceded Madison had been right, that they should get dressed. She'd have his hide if someone saw her naked.

The ladder slid down from the hole above. He climbed up to find a young warrior. With his hand he motioned, and Lonan followed him to the ground.

If he hadn't seen the Skystone around her neck, Lonan wouldn't have recognized Talking Bird. Her body was clean, as was her freshly braided hair. She looked twenty years younger. Her posture was erect and regal.

He must have been gaping because she chuckled. "Skystone not know Talking Bird?" He shook his head and she laughed hysterically. "I trick my people." Her expression sobered. "Talking Bird pretend to be crazy. Better than stares of pity."

Lonan understood her reasoning. With her pretense of insanity, she'd become isolated, made life easier for herself.

"Come, Skystone, let us find a place to talk. I would know more of your story."

They walked toward Fajada Butte. The sun beat down on them, and he could see heat waves rising off the rocks. Talking Bird didn't seem to be bothered by the heat, but Lonan put his hat on to shield his face. At a large bush of some kind, they sat in what little shade it offered.

"How you know evil spirit you seek my son?"

"From the cliff drawings left by your people." He pointed to her turquoise. "Your stone is shown in these pictures. In one, a man is wearing it, and he is struck in the chest by lightning."

She covered her face with her hands and keening, rocked back and forth. Her obvious grief stopped as quickly as it began. Head held proudly, she drew her fist against her breast. "Spirit Talkers bring lightning to stop evil."

"Yes, in another drawing, we see a woman

calling down the lightning, and another with a wild haired woman wearing the stone around her neck." He held out his hand. "May I see the Skystone?"

She removed it from around her neck and placed it in his open palm. His skin tingled with the energy encased inside the turquoise. It was beautiful, smooth and polished from much handling.

He examined the break. "This piece is very powerful, but it is missing two smaller pieces. Its power is still strong, but if reunited with the other two pieces, its strength will be much greater."

The grooves around her mouth and eyes deepened as he spoke. "Many years ago, when the stone broke, a man carried one of the twins far away to keep it safe until needed. This man was Hair of Flame's ancestor."

She nodded. "Yes, the gods told me not to mourn. The piece would return to the people one day."

"The minute Hair of Flame inherited the locket holding the twin, she started having dreams of you, Gold Eagle, and the Elders."

"Ah, Gold Eagle, as well as I and several others, have seen her dreams played out in the skies." Her shoulders sagged. "We did not understand them until now."

****

Madison woke to find Lonan gone. She lay still and looked around the stone apartment, the mat the only furnishing in the room. Evidently this one was used for guests—or prisoners. Considering it was probably $110°$ outside, it was a great deal cooler inside. Not enough to keep her from sweating, but definitely not sweltering.

She sat up. Using her hands, she tried to tame her hair into some semblance of normalcy. Her clip was attached to the rawhide of her hat, so she swept as much of her mane as possible on top of her head.

174

The clasp held it in place.

Where was Lonan? She stood and walked to the one window to look out. In the distance, Lonan sat with a woman. What could they be talking about? From so far, she couldn't tell her age. A little stab of jealousy poked her, making her uncomfortable. It reinforced how precarious their situation was. A short-term marriage, one made only to achieve a mission. Sure, the sex was good—good? Heck, it was wonderful. In just a few short days, she'd become addicted to the man. One touch, and she ached for more of his caresses, but soon she'd return to Texas to find a teaching job. Would she think of him every day and wish things could have been different between them?

She'd been so involved with her thoughts she'd not noticed Lonan and the woman leave the space beneath the small tree. At the scrape of the ladder being lowered, she whirled to see him descending.

He smiled. "Did you have a good nap?"

"Yes."

Gripping her chin, he titled her face up to receive his kiss. "I'm glad. You'll be grateful tonight while on the butte."

"What about you? Did you sleep any?"

"No, Talking Bird came for me. We had a long visit." He took her hand and led her to the mat. "Sit. We need to talk."

"The woman you sat with was Talking Bird? I thought it was a younger woman."

"It seems she's been playing the role of crazy witch since her son's death. It was her way of saving face, not having to suffer the pity or rebuke of her people."

Madison could understand her feelings. It must have been hard to remain here.

Lonan appeared to be deep in thought. Brow furrowed, the lines around his mouth and eyes had deepened. They sat cross-legged, facing each other. She reached out to touch his knee.

"What is it? Did you learn something bad?"

He handed her a small pottery bottle about five inches tall, with a stopper. It was beautifully made. "It's lovely. Did Talking Bird give it to you?"

"Yes, it is for Nukpana's evil spirit. If you can, you're to force him into the jug and plug it quickly."

"Surely you jest." When he didn't respond, the bottom fell out of her stomach. "Did she tell you how I'm supposed to make this happen?"

"No, just that you'd be shown the way."

She could only stare at him, wondering how the hell she'd come to this point. Why couldn't she wake up and this all be a bad dream? If that happened, she'd never have met Lonan. *God, please help me through this.*

He took her hand, and with his thumb, rubbed the sensitive pad on her palm. "Talking Bird said the evil one—Nukpana—will attack you, try to invade your body."

"But why? It's Talking Bird...the other medicine people who have the power, who're able to force him from Rita's body."

"No, sweetheart. It's you."

She shook her head. No, she didn't want to hear this. Nor did she like the despair and worry etched into his face. His mouth was taut, his brow furrowed.

"You, because you are Hair of Flame, you have one of the stones, and have thwarted him several times. You've angered him. And the gods chose you to destroy him." He dropped his forehead to hers.

When he spoke again, his voice broke. "If he enters your body, he'll become more powerful, commit greater evil."

"But...but she has the larger stone. It's more powerful."

He raised his head, his expression unchanged. "Oh, God."

She jerked her hands from his grasp to cover her face. Lilly and Leotie had both told her this, but until now, it'd not sunk in thoroughly. Goosebumps broke out on her skin and she trembled.

Lonan scooted around so he could pull her into his arms. His hands rubbed her arms, warming her as he talked. "Because of three things, I know you'll be successful. One, the gods chose you before you were born. You have one of the twins. And three, with your magic combined with that of Talking Bird and the other ancient Spirit Talkers, evil will be defeated."

Arms around her shoulders, he squeezed reassuringly. "The gods wouldn't have chosen you if they didn't have faith in your ability to succeed."

She knew he firmly believed his words, but she hadn't grown up with the same view of life—of Spirit Talkers, magical stones, and more than one God. But she hadn't grown up believing in time travel, either. If she could pass through time, why couldn't the magic of these people work?

These people? They were her people, too. Though her blood tie was small, she couldn't deny the pulse in her veins and the call of her heart when she was with them.

His lips were against her hair, his voice calmer than the tenseness she felt in his muscles. "I'll be beside you every minute."

His words of reassurance broke through her fears, but did little to allay them. The gods had shown her nothing, she didn't have a clue what to expect, or what to do. "But, I—"

"Trust your inner instincts. Listen to that voice inside your head."

She buried her face in his shoulder, seeking the comfort she knew he couldn't give. *What voice?*

Chapter Sixteen

With Lonan's arm around Madison's shoulders, they stood and watched as the shamans from the other pueblos arrived, each with several warriors in attendance. As the men talked, several shoved their elaborately decorated capes back over their shoulders. They had to be roasting. Sweat dripped from his own forehead, his shirt wet with perspiration.

He watched Madison stare at the men dressed in full ceremonial regalia, faces serious, brows furrowed with concern. Their robes were decorated with feathers or animal fur. Some had primitive beads of turquoise and coral worked in the stitching. Their hair, pulled back in a bun, held a feather or two. It was a switch from seeing them in only loincloths.

Stalking Deer joined the tight group of men. Lonan heard him say, "Flame and guardian." As the Elder talked, all eyes turned toward them, mostly on Madison. She was obviously the topic of their discussion.

"Why are they looking at me like that?" As a group, they started walking in their direction.

He held her steady as they approached. "Stay calm, they are curious about you."

"Easy for you to say." Though she trembled some, she held her ground, and as one by one, they touched her hair and examined the stone in her locket.

Deer Stalker called to Talking Bird, waving her over. As she approached, she bore herself with proud dignity. Lonan grinned at the stunned expression on Madison's face.

"I can't believe that's Talking Bird. Her transformation is amazing." He had to admit, she looked regal with her hair in two lengthy braids. The cloak she wore trailed in the dirt and though old, it wasn't as shabby as the ones the other Shaman wore.

Talking Bird inched closer to Madison while the Elders compared her piece of turquoise with the Skystone. He noticed Madison watched the Indian woman closely, evidently expecting more of her venom, but the older woman's animosity toward her seemed to have disappeared. She even smiled, giving them all an ample view of her rotting teeth.

Madison smiled in return, but quickly turned her head and mouthed, "Her breath doesn't smell any better than before."

Before he could respond, the Elders moved away, then turned their attention to him. They spoke softly and motioned between him and Gold Eagle.

"Gold Eagle wants Hair of Flame for mate." Stalking Deer grinned. "Skystone challenge him with knife. He not give up Hair of Flame."

The men muttered and nodded their understanding.

Gold Eagle sent him a look of fury and disappeared into one of the apartments. Lonan didn't blame the man, his frustration was great, as was his loss of face.

They drew close again and studied Lonan's clothes and all the equipment on him. He kept his pistol hidden and showed them several items from his pack. Of great interest was his canteen.

"To carry water." He opened it and took a drink.

Chief Running Deer took it and at the irrigation canal, emptied and refilled it several times.

Grinning in pleasure, he returned and held up the canteen. "I want to trade for this can...teen." He removed the necklace he wore and offered it to Lonan.

Lonan shook his head. He admired the offering, but handed it back. "Good necklace with much power, but Skystone cannot trade."

Running Deer's jovial face turned belligerent. He shouted several words Lonan didn't understand. Lilly and Leotie hadn't included curse words in his education.

Lonan held up his hand. "Do not be offended. It would be bad magic for items from the future to be found with the Anasazi."

The Indian considered his comment, nodded, and returned the necklace to his neck. Running Deer clasped his friend's shoulder. "Skystone speaks the truth."

Red Bird called, "Come, we must talk." They sat around the low, circular stone enclosure. A fire, used to cook meals, stood in the very center. The stew they'd had for lunch had been tasty, though the meat was slightly tough. It burned low now, mostly glowing hot coals. The aroma still lingered in the air.

"Our visitors come with bad news." Muttering and glances were sent toward him and Madison. When the Elder held up a piece of red hair, Madison squeaked in alarm. With her hand, she searched her head for a shortened strand.

"Oh, my God. It really happened." She shivered, and Lonan put his arm around her.

"When Hair of Flame came to us in our dreams, I cut this piece from her head."

Exclamations of shock raced back and forth among those listening. Red Bird called for quiet, and then turned his attention to Talking Bird. "Come, stand before your people and tell them what is to come."

Talking Bird's voice was sure and steady. Her first words were soft. People leaned forward to hear her. "My evil son has escaped his prison and threatens to destroy the people. We must combine our magic to contain him again." Her voice grew in volume and with her fist, hit her open palm with a smack. "This time we must be sure he can never return." Her last words ended with a wail of anguish.

A Spirit Talker from one of the other pueblos stood. "Talking Bird has brought trouble down on our heads again. She should be sent away." Grousing of agreement traveled around the group

"Silence." Red Bird spit on the ground in disgust. "Talking Bird has suffered much. Did she not help kill Nukpana, her own son?" He looked around. "It is not her fault that our magic did not hold him." Heads nodded in agreement and the grumbling stopped. "This time, we join our magic with Hair of Flame and send him below Mother Earth."

Madison tugged on his arm. "What are they saying?"

"Talking Bird believes with your power and that of the joined Spirit Talkers, they can drive Nukpana into the Underworld forever." He nodded in the direction of the other Elders. "They blame her for her son's deeds, but Red Bird chastised them for causing her more hurt."

Watching Red Bird, she muttered, "Good." She turned back to him. "I thought we had to contain him in a jar or some other vessel."

"That's what I assumed, but Talking Bird says if their combined magic works, his spirit will go below the earth where the Spirit of Darkness will hold him captive for eternity." He took her hand and squeezed. "You must be very careful. The evil one will try to take your stone. Guard it well."

He placed the small pottery urn, about the height of her closed fist, in her hand. "This is a backup plan. If he won't return to the earth, coax him into this bottle, and seal it with this stopper."

She snorted. "I don't see how I can do that. He's not stupid."

"No, but he's greedy. He will do anything to obtain your locket." He pulled her closer and she dropped her head to his shoulder. He lifted her chin to peer into her clear blue eyes. Worry filled their depths. "Have the gods spoken to you, told you how to protect yourself?"

She shook her head vigorously. "No, that's the problem, they haven't. They may never talk to me." Her lower lip trembled. "I don't think I can do this."

****

From where she sat on the low stone wall, Madison watched the people prepare for the trip up Fajada Butte. Torches were soaked in oil of some kind so they'd burn. Water flasks were filled, food stored in pouches, and hot coals carried in pottery containers in case the flares went out. The sun sank in the west, and Madison's stomach churned faster with each inch of its descent.

Lonan had done his best to allay her fears, but his reassurances stuck in her throat like glue. The thought of going up that hill to face Nukpana made it difficult to breathe. Her heart thundered in her chest as she sucked in lungs full of air. *Slow down, Madison, before you hyperventilate.*

She just couldn't go up that tall piece of rock and try to capture an evil spirit. If the gods would speak to her, give her some sign or encouragement, she might find the guts she needed to move forward. But they hadn't said a word. Not one damn word. She was just an ordinary person from Texas, a literary major, for gosh sake. What did she know about magic and containing evil spirits? Nothing,

182

absolutely nothing.

Knees trembling, she watched Lonan work with the others, his movements fluid and purposeful. He must have felt her gaze, because he looked up. Their eyes locked and held as he finished closing his pack. He stood and started toward her.

She covered her face with her hands and lowered her forehead to her knees, trying to block out reality. *Oh, God. He's going to be furious, disappointed, and disgusted with me. He'll never forgive me, either.* She wanted to be brave for him, but...

"Are you ready to go?" She looked up to see him gazing down at her, brow furrowed.

She stood and walked into his arms, the place that offered her the security she so needed. If only they could stay like this... "Lonan, I can't go, I-I just can't go."

Hands on her shoulders, he pushed her away to stare at her. His jaw rigid, he bit out, "You don't mean that, Madison. You're needed."

"Don't you see I'm afraid? I'll hinder the others rather than help."

"Dammit, if you don't come with us, we're wasting our time. You're the key to our success." He took her arm and started leading her to the line already curling up the trail.

She dug in her heels. "No, you have to be wrong. With all the Spirit Talkers together, they'll have enough magic to put Nukpana away as they did before."

Lonan's face was a mask of fury. "You mean you'd let these people go and do your job, the job for which you were chosen before your birth?"

"Lonan, please, I'm so scared. Please understand."

"Understand? How the hell do you think we'll manage without you? Or do you even care?" Madison stumbled back at the harsh tone of his voice and the barely contained rage radiating from his body.

She shook with sobs and shrieked, "Of course, I care." She reached for his arm. He jerked it out of her grasp. "Please understand, I just can't go up there. I'm sorry."

He turned his head and spat on the ground. The insult wasn't lost on her. He turned on his heel and followed the moving line of people.

****

She was all alone. The people who'd remained behind shunned her, leaving her to fend for herself. On shaking legs, she turned toward the cliff drawings. Crying, she stumbled up the hill, falling to her knees and scraping her hands. When she reached the top, she dropped face down in the dirt and wailed out her fear, despair, and total disgust with herself. Lonan would never forgive her. Any love he'd had for her was killed by this action of cowardice and betrayal. *Oh, God. When he returns, he probably won't acknowledge my existence.* There was no need for her to stay. It was best she return, get in her car, and leave the state.

Spent, she pushed herself up, and stared at the crevice where she'd spent the night on her first trip. For a moment, she stood, remembering. Shaking off the nostalgia, she inched her way to the petroglyphs. With one hand grasping the locket, she closed her eyes and raised her hand to the drawings. It hovered there...

Daughter, where is your faith?

She whirled around to see a white fox, not ten feet away. No one else was around. It sat, brown eyes trained on her. Maybe she should be afraid, it could be dangerous. But at this point, she didn't care.

Again she raised her hand.

The gods did not choose a coward to fulfill this

quest. They chose a strong woman with Hair of Flame, guardian of the second twin. You, my daughter, are the chosen one.

The fox came toward her and sat at her feet.

Yes, what you see is true. I am White Fox, messenger of the gods. Close your eyes, daughter, and let the Spirits speak to you.

She did as he instructed, and immediately a blanket of comfort wrapped around her, drying her tears, soothing the fear that overwhelmed her.

Do you feel it, child? This is the healing power of the gods.

She could only nod. A sense of peace washed over her. Images raced through her mind, voices sounded in her brain, and comforting arms held her close.

The gods have not forsaken you. Have faith. They will guide you when the time is right. Go now and walk the path chosen for you.

****

The trip to Fajada Butte and the steep climb up to the top was tiring. Furious, Lonan couldn't focus on the uniqueness of the stairway in its original condition, before time and the elements wore away its usability. Disappointment ate away at his heart and soul. She wasn't the woman he'd believed. The truth hurt like hell. Well, it was better to know now rather than later.

Finally at the top, they rested for a few minutes as warriors started gathering sticks, twigs, and broken branches for fires. He'd been to the top of Fajada Butte twice. It had been an arduous trip up and back down again. Each time, he'd been fascinated by the twisted tree. Here, energy forces were so strong they formed a spinning vortex, a supposed tunnel that transported people to and from different worlds.

In modern times, the tree was much larger. It

amazed him to think the plant had lived for so long. Maybe it hadn't. The one in the twenty-first century could be an offshoot of this one. Tonight, he could feel the power of the vortex. A first for him. On his previous trips, he'd felt nothing. Perhaps it was the presence of the Spirit Talkers.

Talking Bird joined him. "Nukpana will show himself here. He knows about the vortex, so he'll come here to use its energy to travel back to this time."

He worried about Rita. She was old and not up to making a trip up the butte. Though still powerful, Nukpana wouldn't have the strength to give Rita the energy to move quickly. That was why there'd been no rush to get to the top.

The old woman at his side spoke. "You fear for woman who travels with Nukpana?"

"Yes, she is old, and the trip up here will be a great strain on her body. I pray she'll live after all she's been through."

"Maybe, maybe not. Talking Bird does not know."

Lonan knew the name Nukpana meant evil in the Hopi language, but why would a mother give it to her child? Unable to resist, he asked her.

She drew a deep breath. "He was born with the wicked mark." Hand over her heart, she shook her head sadly. "Blood red, it never went away. He was doomed from birth."

Talking Bird fished around in the small bag tied around her neck. When she located what she looked for, she took Lonan's hand and placed a perfect piece of turquoise in his palm. "To give you power to protect your mate. Guard it always."

Protect my mate? She isn't here, she doesn't need protecting.

As he closed his fist over the stone, warmth radiated up his arm. "Is it one of the twins?"

She nodded, and then moved to face the twisted tree, raised her hands to the sky, and began to chant. So, Talking Bird had the second twin, and it had yet to be found in modern time.

Her actions must have been a signal, as the others formed a circle to join in her mantra. Growing up in the pueblo, Lonan had heard similar tunes many times. In their dance, the people shuffled to one side, then back to the other, making the circle larger with each step.

Warriors lit the fires that formed a circle around the tree. There were six Spirit Talkers, six fires—one for each. The seventh fire remained unlit. Madison wasn't here, the circle was incomplete. Offerings were made to the gods, ground grain, flower pollen, and pulverized turquoise.

The chant increased in volume, the wind blew making noise like a lost soul calling for his mate. Its eerie song reverberated through the canyon to return like an echo. Suddenly, the flames in the fires threw sparks, spit ashes, and rose above the heads of the people.

A yell split the air. "Hair of Flame is coming." All movement stopped, all eyes turned toward the rocks where the path down the butte lay hidden. A young woman carrying a torch leaned down to help someone. Madison, chest heaving from her rapid trip, stumbled into the clearing. She scanned the circle, then joined him and grasped his hand. *Thank you, God.* Emotion making his throat tight, he drew her fist to his lips and kissed it.

He bent down to whisper in her ear. "Be strong, stand your ground." She gave him a wobbly smile, and pain at the expression of fear on her face stabbed at his heart. Even in the firelight he could see her eyes were red and swollen from crying. "Do you still have the bottle?"

She patted her jacket pocket and nodded.

A warrior moved into the circle and lit the seventh pile of brush and tree limbs. The fires slowly died down to a steady height, yet the wind continued. It rushed around them, lifting the cloaks of the Elders, tossing dirt into the breeze. It formed a circular motion, surrounded the tree, and began to spin faster, increasing in speed like a tornado.

Talking Bird raised her arms and the chanting stopped. She shouted, "Come to me, evil one. Face your mother, Nukpana, and the people you would betray once again. We knew you were rotten, a corpse of a person, but your search for revenge makes you lower than dung."

Her voice rose in power as she continued to call. The other shamans joined her. "Come Nukpana, come Nukpana."

The top of the butte trembled with vibrations, like aftershocks from an earthquake. Up this high, it wasn't a reassuring sensation.

A growl of anger rushed from the vortex. With it appeared a skeletal face, mouth stretched wide. A terrible stench filled the air. Several warriors stumbled back, but Talking Bird and the other shamans held their ground. Lonan's stomach heaved and he struggled not to retch. He looked at Madison to see that she'd covered her mouth and nose with her hand. The rhythmic chant increased in volume. The hideous face in the current screamed in pain.

Like a cannonball, Rita's body shot out of the whirlwind to land on the ground before them. She barely resembled the woman who'd tried to shoot them at Una Vida. He could only imagine how horrible the trip up Fajada Butte must have been for her. It would be difficult for a healthy man, let alone an elderly person. She was battered, bloody, and twitched horribly, her frame contorting in ways humanly impossible.

"Coward!" Madison shrieked. "Come out. Pick on

someone other than an old woman." She lurched toward Rita, but Lonan grabbed her, pulling her back to the circle.

A low, guttural hiss erupted from Rita's distorted mouth. "Ah, Hair of Flame, you will give me the turquoise to save this old woman's life?"

"Dream on, buster."

Rita screamed in pain as her body bent in half backwards. Lonan cringed at her agony. Sobbing, Madison fought to get out of his grasp.

Talking Bird shouted, "Stop it, evil one." She lifted the Skystone and dangled it for all to see. "This is what you want. Stop playing. Quit hiding like a child. Come out and take it."

With a roar, a black cloud of vapor shot from Rita's mouth. It hovered directly in front of Talking Bird. Rita lay still as a stone. If she survived this, it would be a miracle.

"Yes, Mother, I want the Skystone you stole from me, but I can get it another time, another way." He whipped away and flew to face Madison, his leer a horror to behold. "Give me the necklace, Hair of Flame, or I will take it and destroy you."

Lonan watched as an invisible forced pulled Madison's body. Her feet were planted firmly, but she tilted forward, her locket standing out from her chest as if striving to reach Nukpana. Lonan grabbed her around the waist. With his other hand, he touched the second twin hidden in his pocket.

The face in the miasma jerked over to stare at Lonan. A growl of rage echoed across the canyon.

"You!" His cackle sounded much like that of a hyena. "The stone you have will not protect you or her!" He reeled back to the center, moving forward and back as if trying to make up his mind what to do.

"Come, Nukpana, accept your fate. Let us send you on your way below Mother Earth to live with others of your kind." Talking Bird joined hands with the man beside her. The others did the same.

"No!" His roar shook the ground under their feet. "I'll never be with my ancestors. You called on the gods to kill me, committed me to eternity in a prison." Agony etched his voice. "You showed no mercy. No, I'll not be held prisoner again." He swooped away, back to Rita.

Her body convulsed as the black haze tried without success to re-enter her body. Magic crackled in the air. The wind picked up in force. It whistled around the butte, the chanting barely heard above the roar. Nukpana was weaker.

When Nukpana stuck his evil face in front of hers, Madison trembled with fear. She wanted to turn and run. His stench filled the air, making it difficult to breathe. The noise from the wind and chanting was deafening, making it hard to hear Talking Bird's words. Nukpana's voice echoed in her head, causing excruciating pain. She closed her eyes in an effort to bear the throbbing and shut out the scene unfolding around her.

The pounding was replaced by a sense of ease. *Stand strong, my child. We are with you.* The words of calm washed over her, soothing her nerves, instilling hope that they would survive this terrible confrontation.

She opened her eyes to see Rita's body grow still, and then they lifted to meet the red eyes of the evil one.

He grinned wickedly. With a last spurt of defiant energy, he howled with rage and shot to Madison, hitting her square in the face. The force knocked her down. Cold consumed her, her teeth rattled, she choked, gagging on ashes as he entered her body.

From afar, Madison heard Lonan's shout of, "Noooo!" His grasp never loosened. Before she realized what had happened, her other hand was caught and she was jerked to her feet.

"Yessss," cackled Nukpana. In horror Madison realized the voice came from her mouth.

Her body jerked as the horrible laughter continued to roll from her. Vaguely, she heard Talking Bird and the other shamans as they moved in to form a circle around her, their words as foreign as the entire situation.

Lonan's heart thundered. He wanted to scream, to yell in rage. Why Madison? He was supposed to protect her and had failed. He'd planned to jump in front of her, let the evil one take him instead. Before he could react, it was done. His only hope was that the circle of magic would be able to force him from her.

Bolts of lightning streaked across the sky, illuminating the entire butte. Thunder rumbled in its wake. No sooner had it ended when an arrow of electrical energy struck the ground in front of Madison, creating a small chasm in the earth's floor. Smoke from the singed grass blew away with the still heavy winds. The sky opened. Rain pelted them, making it almost impossible to see.

Madison went limp. Lonan struggled to keep her upright. Like a puppet on a string, the locket rose and sealed itself to her lips. What the hell was happening? A long, guttural scream erupted from her mouth, followed by a blinding spark of light, a black cloud at the forefront. The brightness enveloped the miasma, shot to the gaping crevice, to disappear in the bowels of the earth.

Chapter Seventeen

Lonan scooped Madison into his arms before she hit the ground. Cradling her close to his pounding heart, he found a rock to sit on. She struggled to get loose. "You're okay, sweetheart. I've got you." He kissed her forehead and she relaxed against him.

"He's gone, forever." He prayed to God he spoke the truth. Holding her on his lap, his attention alternated between worry for Madison, and the gaping crack in the earth, fearing he'd see Nukpana rise any minute.

Talking Bird and the other shamans nodded in satisfaction, but continued to guard the fissure. She threw offerings into the wind and thanked the gods as the others stood respectfully.

Madison lurched out of his lap and fell to her knees, gagging and retching until her stomach emptied its contents. She rinsed her mouth with water from the canteen he handed her, took several sips, and then used the hem of her wet tee-shirt to wipe her mouth.

He helped her stand, and with his fingers brushed the wet hair back from her face. Her teeth chattered, but from the clarity of her eyes, it appeared her mind was clear. She tried to smile. His heart jumped into his throat, making speech impossible. Filled with gratitude that she was unharmed, he buried his face in her neck and groaned. "Oh, God, baby, you scared twenty years off my life."

She curled into his body, and hands shaking slightly, he stroked her back. His touch was meant to soothe her, but he wasn't sure she was the one who needed calming. He'd been terrified.

"I'm okay, Lonan. The gods sent a messenger." He stilled at her words. "His name was White Fox. Their words warmed me, made me believe."

"I knew they wouldn't desert you." There were times he hadn't been sure, especially since they took their own sweet time.

At last their quest was over. It was such a relief, he could take Madison home and forget this adventure had ever taken place. No, that would never happen. He'd remember this night until his dying day.

He'd had difficulty believing Nukpana had been restrained. But, the miasma hadn't risen again. "You did it, Madison." He turned her toward the fissure in the ground. "There is Nukpana's grave."

Her face was pasty as she looked at the gaping crack. She shivered. He untied her jacket from around her waist and helped her slip her arms in the sleeves. Hopefully, it would help ward off some of the chill.

"Do...you think...it will hold him?" He needed to get her to warmth before she got sick. As he held her close, his body heat must have eased the chill as her quaking lessened.

With her head tucked against his shoulder, he watched as warriors moved about, scraping up mud to plug the hole. It would take a hell of a lot of muck. Who knew how deep into the earth it went? But the men didn't appear daunted by the task. They worked fast, using their hands to push the wet soil deeper into the gap.

"I hope so, love. If not, it won't be for lack of trying."

"Come, Skystone." One of the women stood before him. "Take Hair of Flame out of the rain."

When Madison stumbled, he lifted her into his

arms. The woman led them down the butte, about twelve feet, deep under the overhang of a jutting rock. A small fire blazed and several blankets lay in the corner. Lonan turned to thank the woman, but she was gone.

Madison was shaky, but managed to stand when he set her on her feet. He removed his backpack and located the rain gear he always carried. "We've got to get you out of those wet clothes."

Shivering, she pulled the T-shirt over her head. Her fingers shook so much, she fumbled with the snap of her jeans. He unfastened them and slid the pants down her legs. Bracing herself with a hand to his forearm, she lifted first one foot, then the other, while he pulled her jeans and shoes off together.

He spread the lightweight blanket from his pack over the poncho before wrapping Madison in one of the Indian blankets.

"Sit down here. Let me rub your feet. They're like ice."

"What about you?" She moaned. "Oh, that feels so good."

"I've got to go check on Rita." He covered her toes and tucked the woven fabric under them. With his thumb, he stroked her cheek. "You're not afraid here alone, are you?"

She looked around. "I don't think so." Her eyes searched his. "Should I be?"

"The fire should keep any mountain lions away."

"What!" She tried to get up. "I'm going with you."

Grinning, he caught her shoulder to keep her seated. "I'm teasing you." He tweaked her nose. "You'll be fine. I won't be gone but a minute."

Before she could object, he hurried out to climb back to the top. Too tired to care if a bear ate her, she lay down on her side and closed her eyes. That'd show him, wouldn't it? He'd feel bad to return and find nothing but her remains. *You're being childish, Madison.* Of course he was teasing her, and he needed to check on Rita. If she had the strength to get up and dress, she'd go too.

****

A chattering woke her. Her eyes popped open to see a squirrel perched on its hind legs, two feet from her. She squealed, scaring the creature. It ran further away, then stopped and looked back at her. Cute little dickens.

Footsteps sounded outside, and the animal scampered away.

Soaked through, Lonan ducked under the overhang and started shucking his clothes. He appeared worn out. His face bore additional lines from his scowl of worry. Using a tee-shirt from his pack, he dried off. She opened the blanket and he joined her on the makeshift bed. Snug in his arms, she rubbed his back and legs to warm them.

"How's Rita?"

"Not good. Talking Bird and another woman are tending her wounds, trying to get fluids in her," he said, his voice tense. "I don't think she'll make it until morning."

"Poor woman." She kissed his chest and rested her cheek against his warm skin. The thump of his heart lulled and comforted her. She grew sleepy. "You missed," she yawned, "our little visitor."

"Let me guess—a spider, a bug?"

"No, it was a small squirrel. Stood not two feet away from me."

He stilled. "Sounds like one of those damn rock squirrels. They're a major nuisance and are destructive to the canyon ruins. We've had a heck of a time controlling them." His chin rested on top of her head, his voice barely above a whisper. "Odd. I'm surprised one would come that close to a human."

Within minutes, he was snoring. It wasn't a

rumbling racket, just a steady hum. Madison grinned as she snuggled against him. His hand found her butt, pulling her closer, flush with his length. She sighed in contentment, but found herself fighting the tears forming in her eyes. Oh, God. She'd fallen in love with this man.

****

The rain stopped in the middle of the night, but their clothes were still damp. Lonan knew they'd dry quickly when the sun rose. Dressed, they climbed the natural steps to the top of the butte, where they were greeted by Talking Bird and the other shamans.

"Skystone. Hair of Flame. Come." Red Bird signaled for them to share the morning repast. They ate a cold meal of bread like a hoecake. He watched as Madison smiled her appreciation to the women.

He'd expected her to be picky, but she ate with relish. He did notice she studied the dark colored flecks.

"You like it?"

"It's not bad at all, especially when you're hungry. It's almost like cornbread, only the corn meal is coarser." She chewed and swallowed, then leaned in to whisper. "What do you think those brown flecks are?"

"Berries or nuts of some kind."

"Ah." She took another healthy bite.

Red Bird stood. Everyone followed suit. They gathered around the crevice where Nukpana disappeared the night before. The dried mud was sunken in places, so warriors worked gathering dirt to make mud to further reinforce the indentation in the earth.

Lonan walked with Madison to see Rita. She'd been made comfortable under a rock overhang, as had he and Madison. The women had washed and cleaned her wounds, but from her jabbering, it was clear she was out of her head. "Has she been like this all night?"

A young woman spoke. "Yes, but she calms when we give her drink." She pointed to a wooden gourd he assumed contained some kind of natural pain medicine. "We give her more now to ease her journey."

"Thank you for your kindness."

"Our people are grateful to Skystone and Hair of Flame." Ducking her head shyly, she returned to her work.

Lonan took Madison's hand and led her out, away from the others. He stood, trying to relax the tension he knew showed on his face. "This is how we need to do things this morning. I will have to carry Rita through the vortex."

He hated they couldn't go together, but Rita wouldn't make it on her own, if she made it at all. Madison's brow furrowed, but she said, "I know."

"As soon as we've gone through, you follow." He tilted her chin up so he could see the expression in her eyes. He saw fear there, and it made his stomach knot. "Don't be afraid, sweetheart. We'll make it. Talking Bird gave me the second twin, and you have the first."

She released her bottom lip from between her teeth and attempted a smile. "I'll be right behind you."

Deer Stalker called them over to where several men were working. "We make a carrier for the old woman. It will make your passage easier." Lonan had to agree. Using a blanket, they fashioned a sling similar to a huggie sack for a baby.

Before they put it on him, he took Madison in his arms. Voice hoarse, he whispered against her hair. "I'll be waiting on the other side." His hands cupped her face. He saw that she struggled to keep her lips from trembling. "Be careful, love."

She laid her cheek against his chest. "I will. You too."

He scanned her face one last time, then took her mouth in a hard and thorough kiss. She clung to him as his lips slashed across hers with desperation, longing, and promise.

When he stepped back, he held her steady, both gasping for air.

"You know what to do?"

She nodded. "When I hit the ground," *if I'm still alive,* "relax and roll to soften my landing."

He smiled and then nodded to the warriors. With Rita moaning, they gently placed her in the sling, fit it over Lonan's left shoulder, and under his right arm.

"You are comfortable, Skystone?" Deer Stalker pulled on the knots to make sure they'd hold.

Lonan moved to adjust it to fit better. "It is good, Deer Stalker." He clasped the Indian's forearm. "I thank you for your help. We will remember you," he nodded to Red Bird and the others, "with honor."

With a last glance back at Madison, he winked, then walked closer to the vortex.

Truthfully, Madison didn't see anything other than a very twisted tree, but as Lonan drew nearer, he was caught in an invisible coiling wind that drew him inside its motion. Movement out of the corner of her eye caught her attention. It was a little rock squirrel. He moved from behind a large boulder to watch the goings on with interest, chattering as he did so. Lonan and Rita were in the eye of the vortex now, spinning faster, and faster, the wind gaining in strength. Suddenly the squirrel, along with dirt and debris, twirled around with them. All she could do was gape. It was beyond anything she'd ever seen. In a flash, they vanished. The whole thing reminded her of the old *Star Trek* series and the expression— "Beam me up, Scottie."

Talking Bird smiled, nodded with satisfaction, then turned to Madison, motioning her forward. The old woman looked at her for a long time, touched her skin, her hair, and then embraced her. The gesture deeply moved Madison. Not enough to want to stay, but it was a moment she'd remember forever. Tears pricked her eyes as she looked around at the proud people and the untouched land from over a thousand years ago.

On impulse, she removed one of her amber earrings and placed it in Talking Bird's wrinkled palm. The Indian picked it up by the wire, shook it, watching it dangle and reflect the sun's rays.

Those standing around whispered, she supposed in awe of the gift. The old woman's face split with a radiant beam. Even her rotten teeth didn't detract from the joy in her expression. Madison hated to give one of the pair away, but she knew Great-grandmother Evans would be pleased with her kindness.

With a sigh, she looked toward the twisted tree. Lonan would be waiting for her. She better get on over there and catch her transport. She swallowed a giggle. God, would her life ever return to normal?

Talking Bird prodded her in the back, sending her stumbling toward the vortex. Feet like lead, she moved to stand before the whirling mass, waiting for that pulling she'd observed with Lonan. It didn't happen, though the swirling was plainly visible. Maybe she just wasn't close enough. She glanced back at Talking Bird, who made shooing motions with her hands, smiling with encouragement.

Her heart pounded in trepidation. *Okay, girl, get a grip on your fear. I'm coming, Lonan.* Grasping her locket, she ran the few feet to the vortex. Just before she jumped, she shut her eyes.

Her feet hit something as she landed, jarring her knees, hips, back, and rattling her teeth before propelling her backward. From far away, someone moaned. Oh, poor Rita. Her voice a croak, she called, "Lo...na...nnn." The effort increased the pounding in her head. She tried to open her eyes. The bright sun shot pain right to her brain. Nausea hit in a wave, her stomach heaved, she couldn't move. Darkness surrounded her.

****

Lonan feared their touchdown would be a rough one, but they were spit out of the vortex like gum from a teenager's mouth. His butt hit the ground. With arms tight around Rita, they skidded several feet. Before they came to a standstill, something flew by them to land several feet away. The critter rolled several times, and lay stunned before getting on its feet and scurrying for cover.

Shit, it was one of those damn rock squirrels. It'd probably breed like a rabbit and they'd have to wipe them out to preserve the ruins. Maybe it wasn't a female. Maybe it wouldn't find a mate in these parts. Yeah, right. Maybe he should take out his pistol and shoot the pest.

He looked down at the woman in his arms. No, he didn't want to disturb her with a gun going off near her. Thank God, she still breathed. Carefully, he untied the blanket, settling Rita on the ground.

From his backpack, he removed the portable two-way radio he always carried. He was torn. Should he go ahead and contact Joe? No, he'd wait until Madison arrived before he made the call.

His Indian friends had been terribly interested in everything he carried in his bag, but after the confrontation with Running Deer, and Red Bird's orders, no one challenged him again for trades.

He rubbed the edge of the rough-textured rug wrapped around Rita between his fingers. It was bad enough that he had this fine example of ancient weaving, which should be in a museum somewhere.

He couldn't imagine what the world would have thought if they'd found modern camping equipment in the ruins below. Tomorrow would be soon enough to worry about how he'd explain where the blanket came from. He looked again at the twisted tree.

Where was Madison? He stood and approached without getting too close, waiting. Thirty minutes later, he was alarmed. What the hell was holding her up? He knew she was afraid, but didn't doubt for a minute that she'd jump, knowing it was her ticket home.

He paced the rough ground, anxiety increasing by the second. The squirrel stuck its head up behind a rock and chattered, the noise grating on his nerves. His finger itched to take out his revolver and shoot the thing.

He yanked his hat off, beating it against his leg in frustration. Dust flew around him. His heart raced as adrenalin pumped through his body. He needed to move, go get her, do something to ease the sinking in his stomach. What happened to prevent Madison from getting back? He looked from the twisted tree to Rita. His gut told him to jump back into the spinning air and go after her, but his conscience ordered him to take care of Rita first.

He flipped the switch on the radio. "Stone here. I'm on the top of Fajada Butte with Rita Santiago. She's seriously hurt. Send Joe Redhawk with a chopper."

"Judy here. I'm on it. Stay on the horn." If he wasn't so worried, he'd chuckle at the pop that ended the call. Judy and her gum.

Five minutes later, the radio cracked to life. "Joe will be in the air within ten minutes. You okay, Lonan?"

"Yeah, I'm fine." At least he would be when Joe got here to take his prisoner and he could return for Madison. It couldn't be soon enough. He was

201

tempted to leave Rita, now that he knew Joe was on the way, but he couldn't do it in good conscience.

Lord, I pray she's okay. She'd been thrust into his life when he'd not been in the market for a woman, much less a wife. Without realizing it, she'd wormed her way into his heart. He shook his head in disgust. A fine protector he was. If she was hurt or dead, it would kill him. Surely the gods wouldn't allow that to happen. They'd forecasted a great love between them. For the first time, he allowed their prediction to give him hope. Did he love her, want her with him always? Did she love him? Hell, he didn't know how he felt about her, but knew he wanted her safely back in the twenty-first century.

He heard the sound of the chopper in the distance, each whoop of the blades increasing his impatience. Standing in the flattest area atop the butte, he waved so Joe would know where to land. As soon as it touched the ground, two EMTs jumped out with a stretcher. In no time, Rita was loaded and they were ready for lift-off.

Lonan, bent over walked to the door. "I'm not coming."

"Why the hell not?"

"Madison didn't make it through. I've got to go back for her."

Joe looked at him like he'd lost his marbles. "What are you talking about? Is she up here somewhere, hurt?"

"I don't have time to explain or argue." He started to turn.

"Wait. You've got to come in to file a report. If you're still so hot to get back up here, I'll give you a ride, but at least tell me what's going on."

Lonan didn't want to listen, but supposed he needed to explain what happened so Joe could inform the council. It wouldn't take him long to type up his report. Report hell—what would he say?

People would think him nuts if he told the truth.

"No more than two hours."

Joe nodded and Lonan climbed in the craft. As it lifted into the air, the rock squirrel crept out to watch them. Lonan shook his head. Curious little bugger.

****

Madison woke, opened her eyes a slit and quickly closed them. The light hurt too much. Someone had placed a wet cloth over her forehead and it felt good against her hot skin. Where was Lonan? Without moving, she called, "Lonan."

She heard the sound of voices, mostly women, a few men, but none sounded like Lonan. Actually, she couldn't understand a word they said. Fear clutched at her throat. She cried out. "Lonan, please, where are you?"

Comforting hands touched her arms and smoothed her hair back from her face. The cloth was lifted from her forehead and she opened her eyes to see Talking Bird bending over her, sympathy drawing her features.

"Noooo! Lonan. Oh please, God, please let this be a dream." Sobs wracked her body, making it ache in places she hadn't known she was injured. She tried to sit up. The pounding in her head caused her stomach to heave. She threw up in the bowl Talking Bird held for her. Another woman helped her ease down on the mat.

Red Bird stood at her feet, brow wrinkled in a scowl. Slightly behind him was Gold Eagle. His face held an expression of triumph. Madison screamed, "Never." All eyes turned to him, and the women shoved him out the door.

Another cool rag was placed over her forehead and eyes. Why wouldn't the vortex take her? Lonan was at home, waiting for her to arrive. Tears rolled down her cheeks, trickling past the lobes of her ears to hit the mat.

Though she couldn't understand her words, the Indian woman's soft talking soothed her. She would sleep, get well, and find a way to return to Lonan.

Chapter Eighteen

Joe's two hours turned into four. Lonan was beside himself with worry, impatient, and growing angrier by the minute. Rita had been taken to the hospital in Farmington, her wounds treated, then immediately airlifted to Albuquerque, where she was met by her husband and son. Since her crimes were committed on Indian soil, she'd be arraigned by the Tribal Council. They'd probably charge her with second degree murder, assault, as well as breaking and entering.

Now he sat before the emergency-called meeting of the Tribal Council.

"Lonan Stone!" His name boomed through the room.

He jerked at the sound to see all eyes on him. "I'm sorry. My mind was elsewhere—on my wife." He couldn't keep the condemnation from his voice.

The Chief Elder, Tom Lone Eagle, nodded. "We understand your impatience, Lonan Stone, but first you must tell us all what took place when the gods whisked you away to the time of our ancestors."

With a sigh of exasperation, he repeated the entire story for the third time—once to Joe, then to the Tribal Police Chief, and now the Council. When he finished, the room grew quiet.

Tom Lone Eagle turned to the spiritualists in attendance. Both of his grandmothers were there, along with others. They formed a circle to quietly offer a prayer to the gods. When they finished, they put their heads together. Then Leotie joined Lone Eagle on the small raised stage and asked to speak.

"What Lonan has reported, we've seen in our dreams. The wind, lightning, and the mud-filled crevice." She looked to the others for confirmation. They nodded.

His grandmother asked. "Is it true that you have the second twin?"

"Yes, Grandmother."

"May we see it?" asked Lone Eagle.

Lonan stood and carried it to him. The old man fingered it, rubbing the soft stone.

"How did you get it?"

"Talking Bird, the witch woman, Nukpana's mother, gave it to me."

The older man nodded. "It must join the mother stone."

Lonan snatched it from his hand. "Not until I have my wife back safe."

The elder's brow wrinkled and he slammed his fist on the table. "You would defy me," he waved his hand, "this council, take the chance of being shunned by our people?"

"Yes, I would. I will. I'll not leave Madison there to fend for herself."

"She is being taken care of, Lonan." The words came from Lilly. "When she recovers, she will go to the petroglyphs and pass through."

His heart lurched. "Recover? What do you mean?" He turned to Leotie. "Grandmother—"

She raised a hand. "Hair of Flame is not seriously hurt, my son. Some scrapes and bruises," she shrugged a shoulder, "possibly a concussion."

A concussion? Not seriously hurt? "Why couldn't she make it through the vortex?"

"It is possible the vortex was full, that it had no room for Madison." Leotie turned to the other spiritualists, and then back to him. "We had no idea this would happen or we would have warned you."

Anger and frustration shook his frame. Hands

fisted at his side, jaw rigid, he bit out, "I will not leave her there to think I don't care. I'm her protector, though I've done a piss-poor job of it so far. I'll return to bring her home." He dared anyone to challenge his decision.

The old man grinned. "Ah, so the gods were right. There is great love between you."

Lonan had never blushed in his life, but he felt the heat rise to his cheeks standing before his people. "That is no one's business but my own." He looked to his grandmothers. "What kind of man would I be if I didn't go back for her? I would lose face with myself, with my people." He waited for someone to object, but no one spoke.

Finally, Lone Wolf grinned and bobbed his big head. "It is good and as it should be. Go in peace, my son. May the gods be with you."

****

Madison woke to find a small child watching her. The minute she opened her eyes, the tike ran off. She returned with Talking Bird and another woman. Madison watched as Talking Bird took a pinch of a dried mixture and mixed it with water. They knelt on each side of her, carefully lifted her shoulders, and poured the noxious brew down her throat. The next time she woke, she felt a little better.

She was dying to pee. Trying to make them aware of her discomfort, she patted her lower tummy while scowling. Both nodded understanding and helped her rise. The movement increased the pounding in her skull, but she could manage. It was the urge to retch that made her remain still, sucking in deep breaths of air. No, she couldn't vomit. The heaving would kill her head.

It took forever to reach the latrine and return. She lay down on the mat, grateful to be prone again. The women dosed her again. What did they use to control pain? Most early cultures had herbal medicines. She pondered the possible source. Within a few minutes her pain eased, and her eyes closed. Her last thought was, *Lonan, please come for me.*

Talking Bird woke her late in the afternoon. She held a small bowl with a soup of some type. The aroma made Madison's stomach growl loudly. The older woman laughed as she helped her sit up. She took small sips of the liquid, letting it settle in her stomach before trying more. Though her head continued to ache, the pain was nothing like it'd been before. The broth remained in her stomach, so she drank the rest.

Smiling, she handed the bowl to Talking Bird. "Thank you."

The Indian nodded and sat the container aside. She stood holding a hand to her. Madison took it and carefully rose to her feet. She remained unmoving for several minutes until the dizziness passed.

As they stepped outside, it took a moment for her eyes to adjust to the fading sunlight. The air smelled fresh, clean, though cooking odors wafted on the breeze to blend with the scent of juniper bushes. The air grew cooler with the setting sun. Holding on to Talking Bird, she walked slowly to the walled sitting area and sat. People approached, smiled, and said something in their language. She returned their greeting with a nod.

She startled when Stalking Deer stopped before her. He handed her a blanket and mimicked wrapping it around her. She followed his instructions and welcomed the warmth. She smiled and nodded her thanks. He grunted and walked away.

Everything was peaceful as the women went about their work. The children played while the men hovered in groups to talk. If only Lonan were here. She was lost without him. Tears gathered in her eyes. She struggled to stifle her rising sobs. *Stop it, you fool. You're stronger than a sniveling baby.*

Shouts echoed around her. Her ears caught the word the Anasazi used for Lonan, the one that she thought meant Skystone. She covered her ears to lessen the pain the sound waves produced in her head. Men ran toward the cliff behind Una Vida. In a wave, the women came to her. Several helped her to stand. What was going on? She gasped for air. *Could it be? They called Lonan Skystone.*

Walking carefully, holding on to Talking Bird for support, she followed the happy women. The crowd of men parted to allow a tall man to pass through. The sun was behind him, so she didn't recognize his face. But, his bearing, the catlike stride was Lonan's.

Arms outstretched, she cried. "Lonan!"

Lonan heard Madison call his name. He located her amid the women, and quickened his pace until he stood before her. He took inventory of her injuries, afraid they were worse than he'd been led to believe.

He shortened the distance between them. Careful not to hurt her, he enfolded her in his arms. "Madison, are you all right?" His voice cracked as he whispered against her hair. "Grandmother said you'd suffered a concussion."

Head on his chest, he felt Madison's tears dampen his shirt. Her fists gripped handfuls of the material, holding onto him. "I've been so sick, but I planned to go to the petroglyphs as soon as I could."

He tilted her chin up to kiss her—a soft, comforting meeting of lips. Her breath smelled of some kind of herb, not necessarily unpleasant, but not good either. "That's what everyone tried to tell me you'd do, but I wouldn't wait."

Red Bird, accompanied by Stalking Deer, joined them. Stalking Deer said something to Lonan.

He turned to Madison. "They want to hear about

my journey. Do you feel well enough to stay up a while longer? I have much to tell them."

She smiled up at him. "Yes. With you beside me, I'm fine." As Lonan led her to the stone circle to sit down, he watched to make sure she didn't tire. He didn't want to turn loose of her, but he needed to relay to the people what had transpired.

Talking Bird came to sit on the other side of Madison and handed her a cup of something to drink. He assumed from Madison's expression, it wasn't tasty, but she finished it off. Probably something to ease her pain. The brew was the source of the smell on her breath. It fascinated him that the early people knew ways of treating different conditions with herbs, tree bark, roots, and other items from nature.

Red Bird stood. "We would hear of Skystone's travels."

He told them how Rita, when she recovered, would be turned over to the Tribal Police to determine her punishment. Red Bird nodded and sat down. Lonan continued. "Though the woman committed evil deeds, it was the spirit inside her that was the guilty one. The council will take that into consideration."

"This is good," said Red Bird. "What about your mate? Why would the vortex not take her?"

Madison's eyes were drooping. She'd be asleep in a minute. He supported her with one arm around her waist. "It is believed the vortex was full and didn't have room for another soul at the moment."

Heads bobbed in understanding.

"How do you know this?" asked Stalking Deer.

"My grandmother talks to the spirits. They told her."

Lonan carried Madison to the apartment she'd been assigned, one downstairs so she wouldn't have to climb ladders. When he placed her on the mat, she woke.

She reached for him. "I'm so thankful you're here."

He lay down and gathered her close. "Me too, love. Me too." This woman was everything to him. He'd desired her the minute he saw her, but with the desire love had grown. He wanted her for a lifetime, to bear his children, sit with him to watch the sunsets. Did she love him? Would she be content to live in this barren land with no large towns within a hundred miles? As much as he loved her, they might not have a future together. It was best to steer clear of that topic until they were home and issues with the Tribal Council and Police were settled.

"Where did you hit your head?" She took his hand and moved it to the top of her cranium, just behind where the soft spot would be on an infant's head. There was a large knot where the broken skin had begun to scab over. "What happened, anyway?"

"I wasn't feeling the pull, but could see the swirl." She shrugged. "So I just ran and jumped in the middle, feet first. It spit me out like I tasted bad."

He couldn't stifle the chuckle at her expression. He quickly sobered. Lord, she could have broken her neck. "You're lucky you weren't killed, or paralyzed."

"I was unconscious most of the trip down the mountain. Probably a good thing, because the few times I was awake, it was rough going. They made a travois-like thing with a man at each end. Even so, I got jostled a time or two."

"Can you tell a big difference in how you feel now?"

"Oh, yes. Of course, I may be drugged. I don't know what was in that bitter stuff they've been pouring down me, but it's helped the pain and made me sleep."

"These early people have many herbal remedies.

It's probably made from some kind of tree bark." What a shame they didn't have cures for diseases and malnutrition. Though they had grain, some vegetables, and raised turkeys, their diet lacked protein.

He felt Madison relax in his arms, her voice barely above a whisper. "Lonan?"

"Mmmm?" She was half asleep and still wanting to talk. "Go to sleep, sweetheart."

"Okay." She sighed. "I love you, Lo...nan." Her words ended with a gentle snore.

His heart stopped. She loved him? A sharp pain pierced his chest, but it was one of joy. He wanted to wake her, but she needed her rest so they could go home the next day.

Lines etched Lonan's brow. What she could see of it in the light just before dawn. "Are you sure you're up to this? It could be bumpy, and I don't want you hurt any more than you are."

"I'm fine. My head hurts some, but it's not something a couple of aspirin won't cure." She hadn't had any more of Talking Bird's brew since last night, before they'd gone to bed, probably no later than ten o'clock p.m., so she'd welcome a couple of analgesic pills right now.

He opened his pack and pulled out a bottle. "Here, take a couple of these."

She snatched them from his hand and poured three into her palm. He opened a canteen and handed it to her.

"If you're sure you can manage the trip, we better get a move on. I'd like to leave before everyone is awake."

Madison did, too. She'd said her good-bye to Talking Bird on Fajada Butte before busting her head. Not up to par physically, her emotions were too fragile to go through it again. They folded their blankets and placed them on the sleeping mat before leaving the apartment.

Outside, the gray dawn made it easy enough to see where they were going. They'd just reached the center of the yard, when a burst of flame made them jump back in alarm. Two warriors ran to the foot of the hill below the petroglyphs with blazing torches, and extended them to light the one of the next man in line. The action continued until a double trail of fire wove up the path.

Madison felt the tears well in her eyes and sadness tightened her throat. She glanced at Lonan. His jaw was rigid as he tried to keep his emotions in check. He took her arm, and they moved forward. Not a word was uttered, no children cried as they started their trek upward.

At the top, Red Bird, Deer Stalker, and Talking Bird, wearing the amber earring, waited for them. Both Elders clasped arms with Lonan, and they nodded to her. Talking Bird touched each of their faces.

Madison released a sob. Before she could utter another sound, Lonan had his arm around her and one of her palms on the cliff drawings. She released a screech as the light enveloped them.

****

Their landing had been easy enough. He guessed practice made perfect. He made sure their descent down the hill was a slow one. Madison didn't need another fall or an additional knot on her head.

He hustled her into the truck and headed for the road that left the park. When they reached the check station, he honked and roared on through. He grinned at the shocked expressions of the two rangers on duty as they flew by.

Madison leaned against the doorframe, eyes closed, so she didn't see them bypass the road leading up to his house. Ten minutes later, she sat up and looked around.

"Why aren't we there yet?" She turned and searched behind them, then fixed him with a glare. It must have hurt, because she winced. "Where are we going?"

"To the hospital in Farmington to get you checked out."

"I don't need—"

"Don't argue because it won't do any good. We're going, and that's final."

She crossed her arms across over her chest and scowled, giving a good imitation of Chief Sitting Bull. He grinned. "Calm that temper, Hair of Flame."

At a loss for words, she opened and closed her mouth, then clamped it tightly shut. He drove another fifteen minutes, whistling while maneuvering the two-lane road. From the corner of his eye, he could see the smoldering looks she threw his way. He didn't say a thing, just grinned. Thirty minutes later, her lips were twitching.

She harrumphed. "You might've won this round, but there's always the next one."

"I look forward to it." He pulled into the hospital's parking lot, and drove straight for the emergency room entrance.

"You will not take me in there like a car wreck victim. Park this thing, and I can walk a short ways."

Lonan looked behind him to see a car pull in. It could be a real crisis, not that Madison's wasn't, but it wasn't life-threatening. He pulled up and found a parking spot. As they walked to the entrance, a man and a nurse helped a hugely pregnant woman into a wheelchair. The woman's moans were hard to ignore, causing Lonan's gut to twist. The nurse wheeled her away while the husband parked the car.

Madison fixed him with a stare. "Okay, you were right. Thank you for bringing it to my attention."

Pregnant women scared him. The thought of Madison big, and in pain, terrified him.

Inside, they filled out paperwork and were then ushered into a curtained stall. "I don't see why I have to get undressed," Madison groused. "It's my head, not my body."

"I don't know either, but that's what he said to do, so let me help you." She tried to hide the fact she was worn out, but stood still and allowed him to undress her. He tied the hospital gown at the neck and at the waist, and she carefully lay back on the cot.

Several hours and x-rays later, a doctor came into the room. He gave Madison a thorough exam, eyes, reflexes and then sat in the second chair in the cubical.

"You have a minor concussion. Your headache will continue for several days and then ease up. If you get dizzy, nauseated, or have difficulty with your motor skills, come back immediately." He wrote out a prescription, handed it to Lonan, and then turned to Madison. "Young woman, I hope you'll be more careful in the future. The park EMT faxed a copy of her report of your first knock on the head."

The doctor stood and shook Lonan's hand. He patted Madison on the shoulder. "You take it easy for the next couple of days. No arduous activity."

Madison was dressed and ready to leave. He took her hand as they left the emergency area. A young man burst from two metal swinging doors. Dressed from head to foot in green paper garments, he yanked off his facemask. Four older people jumped up and rushed to him. "It's a boy," he shouted and then dropped face down in a dead faint.

Madison stopped at the outburst, and then added, "Poor man."

Poor man is right. He's probably broken his nose. They watched for a minute as orderlies tended to him, and then they walked to his truck.

Seeing the man's response wasn't terribly reassuring, considering someday he and Madison might have kids. Would he fall apart like that? He'd have to find out when Madison was due for her next birth control shot.

"Hmmm. I wonder what the doctor considers strenuous activity."

Chapter Nineteen

Madison was sick and tired of lying around. Her head no longer hurt, yet Lonan hovered over her constantly. His attention was nice, but it wasn't the attention she craved. Oh, he made love to her with a scorching passion that left her breathless and sated, but the rest of the time he treated her like a piece of fragile china. More importantly, he'd not said the words she longed to hear. Sure, he called her 'love' all the time, but he'd not said, 'I love you, Madison. Stay with me and be my wife.'

Tomorrow, he'd return to work full-time and they'd yet to discuss their future. Every night, she wanted to bring it up, but didn't have the guts. Maybe he didn't want a future with her, she'd just been a means to an end. No, she didn't think Lonan would intentionally use her that way, but he'd been forced into a corner. She couldn't stay here with the man if he didn't care for her as much as she cared for him. She had to hear those words, know the commitment was genuine.

As instructed by Lonan, she was lying down, supposedly to take a nap. It was easier to do it than argue with him. His every action said he cared about her, but how much? She couldn't sleep, and flipped through magazines. A couple of her favorite Shakespeare books sat on the bedside table.

The weather, though hot while in the sun, was almost comfortable when in the shade, because of the low humidity. It was nice enough inside to turn off the air conditioner and use the ceiling fans. The house was designed to take advantage of cross breezes to keep them comfortable. Still a little warm, she rose from the bed and opened the patio door another couple of inches. The smell of juniper drifted into the room. With a sigh, she retraced her steps to the bed and lay back down.

The doorbell rang and she heard Lonan's steps as he walked across the tile floor. "Hey, Joe. Come on in. How about a beer?"

"I'd love one. I've been in the sun most of the day and it's hot as the devil out there. My throat's so dry it feels like I've swallowed a truck load of dirt." She listened as their footsteps left the hall and they moved into the kitchen. "How's Madison?"

"She's doing fine. Good enough that she's resisting my fussing and coddling. Guess I'm going to have to stop."

All right! It's about time, thought Madison. The refrigerator door opened and she heard the clank of beer bottles. "Let's take these out on the patio."

Lonan's voice was deep, but didn't have the bass rumble of Joe's—a big voice to fit a big man. "As soon as Madison's well enough, you need to come over and pick the puppy you want."

"They can't be ready to leave their mother yet. Last week, you said they'd be ready in six weeks."

"True, but I have a line of people wanting one and want you to have first pick."

"Hans is the papa, right?"

"Yep, and Star is the bitch. You can already tell they're smart little buggers. Three females and two males. If you want one, you better come over and pick the dog you want."

They were quiet, guzzling their beers, she supposed. "Well, you want a puppy or not?"

"Yeah, I want one, but don't know if I can take on a pet right now. Who'd take care of him while I'm at work?"

"Your wife, of course. She like dogs, doesn't

she?"

She got up and padded to the patio door to join them outside.

"Yeah, I think she does. The problem is, I don't know how much longer she'll be here."

Never one to beat around the bush, Joe muttered, "And why the hell not?"

"She doesn't belong out here in the sticks. She needs to be in a big city where she can use her degree, play in an orchestra, go to the theatre if she wants."

Madison's heart sank to her toes. Hand poised at the sliding screen, she eased away from the door and rushed into the bathroom. She drew a tub full of water, turning the faucets on full to cover the sound of her sobs.

Joe snorted. "Hell, man, it's not like New Mexico is primitive and unsettled. She can do the things she loves here."

"Where? Out there on the mesa?"

Joe shook his head. "You love her, don't you?"

"Yeah, I love her, but damn it, I've told you—"

"Have you even asked her what she wants?" He shook his head. "You're a fool, Lonan Stone."

Maybe he was a fool, but he wanted Madison to be happy. And he didn't think she would be as a park ranger's wife. She'd said she loved him, but she would grow to hate him, tied down out here. He'd give anything if circumstances were different, but they weren't. His life was in Chaco Canyon with its Indian culture, and hers was with the literary crowd. The two didn't mix. Did they?

Joe stood, breaking his concentration. His parting words stuck like an arrow. "Most people never experience a love like you and Madison share."

"I—"

The big Indian held up his hand. "You can deny it all you want, but there's not a soul around here that can't see the love and attraction between you guys. Most people don't get a second chance at a love like that."

He set his empty beer bottle on the table, stood, and stared down at him. "You better give it some serious thought, friend."

Lonan heard the front door close and the roar of Joe's vehicle. Popping the cap on another beer, he guzzled half of it down in one swallow. *Getting drunk won't solve your problems, friend. You've got to make a decision.* Joe was right. She deserved to know his feelings and give her enough credit to make her own choice. He'd talk with her tonight, after dinner while they watched the sunset.

Inside, he walked softly to the bedroom in case Madison was asleep. She lay with her knees drawn up almost to her chest, his pillow hugged to her face. He'd never seen her sleep that way before. Not that he'd had the opportunity to watch her often. She looked so fragile lying there and vulnerable. God, he loved her, hoped she'd stay with him, but he wanted her to be happy and be able to use her career and skills.

In the bathroom, he noticed the tub was full of water. He reached down to pull the plug and noticed the water was still warm. Had Madison filled it and then decided to go back to bed? Maybe she was hurting again and didn't want him to know. She was pissed because he made her follow the doctor's orders and took every opportunity to let him know her displeasure. Tomorrow, she could do as she pleased.

He walked back into the bedroom and sat on the side of the bed. A hand to her forehead, he asked, "Sweetheart, you feel all right?"

She mumbled into the pillow. "Mmm, feel fine...just sleepy."

Brushing her hair back from her face, he leaned

down to give her a kiss on the cheek. "I'm going to run to the camp store. I'll be back in two hours." She rolled to her back and pulled his head to hers, taking his lips in a kiss that tasted and teased, making his nerves sizzle. *Lordy, he better get out of here or he'd never get to the store.* Not that he'd complain, but he wanted tonight's dinner to be special.

Groaning, he pulled away. His body said stay, but they needed wine to go with the lasagna they were making tonight. And candles, he wanted to have candlelight. He kissed her nose and forehead.

"What's wrong with your eyes? They're red and puffy like you've been crying."

"Really?"

"Yes, really. Are you upset about something?"

"Oh, it's that bath oil. The minute I poured some in the water, I remembered it aggravated my allergies. I took an antihistamine. They should be back to normal soon."

"You better dump that stuff in the trash and get something else."

"I'll throw it away as soon as I get up."

"I've already let the water out of the tub, so that should help. You need anything at the store?"

"No." She wrapped her arms around his neck. "But I need another kiss."

This meeting of lips was softer, sweeter, and poignant. It unsettled him for some reason. But then she smiled. "Be careful."

"I will." He stood and headed for the door. "You rest up, because tonight you're officially well and I intend to love you until sunrise." They'd made love several times since they'd returned home, but he held back in fear he'd hurt her. Now they could both give in to the intensity of their desire.

A smile stretched her face. "I'll look forward to it."

When he reached the door to the carport, he

heard her add, "Good-bye, Lonan."

****

Lonan whistled all the way home. He'd found several good bottles of wine at the camp store. Usually, the bottles were picked over, but they'd just received a new shipment. A box of tall candles sat on the seat beside him.

As he pulled up to the house and saw Madison's car was gone, dread washed over him.

He pulled in and parked. Leaving the groceries in the truck, he tore through the house, looking for signs she'd be back, but her clothes were gone, as was her violin.

"Son-of-a-bitch!" He kicked the bedside table, knocking it over. The glass lamp hit the floor and shattered. Then he saw the note on his pillow. He snatched it up and quickly scanned it, then read it again.

Dear Lonan,

I'm sorry to leave like this, but our lives are so different.

When I arrive in Houston, I'll find a lawyer and file for divorce.

I'll never regret coming to New Mexico, meeting Skystone and the people, and will treasure every minute we shared. I hope your memories of Hair of Flame will be fond ones.

Madison Evans Stone

Lonan wadded the paper into a ball and tossed it in the pile of glass on the floor. Anger shook his frame, yet his heart hurt. He was a damn fool. By waiting too long to tell her of his feelings, he'd lost her. Well, good riddance.

Pulling his shirt off, he strode to the bathroom, turned on the faucet and splashed water over his heated face and neck. He scrubbed dry with a towel, hung it on the rack, and then yanked if off, stuck his nose against it, and sniffed—no perfumes, only the soft, subtle smell of laundry detergent. He took a deep breath and looked around the small bathroom. There was no bath oil. Madison had lied to him. She didn't have allergy eyes, she'd been crying. Her kisses this afternoon said good-bye.

Why? What had happened to upset her? Everything had been fine that morning. Back in the bedroom, he sat on the bed, and dropped his head into his hands. The little bitch should've had the guts to tell him to his face she was leaving. He should've had a chance to tell her how he felt. Damn it to hell! He could have told her days ago how he felt. Why hadn't he?

The breeze from the patio door caught his attention. He stared at it for several seconds. She'd heard him and Joe talking. What had been said to make her run? He picked up the balled up letter and read it again. It didn't make any more sense than it did the first two times. She said she loved him, but she needed to hear those words from him. *Fool, fool, fool. You've lost her because you waited to long to share what was in your heart.*

****

Madison should have been crying, but instead, she drove with a dead calm and purpose. She'd go home, get a job, and get over Lonan Stone. No, she wouldn't, but she'd go on with her life and be a better person for having known him. But, she'd miss him, and Chaco Canyon—its beauty and history.

She stopped at the motel in Sotol and collected her box of papers and photographs. Back on the road, she drove past Albuquerque, where she turned southwest, headed for Texas. Around midnight, worn out, more from stress than activity, she pulled into the first motel that caught her attention in a tiny town on the Texas/New Mexico border. The room wasn't fancy, but clean. She fell into the bed fully clothed, and by 8 a.m., she was back on the road.

At midnight, she parked in the lot beside her apartment. The only things she carried inside were her family papers and violin. Before she'd left Houston, she'd turned the air up to 85 degrees, so she slid the lever down to 70, felt the compressor kick in and cool air rush from the vents. It'd be two hours before the place cooled off.

After a quick shower, she fell into bed and stared at the ceiling. Her locket lay on the bedside table. She picked it up and slipped it over her head. Finally back on familiar turf, she let go, and the tears flowed. Sobs wracked her body, her wails echoing around the room. Fearing her neighbors would hear, she muffled the sounds with her pillow and howled until she could cry no more, and then slipped into a dead sleep.

Pounding on the door woke her. "Madison, I know you're in there. Open this door and talk to me."

It was Lonan. She sat straight up in bed and pulled the sheet up to her chin. Harrumph! She might open the door, and then she might not. The pounding continued. She swung her legs over the side of the bed, stood and padded to the bathroom. After she peed and washed her hands, she brushed her teeth and washed her face.

"You know, I can kick this door down."

She brushed her hair. Let him wait.

"I'm tired, Madison. I drove straight through without sleep." He beat again. "Or food."

Oh, now that hurt. She couldn't stand to think of him weaving on his feet, stomach growling. Her front door had a transom above. She grabbed a Pop Tart from the pantry, opened the casement, and tossed the pastry through.

Ear against the door, she couldn't smother her giggle as she heard him ripping the package open.

She jumped back. "It would go down better with a cup of coffee."

"Why are you here, Lonan? Since I'm a literary person, I won't fit into your life in the boondocks, and with your people." She stifled a sob. "Plus, you don't love me. If you did, you'd have told me by now."

"Open this door, we're drawing a crowd." He spoke to someone in the hall. "She's my wife and I'm not leaving until I talk to her."

She heard someone talking but couldn't make out their words, and then jumped when he knocked. "Madison, open up now, or I'm going to kick this door in."

"You wouldn't dare."

The door shook as a booted foot hit the century-old wood.

"Okay, okay. You can come in, but say your piece and leave." Though the hurt remained, compassion overrode the emotion. She stared. His face was drawn, his yellow eyes, flashing with anger, were red from fatigue. Black stubble covered his chin and jaw. He carried a small duffle bag. Moving back so he could enter, she said, "I'll make coffee and fix you something to eat."

"Do you mind if I take a shower?"

"No." She waved toward the bathroom. "Go ahead. Towels are in the tall cabinet."

She quickly dressed in shorts and T-shirt, but remained barefoot. It didn't take but a minute to make the bed.

Breakfast? What the heck could she cook with nothing in the refrigerator? She searched the pantry. All she had was Pop Tarts, Pancake Mix, and Cereal. Unfortunately, she didn't have any milk. Looked like they'd have sugar with their coffee.

It didn't take Lonan long to shower, shave, and dress. He walked into the bedroom and tossed his bag onto her bed. She bristled, but clamped her mouth shut. Let the man eat, then she'd lay into him.

She handed him a cup of coffee.

"Thank you."

"You're welcome. Sit down. Hot breakfast coming up." She placed a plate with two boxed strawberry pastries in front of him.

He arched an eyebrow and his lip twitched.

"They're warm and happen to be all I have at the moment. I haven't had time to go to the store."

She sat down with him and started munching. They weren't too bad when heated.

When he finished, she removed their plates to the sink and refilled their cups.

"Okay, say what you came to say and then go."

He cleared his throat. "I want you to come home, for us to build a life together."

"We don't have enough in common to make it work, Lonan. After all, I'm the literary type who needs the theatre, bright lights, and a university."

He reached for her hand, but she moved it under the table to her knee. "You misconstrued what you heard on the patio. I was telling Joe my fears, not my conclusion. He knew I loved you and said I'd be a fool to let you go. I knew it too, and didn't plan on letting it happen."

"Then why did you? You never once told me you loved me."

He rubbed the back of his neck. "That afternoon I left, I went to get wine and a box full of candles. I'd planned to tell you over a romantic dinner."

Her heart lurched. Was he telling the truth?

"You don't believe me? Woman, I've got the candles and wine in my truck to prove it."

Why, the man was getting mad at her. How dare he? She was the injured party here.

"How the hell do you think I felt when I drove up to find you gone? And why the hell did you just

226

leave a note? I didn't picture you as a coward, Hair of Flame," he spat out. "You should have faced me, told me you were leaving."

Should she believe him? The phone rang. She kept him in her line of sight as she picked it up on the fourth ring. "Hello."

Her sister's voice vibrated over the line, loud as it always was when she was excited. "Are you all right, Madison?"

"I'm fine, Rosalie."

"Your neighbor called and said a man was trying to get into your apartment. She said he claimed to be your husband."

"Rosalie, I'm—"

"Uncle Dan is on his way over there."

Madison groaned. "Sis, why did you call him?" Her uncle was a bull of a man and wouldn't leave until he was satisfied she was all right.

"He should be there in five minutes, and I'm not far behind."

She hung up and sank into a chair. The door shook with her uncle's knock. "Young woman, what in thunderation is going on over here? If you don't open up, I'll shoot the lock off and let myself in."

She shot from the chair. "I'm coming, Uncle Dan. Don't you dare put a hole in this door." It was an antique, and the only thing beautiful about her apartment.

Lonan stood. "Your uncle, the Texas Ranger, I presume." He didn't look in the least nervous that an armed man was coming in to protect her. She snorted. Men!

"It's unlocked."

He barged through like a bull. "Dammit, how many times have I told you to keep this place locked up as tight as a drum?" He whirled to Lonan. "And who the hell are you?"

Lonan took out his billfold, flipped it open, and

handed it to her uncle. He looked at his I.D., handed it back, and then offered his hand. "Dan Dyson, Ranger Stone. Now what are you doing in my niece's apartment?"

"I'm her husband. She's upset and left me without a word, just a note. I've come to bring my wife back home."

He rocked back on his heels while eyeing Lonan. "And just exactly why did she leave?"

Lonan held up a hand. "I would never hurt her, if that's what you're thinking."

"Good thing for you." He turned his steely gaze on Madison. "What's going on here, Missy? Are you married to this man?"

Before she could answer, Rosalie flew through the door and skidded to a halt at the sight of Lonan. "Married? You got married and didn't tell me?"

"Hush, Rosie." Uncle Dan's expression brooked no argument. Madison couldn't hide her grin as Rosalie shut her mouth and struggled to keep it closed. "Now, answer me, Madison. Are you legally married to this man?"

She took a deep breath, and exhaled. "Yes."

He nodded and pursed his lips. "Do you love him?" Before she could utter a word, he belted out, "And don't lie to me."

"Yes, Uncle Dan, but—"

He turned to Lonan. "Do you love my niece?"

"Yes, sir, I do."

"Then what's she upset about?"

"We married under unusual circumstances." He shrugged. "I was too stupid to tell her how much I loved her." He turned to Madison. "You should have known how I felt. I showed you in every way possible."

"Son, you don't know much about women, do you?" He included Madison in his stare. "You've admitted you love each other. Now work this out.

228

Your aunt and I will expect you for supper tonight at 6:30, and you better be the image of conjugal bliss."

He took Rosie's arm. "Come on, let these two work things out."

Lonan closed and locked the door behind them, and then turned on her. "Are we going to work this out?"

"I don't know. I've got to think about it. Come back this afternoon."

"I'm not leaving, Madison. While you're thinking, I'm going to get some sleep." He stalked from the room, with her on his heels. She watched as he stripped down to his shorts and climbed into her bed as if he belonged there. At the sight of his bronzed body, damn if her mouth didn't water. "Come take a nap with me, sweetheart."

"Dream on, buster." She flounced from the room.
****

Lonan woke to find Madison lying on her side, asleep next to him. Actually, she was as far away as the bed would allow, but his arm could easily reach her. He lay still though, and watched her sleep, the rise and fall of her chest, dark lashes fanning across her upper cheekbone, and that full mouth he loved so much slightly open. Her hair sprung out from her head and lay in curls all over the pillow.

He'd made up his mind. She'd not leave this bed until she realized he loved her. The bedside clock said 3 p.m. Hopefully, it wouldn't take too long to convince her. Her uncle didn't appear to be the type to be kept waiting.

With one hand under her head and one on her butt, he pulled her closer. She murmured, "Morning."

Maybe this would easier than he'd thought. "Morning, sweetheart."

Her eyes flew open, then grew wide. She shoved at his chest. "Let me up."

"If you didn't want me to touch you, why are you in this bed with me?"

"Because I was tired and the couch wasn't comfortable." She tried to wiggle away from him. "Let me up, Lonan."

He pulled her closer, his mouth flush with hers. "I love you, Madison." He nibbled at her lips. "Forgive me for being a bumbling fool and not doing things the right way." Tears leaked from her eyes and he caught them with his tongue. "I want you to stay with me forever, but I want you to be happy and use your education. I was afraid you'd grow tired of our isolated area and begin to hate me."

"Really?"

"Yes, really." He nuzzled her neck.

She sniffed. "Hate you? Never. I love Chaco Canyon. I could teach in Albuquerque two days a week and be home five."

Hope flared in his chest. "What about your music?" His heart thumped with anticipation as he waited for her answer.

"I can give lessons on the reservations, maybe the schools."

He released a sigh of relief. Pride engulfed him. "That would make the people very happy. They'd be grateful to have you share your talent."

She pulled back and corrected him, "Our people."

His throat tightened. He pulled her closer and whispered in her ear. "Yes, our people, love." His hand caressed her back and moved down to cup her buttocks. "Am I forgiven?"

"Say it again."

He hid his grin in her neck. "I love you, Madison. I think I have from the moment you grabbed me around the neck on the cliff, after your first trip to ancient Una Vida."

"Really?"

"Yes, really."

She wrapped her arms around his neck and gave his hair a couple of yanks. "You better have wine and candles in that truck of yours."

"I'd go get them, but I'm afraid you'd lock me out again."

She threw her leg over his, bringing her heat flush with his arousal. He groaned and thrust against her. He rolled to his back with her straddling his body. "I want you, woman."

She wiggled against him. "I know." In one swift movement, she'd drawn her tee-shirt over her head and tossed it aside. He sat up and teased the flesh above her breasts with his fingers, stroking over her shoulders, then back down to circle her taut nipples. Her breath hitched. She let her head drop back, offering her breasts up for closer intimacy. She tried to take her bra off, but he caught her hands and used his mouth to further torment her.

"Lonan, please." He rolled her to her back and quickly removed her bra. She pushed her shorts and panties down, kicking them aside and reached for his shorts. "I want to see you."

He lay back, watched her eyes, sucked in his breath, and trembled as she stroked his body. "You're a beautiful man, Lonan." Her lips followed the path of her hands. She nipped at his waist, swirled her tongue in his navel, and nibbled her way down his legs and back up taking her time at the juncture of his thighs. When she poised above his sex, her mouth ready to touch him, he shouted, "No," and pulled her up for his kiss.

His hand slipped between them and found her sex moist and ready for him. He rubbed the slick folds until she squirmed. Hands on his chest, she lifted her hips to take him inside. Slowly, she inched down until deeply seated. He set his jaw, determined to remain still, to let her set the pace. She rocked, he held her thighs and joined the motion as they moved, setting a rhythm that pleasured them both, searching, seeking until their world burst and they gasped out their pleasure.

They lay entwined on the bed, covers strewn on the floor. "You're coming home with me, aren't you?"

"It'll take me a week or so to get a mover to pack up my things."

He stilled. "You plan to bring everything in this apartment?" There'd never be enough room for all her stuff and his too.

She sat up and looked around. "I'd like to bring this bed and my vanity. We could probably use the chest too."

"Okay." Lord, there'd be wall-to-wall furniture.

"I know it'll be a tight fit, but we could put it in the spare bedroom."

It might work, he thought.

"The only other furniture I want is the dining room table, Mama's grandmother's china cabinet and the dishes inside. A few pieces were Texanna Dyson's."

Lonan smiled. Their home would be a blend of cultures, as their children would be.

Chapter Twenty

Lonan heard Madison's car as she drove up the isolated road. It'd been three weeks since he'd left Houston, now an approved member of Madison's family. He smiled at the memory. They were a rowdy bunch, much like his own. The car screeched to a halt before he was fully out the door. She flew from the car and jumped into his arms, legs twined around his waist. "Oh, I missed you!" She planted kisses all over his face before finding his mouth.

Between kisses, he managed to get out, "I missed you too, sweetheart."

She dropped her head to his shoulder. "I can't believe I'm finally here." She unwound her legs and he set her on her feet. Face alive with enthusiasm, she looked at the house and the trees and rocks that surrounded it. Her gaze stopped on an addition to the yard and her mouth fell open. She whirled to face him. "My God, what is that?"

"Why, it's a wedding gift, my dear. From my cousin, the one who made the big wooden bear."

She shook her head. "You need to break that man's chain saw, or find him another art field."

Laughter burst from his mouth. "It is a sight isn't it?" This statue was the tall grizzly's mate. She stood on all fours, snarling up at the male. "I shudder to think what he'll give us when we have our first child."

Covering her mouth, she giggled. "I'm buying the man a modeling set, or how about a welding torch. Scrap metal is being made into interesting yard art these days, if you're interested in that kind of stuff."

She was so cute. He squeezed her shoulders. "Come on. Let's get your car unpacked so you can shower and have dinner. I've cooked for you, madam." *And have plans for our evening, I might add.*

****

The warm shower refreshed her. Now she was ready to eat whatever Lonan had cooked for her. Her stomach growled at the heavenly smells coming from the kitchen. Wow! A hunky husband, and he could cook, too.

She layered on freesia-scented lotion, slipped into new bikini panties and bra, both deep lavender. She loved the color as well as their silky feel. Wearing white shorts and a purple sleeveless blouse that hit her at the waist, she stepped into sandals. Her hair was wet, so she pulled it up on top of her head and held it with a large clasp, then pulled a few curls loose around her face. A touch of lipgloss, and she was finished.

When she stepped out of the bathroom, the hallway was dark. "Lonan, what's wrong with the lights?" Her eyes adjusted and she could see a glow coming from the living room. He met her at the end of the hall, and held out a long-stemmed red rose. With a flourish, he led her into the living room. Candles glowed everywhere. On the mantle, the floor, the end tables, and on the large coffee table set with placemats for two, with pillows arranged on the floor.

"Your romantic dinner, my love."

Her heart jumped up into her throat. "Oh, Lonan, it's beautiful. Thank you, darling."

He lightly kissed her lips. "My pleasure. Now, come sit down while I serve you." She watched his retreating form. His denim shorts cupped his tight butt, and his white polo shirt emphasized the

234

whiteness of his teeth when he smiled. She sighed. *Oh my, I love that man.*

Lonan returned with small salads. He placed them on their mats and then eased down onto a pillow, sitting cross-legged. "Would you like some wine?"

"Yes, I'd love some."

He filled their glasses half full. "A toast." She raised her glass. "To us. May our love be as great in fifty years as it is today."

She tapped her glass to his. "Here, here!"

****

Madison looked around at the guest bedroom. Her bed and chest were a tight squeeze, but the golden oak looked pretty against the coffee-and-cream-colored walls. The vanity occupied a niche in their bedroom. It was bigger and she could use the dresser with its big mirror. Lonan hadn't been too sure about the color she'd picked out for the walls, a shade between olive and gold called antiquity, but liked it once it was on the walls. He accused her of choosing it because it looked good with her hair.

She'd painted the living room and one wall in the kitchen a color between rust and orange called jalapeno, as it blended so well with his Navajo rug. She'd learned why the piece of art was so important to him.

The night of their candlelight dinner, they lay entwined on their bed, relaxed, discussing whatever came to mind. "Lonan, tell me about the rug on the wall."

It took a while for him to start talking. "My best friend, Glenn Black Raven and I joined the service at the same time. Somehow, we were able to stay together through training and were sent to Afghanistan in the same unit." His breathing grew harsh. Madison wished she'd not asked him.

She cupped his face. "Don't tell me if it hurts too

much."

He captured her hand and kissed the palm. "I need to tell you. Maybe it will help my heart heal."

"Take your time." She cradled his head on her shoulder and stroked his back.

"One day while on patrol in the mountains, we were ambushed. Our men were screaming, falling like flies. We returned fire as we ran for cover." He rolled to his back and took her with him. "I covered Glenn while he ran to get over a small rise. Someone yelled, 'Stone! Haul ass.' It was Glenn. As I took off running, Glenn had reached the top of the mound and turned to see if I was coming. Before he could turn and jump behind the small hill of dirt, a bullet caught him in the chest."

Lonan's big body shook. His arms locked around her and she tried to hold him with her arms and legs about him. "Shhh, don't talk anymore."

"Got to." He struggled to get the words out. "I'll never forget the blood that burst from his chest or the look on his face—one of shock, denial. I reached him, jumped over the hill and landed on my back, cradling Glenn to my chest. I started screaming, 'Medic! Medic!' and ripped his shirt open. Blood pulsed from a gaping hole. I rammed my fist inside his chest to try to keep him alive until the medics arrived." He shook his head. "Dammit, if he hadn't turned and called to me, he'd be alive today."

Tears pooled in her eyes at his suffering. "Lonan, you know you'd have done the same for Glenn, looked back to make sure he made it." She kissed his wet cheeks, his lips, and held him. His shaking eased. She thought he'd fallen asleep. When she moved to lie at his side, he whispered, "The blanket is a healing gift from Glenn's mother—to heal my heart."

Madison felt weepy just remembering, but in the past week, she'd seen Lonan staring at the blanket, and once she saw his lips curve into a smile. Maybe Mrs. Black Raven's gift was doing its job.

Lonan worked until 8 p.m. this week, so she had plenty of time to piddle around the house. She'd cleaned, dinner was partially made and in the refrigerator. The week after she'd arrived, she'd sent applications to the University of New Mexico and a private faith-based university. Yesterday she'd received an interview request. They needed someone to teach English Literature three days a week, but maybe she could talk them into scheduling so she'd only have to stay for two days.

She grabbed a Dr. Pepper from the refrigerator, a couple of magazines, and her favorite book of Shakespeare's works. Her sun hat hung from a peg by the back door. Rather than listen to Lonan fuss if he caught her without it, she plopped it on her head. Outside, she set her reading material and her soda on the table beside the chaise lounge and turned to check the geraniums she'd planted in five-gallon clay pots. Standing between the two pots were several wine bottles with candles and wax dripped down the sides. They weren't attractive, but served the purpose of adding light and romance to the patio.

The plants were fine, the dirt moist but not soggy. With the water hose, she washed the dirt off her fingers, and shook them dry. She moved the chaise out of the sun and positioned it to recline at a forty-five degree angle. Drink in hand, she stretched out and pulled the tab on her drink. The carbonation bubbles teased her nose and she struggled not to sneeze.

Her literature book was marked to *Romeo and Juliet*. She slipped the paper marker in the back of the book and started reading. How could people not enjoy the works of this master? The words fell together so smoothly, the prose beautiful.

With her finger marking the page, she laid it

across her abdomen and closed her eyes for a minute. It was fairly heavy and the weight felt comfortable against her. In a haze between sleep and consciousness, her mind drifted. She stood by the cliff art, wind whipping her hair around her head. White Fox spoke, but she couldn't understand him over the noise of the air current. "I can't hear you." As if he'd snapped his fingers and said hocus pocus, the air stilled.

Hair of Flame, your job is not finished. The people are still in jeopardy. Nukpana is still on the loose, the earth did not hold him. You must capture him and confine him forever.

"But how?"

The gods will show you the way.

"They better, because this evil spirit business isn't fun."

She yawned. "You've never been in my dreams before, White Fox. Why now?"

It wasn't necessary before.

"Oh, okay."

There was a light breeze that tickled the hairs on her arms. It carried the scent of juniper and something else that wasn't pleasant.

A voice rumbled through her head. *He is here! Do it now!*

****

Lonan made one last turn through the campground. He'd had to give a citation to a man from Boston for starting a fire in an undesignated area. He'd leave word for someone to check back on the camper tonight.

It felt good to be working again. He'd enjoyed having time with Madison, but the park was his job, one he loved. Madison didn't seem to mind him leaving. She stayed busy painting and moving furniture around. He had to admit, the house did look nice. He was proud of the way she'd decorated the living room around the colors in his Navajo rug.

On Saturday, he and Madison had driven to visit with Glenn's mother. The older woman welcomed Madison with open arms and hugged him tightly. "It's about time you came. I'm glad to see you happy." She patted his cheek. "The hole in your heart is healing." He could only nod. She smiled. "Good. The one in my heart is, too."

It was almost time to go home. For the past hour he'd been counting the minutes until he got off, which was unusual for him. Before Madison came along, he'd worked overtime, but he didn't any longer unless needed.

Something nagged at the back of his mind, and he didn't have a clue what it was. He'd been tempted twice to call Madison and see if everything was all right, but decided she wouldn't appreciate being checked on. Still, unease niggled at him. *Get a grip, man, you're being sappy.*

Madison had settled in and seemed happy. He was pleased she'd received responses to her applications for teaching positions at the University of New Mexico and a private college. He'd hate her being gone overnight, possibly two nights, but if it cinched her contentment, it would be worth it. Maybe it would be possible to arrange his schedule so he worked those nights and could be home during the day when she didn't have to work. There was so much of the country he wanted to show her and more family for her to meet.

Madison's Uncle Dan was a real character. How he'd gotten his sweet wife to marry him, Lonan didn't have a clue. Maybe it had something to do with knowing more about how a woman's mind worked. He liked them both, as well as Madison's sister, Rosalie. They'd all be coming out next year when the new Skystone exhibit opened at the museum. Madison had volunteered to leave her

239

locket on loan for two years. He'd have to find something for her to wear until she got it back.

It was 8 p.m. He was headed home. Wonder what Madison had fixed for dinner.

****

Startled, Madison's eyes flew open to see a rock squirrel standing on hind legs to the side of her right knee. "Scat, get out of here."

The squirrel bared its teeth in what resembled a smile gone astray, that metamorphosed into the evil face of Nukpana. Madison didn't think. With a screech, she backhanded the creature with her book, knocking it against the adobe wall near her geraniums.

"Holy Molie!" She jumped up to look at the animal. The creature was stunned. Fearing it would get up to attack her or run away, she picked up a wine bottle and pounded. "Take that, that, that!"

Breathless with relief, she looked at the squirrel. It wasn't going anywhere, but its mouth opened and miasma began to rise. She jumped back with a squeal. *Think, Madison, think!*

Her eyes lit on the container of geraniums. Hand poised to give the squirrel another whack if necessary, she yanked the red flowers from the pot, tossed them aside, and turned it upside down, dirt and all, on top of Nukpana. She twisted it and pushed until the edges were flush with the cement floor.

Satisfied, with her handiwork, she looked around to find something to stuff in the drain hole in the bottom. The bloody wine jug caught her attention. She yanked the candle out and shoved the neck as far down as it would go in the couple of inches of dirt left in the underside. It was jammed in so tight, it would be impossible for anything to come past the edges, but just to make sure, she located the lighter Lonan kept on the window casing. She clicked until flame shot out. Holding it under one end of the candle, she melted and dripped a ring of wax around where the container and bottle met.

That done, she sat down, exhausted and shaking. She watched the overturned flowerpot to see if anything would happen. Five minutes later, it dawned on her that Nukpana's miasma could rise out from underneath the vessel. What could she use to form a barrier? She looked around outside and noticed the fresh caulking on the windows. Where had Lonan put the caulking gun? Under the kitchen sink. She calculated how long it would take her to get the gun and get back. The animal hadn't revived or the pot would have been shaking. Dare she take a chance and run get it? She didn't have a choice. If the bottom wasn't sealed, Nukpana's smelly mist could ooze from the bottom.

First she had to make sure it was weighted down. She noticed several nice sized rocks just off the patio. They should do the trick. Making a dash for the small boulders, she grabbed two and set them on top of her makeshift prison. Reasonably sure they'd hold the squirrel securely inside, she ran into the kitchen, grabbed the caulking gun and rushed back out.

There was an art to caulking, and she hadn't developed the skill, but she didn't need it to look pretty. She made one pass around the pot, and then another, making the line as thick as possible. Then with her fingers, she smoothed the paste out making sure it sealed around the bottom of the container and where it connected to the cement. For extra measure, she put some around the neck of the wine bottle, over the wax.

Satisfied that she'd done everything she could to contain the evil one, she pulled the recliner closer to the pot and sat down. She watched as bit by bit, the wine bottle filled with the dark haze of Nukpana.

Her eyes wouldn't leave her prisoner's cage, not until Lonan got home to help her.

****

Lonan walked into the kitchen with no delicious odors wafting through the room. The house was dark, though the sun hadn't quite set. It was still a good ways above the far mesa.

"Madison, where are you, sweetheart?"

"Out here on the patio."

Her voice sounded tired and mournful. "I'm so glad you're home."

He stepped outside, apprehension tensing his muscles. "Is something wrong?" She stepped into his arms and he held her close. Over her shoulder he saw something, he wasn't quite sure what. He didn't want to hurt her feelings, but... A large clay pot was turned upside down, with the neck of a partially waxed wine bottle stuffed in the hole. Some kind of white goop ran around the vial's neck and the base of the clay pot. Two rocks sat on what was now the top of the creation. He looked around and noticed the geraniums and dirt scattered around the patio. His eyes returned to the object. God, it was ugly. "That's not some kind of new artwork, is it?"

Chapter Twenty-One

Madison jerked back and slapped him on the chest. "That's not the least bit funny!"

"Ouch!" Her whack didn't hurt, but her trembling alarmed him. He caught her shoulders. "What's the matter with you?"

"I've been sitting here for four hours in the heat," she motioned toward the 'object', "making sure Nukpana couldn't get out of this makeshift jail."

Nukpana? He bent down to examine the wine bottle closely. A black smoke swirled around inside. *My God!* No wonder he'd been apprehensive earlier. Madison had been in danger and he'd not been here to help her.

He straightened, and cupping the back of her head, drew her into his embrace. Hands on her back, he stroked and pulled her closer. Lord, she could've been killed. Anything could have happened. "You did good, baby. You did real good."

She sighed against his chest. "I've been so afraid he could escape. I was afraid to leave for a second. Can you watch him for a minute? I'm dying to go to the bathroom." Without waiting for an answer, she left his arms and rushed inside.

He took her seat on the chaise and studied the bottle. "So, Nukpana, we meet again. I think Hair of Flame out-foxed you, old boy." He chuckled. "With a flower pot and a wine bottle." Lonan couldn't hold the laughter inside. Chuckles turned into guffaws.

When Madison came back out, he was wiping tears from his face.

Hands on her hips, she snorted. "Well, I'm glad

you think this is so funny. I've had a miserable day, not to mention I was scared out of my mind." She did look bedraggled. Her fair skin was slightly sunburned, with dirt and caulking smeared on her clothes and face.

Trying to stifle his chuckles, he held out a hand. "Come sit with me. Tell me what happened."

She eyed him for a second. "Come on, I'm through laughing, and I certainly wasn't making fun of you."

She settled on the chaise beside him. "I was reading and started dozing off, but heard White Fox's voice." She relayed what had taken place—from the messenger's voice, to her using her Shakespeare book to backhand the rock squirrel. It was the picture in his mind of her bludgeoning it with the wine bottle that set him off again. It didn't take much imagination to see her yanking the flowers up by the roots and stuffing the neck of the wine bottle in, either.

His hysterical laughter made her giggle. "Stop it, now. What are we going to do with him?" She shivered. "I don't think I can sleep with the thought of him being out here on the patio, and his cage may not be very secure."

"Was there still plenty of dirt in the pot when you covered him?"

"Yes, about half full."

"Good. The only way Nukpana can get lose is if the squirrel is still alive, which I seriously doubt, and could move enough to loosen the grout." From the pounding the creature had taken, Lonan doubted it had an inch of life left in it. It's a wonder she didn't crack...shit...the bottle. He jumped up to inspect it closely.

She joined him. "What are you looking for?"

"To make sure you didn't crack the bottle when you bludgeoned the squirrel."

"Oh, God!" She jerked back and covered her mouth.

"Settle down, now." He didn't see any cracks, but carefully ran his hand over it to make sure before straightening. "I don't think he can escape, but I'm like you. I don't want to take a chance." He threw his arm across her shoulders and turned her head up to his for a quick kiss. "The people will be proud of you, sweetheart. You more than deserve the name Hair of Flame, and your Badger Fetish."

How could they have been fooled into thinking they held him fast in the earth? All number of animals, bugs, worms lived in the soil. And then, the squirrel being tossed out of the vortex with them. He shook his head. They'd been careless, and Madison could have been infected by the rotten soul. His eyes turned skyward. *Thank you, God, for sending White Fox to watch over her.*

"What are we going to do with him? I'm starved and worn out."

"You leave that to me. Go in and take a long soak and when you finish, he'll be taken care of. We won't have to worry about him any longer."

"Are you sure?"

"Yes, love."

"Thank goodness."

Madison didn't know how Lonan had taken care of Nukpana, but when she finished bathing, he'd cleaned up the mess on the patio, everything, that is, but the white ring of caulk. He'd even stuffed her geraniums back into what little dirt was left in the pot.

The following day, he delivered the evil one to The Tribal Council. Their Spirit Talkers, including his grandmothers, had been called, and a solution worked out for Nukpana's resting place.

Madison didn't want to know where they'd put him. She felt safer not knowing, which was probably stupid, but...

Madison couldn't keep her eyes off her husband. The only time she'd seen him dressed up was at their wedding. Tonight, he wore a dark suit over a light blue silk shirt open at the neck. Hubahuba. Handsome didn't completely describe him. He was that, but he exuded an air of raw animal appeal. Her shiver wasn't nerves. Her stomach flipped and heat shot to her toes. It was lust, pure and simple—pride and love, too.

"You ready to go, sweetheart?" His gaze traveled from her strappy high heels, to the top of her head. "Turn around." She twirled for him. "Beautiful." He tilted her chin. "You know I love for you to wear this dress and shoes, don't you?"

"Yes, I do, that's why I wore them." It was a black crepe ballerina length that dipped low in the back and emphasized her derriere.

He kissed her softly on the lips, "Thank you," and then dropped a hand to her hip, where it moved to cup her butt. His brow furrowed. "I don't feel a panty line. You're not bare under there, are you?"

"Nooo. I noticed your interest in the mannequin in the store window yesterday—you know, the one wearing the black thong."

His eyes lit and he grinned. "You didn't?"

"I did."

"Hot damn! Let's get out of here and get this show over with."

She picked up her evening bag and they left the hotel room. It had been one year since Nukpana had been contained. Tonight, the Albuquerque Museum of Arts and History would open the new Skystone Exhibit. At the urging of the Indian Affairs Council, anthropologists had re-examined the artifacts found with the bones of the woman wearing the Skystone. They'd uncovered several interesting items. And her locket would be on display with the mother stone and the second twin. She'd agreed to leave it for two years.

Being without it would be hard, she'd feel naked, but Lonan had bought her a beautiful amethyst and amber pendant set in gold with matching earrings. Now, unable to resist, she reached up to touch the stones. She'd been thrilled when he'd presented them to her.

Yesterday, they'd just dropped her locket off at the museum, and returned to the car. Lonan reached across her lap to open the glove box and withdrew a velvet jeweler's box. He flipped it open to reveal her remaining amber earring suspended in a circle of amethyst.

"Oh, Lonan, it's beautiful," her voice cracked, "and Great-Grandmother Evans's earring. I thought I'd lost it."

He just grinned and removed the necklace from the box. "Lift your hair for me."

She complied, tilting her head forward as she did so.

"There."

Flipping the visor down, she gazed at her reflection in the mirror. It was the most stunning piece of jewelry she'd ever seen. She twisted her head to watch the amber in the center dance with each movement.

"Do you like it?"

"Do I like it?" she squealed. "I love it!" She leaned toward him, pulled his face to hers, and kissed him. "It's magnificent. Thank you, darling."

Now, as they walked through the revolving door of the hotel, they left the cool air for the heat of outdoors. As they stood waiting for their car, she tucked her arm through Lonan's.

He looked down. "Are you nervous?"

"A little. I've given talks in lecture halls, but this is totally different."

"You'll do fine." Their car arrived, and he ran around to the driver's side while the attendant held her door. They fastened their seat belts.

Madison relaxed against the seat. Butterflies tickled her stomach. "I hope so. This is a big moment in all our lives."

****

Lonan stood back and watched his wife with pride as she stood at the podium in the lecture hall and talked about her family history. She was a natural, and didn't appear at all nervous. Using a Power Point presentation, she showed pictures of her ancestors and some of the old family documents. When she flashed pictures of her great-grandmother wearing the locket, they leaned forward in their seats to better see.

"That concludes my presentation, ladies and gentlemen. If you have any questions, I'll be near the Skystone Exhibit and will be happy to talk with you."

The room thundered with applause and she waved as the curator took over the microphone. "Thank you, Mrs. Stone, for your talk, as well as for leaving your locket with the museum so people can see all three pieces together." Madison nodded and more clapping echoed around the room. "Now, ladies and gentlemen, if you'll move to the exhibit hall, we'll begin the unveiling ceremony. Please help yourself to the refreshments and enjoy the display." The man got a little choked up. "It is splendid. I never dreamed the stones would be reunited. It's a miracle."

As soon as she exited the stage, Madison was surrounded by people. She shook hands with the patrons and visited. When she caught his eye, Lonan stepped in to whisk her away. He eased through the group. "Excuse me, folks, Madison is needed at the exhibit."

"Am I really needed or did you make that up to rescue me?"

"They won't do the unveiling until you and I arrive, plus our families are waiting." Madison's sister, Uncle Dan and his wife, along with several cousins made the trip. His family had embraced the newcomers and they stood together, talking like life-long friends.

Mr. Rodriguez, President of the Museum's Board, stood patiently. He had the honor of lifting the black cloth that covered the glass case that rose five feet from the floor. It was probably thirty inches square.

Madison clutched his arm as they drew nearer to the display. "For some reason, I'm nervous. Do you know what else they found stored away with Talking Bird's bones?"

"No, but I'm sure it's not something you should fear or worry about." He squeezed her hand. "Buck up, woman. You're Hair of Flame."

She stood taller, shoulders back. "That's right. What is there to fear? Nukpana is imprisoned forever, the mother stone has been reunited with her twins, and they're safe behind that tempered glass."

Mr. Rodriguez beamed. "Ah, here they come now, our guests of honor." Lonan escorted Madison around to stand beside the older man. "Before I unveil our treasure, I want to say that it was Park Ranger Stone who suggested to the Council that we further investigate the container where the Skystone was found along with its owner's remains. If not for him, we'd not have the additional items to share with the world. He also found the second twin while exploring on top of Fajada Butte."

Madison looked at him. "Additional items?"

He whispered. "I don't have a clue what they found. No one's told me." He looked over at the Council's Chief Elder. His eyes gleamed with pride as he nodded.

"Ladies and gentlemen," he pulled the black cloth away, "the Skystone Exhibit." Gasps rushed around the room. The Skystone was the focal point, with her necklace and the second twin as accents. Light glinted off the mother stone, and for those who'd never seen it, it had to be an extraordinary sight.

Madison had seen it several times, but could only stare in wonder. Seeing her locket grouped with the other stones touched her deeply. It was as if a soul from another time called to her. Tears gathered in her eyes and she grasped Lonan's hand as they stepped closer for a better look.

Mr. Rodriguez continued to talk, but the roar in her ears was so intense, she barely heard him. Music, the music of the people, the flutes and drums, and the sing-song chanting that accompanied them. For a moment she was back at Una Vida, atop Fajada Butte.

Her gaze moved from the turquoise to the other objects on display. "Ah..." She stifled the cry with her fist. There, atop the small bag made of human hair Talking Bird had worn around her neck, lay her amber earring, even more stunning for having been handled with loving hands for years. The old woman must have treasured the bauble. Madison remembered her holding it up to watch it dangle, a smile of delight stretching her mouth. The wire hoop was gone and only the hole where it had once been remained.

Lonan caressed her neck, and whispered in her ear, "It wasn't a dream, sweetheart. If we needed proof, which we don't, it's there before us."

"It's all so surreal," she said, unable to take her gaze off the artifacts. "Look at the tall pot. It wasn't here before. I don't remember seeing any pottery like this." It was black on white, painted with geometric designs.

"This style of pottery wasn't made until later. I think it was made around 1250 A.D."

She was curious. Why had they added the earthenware to the exhibit?

Lonan's arm snaked around her waist. "Let's step aside and let the others get a closer look."

When at last the line dwindled, Madison joined her aunt and uncle. The older couple studied the artifacts with rapt attention. Aunt Kate hugged her and then stepped back, leaving her hands on her forearms. It was a habit her aunt used with them as kids, to make sure they were listening to her. "What an accomplishment, Madison, to have traced the history of the locket this far back. It's a real honor to the family."

"Thank you. I think I'm still in shock. So much has happened in so little time."

Uncle Dan continued to look, but tossed her a smile. "You did good, Missy. Your mama would be real proud."

Rosalie leaned down to get a better look at the bag. "I can't believe they cut their hair to make stuff with." She shivered. "Just thinking about wearing something made of human hair gives me the willies."

She peered closer, turned back to grab Madison's hand, and tugged her closer to the glass. "Missy, look at that piece of amber. It looks just like one of Great-Grandmother Evans's earrings, doesn't it?"

Madison gasped, and quickly covered her necklace. She moved in beside Rosalie. "It sure does. Almost identical. Isn't that strange?"

Uncle Dan, a head taller than everyone else, bent and studied the earring. "Sure looks like something modern, but with stone, it's hard to tell. Just look at Missy's locket. It doesn't look old."

His attention returned to the pot. He scratched

his chin.

"For the life of me, I can't figure out what the heck that wax-covered wine bottle is doing in that pot."

Epilogue

Madison sat on the low stone wall at Una Vida with Lonan at her side. They were pressed hip-to-hip beneath the warm blanket, arms linked to share body warmth. Chu'a, Lonan's German shepherd pup, lay at their feet, muzzle on his crossed front paws. The fire in the center sizzled, sending hot sparks dancing on the wind. It was the end of October, the last of the campfires until next spring.

Sam Spotted Elk, Lonan's grandfather, prepared to speak to the visitors, some with children of varying ages, and others just couples, both young and old. He stood, waited for quiet, and started chanting. Two teen boys accompanied on the drums. Slowly, Sam danced around the fire to the ancient rhythm. Every eye remained on his tall body as, hands in the air, he sang, offering a prayer to the gods.

Then total silence. Everyone waited expectantly. "Tonight, I will share the legend of the witch woman." He paused for a moment as he made eye contact with the listeners. "She called to the gods to destroy her evil son, and they killed him." Sam walked up to a boy, probably around ten years old. "Have you seen the witch on the cliff drawings?" Eyes round, the kid nodded. "Ah, how about the rest of you? Raise your hands if you've seen her." Hands went up all around the circle.

"Her name was Talking Bird. Her son, Nukpana, inherited the Skystone from his father. But, he used the stone's magic to work evil, to destroy rather than to heal. Talking Bird was a very powerful Spirit Talker. She called on the gods, and they sent lightning from the sky." He raised his hand to the darkness above them, and back to hit himself in the chest. "It struck him in the heart, killing him and splitting the Skystone. His body was burned, and his ashes confined to a small clay bottle for all eternity." Sam's shoulders sagged. "But one piece of the turquoise disappeared. Legend says an eagle flew down, picked it up, and carried it away."

Arms stretched heavenward, he released a sad cry. It echoed off the rock walls. "Talking Bird mourned for her son. Her grief made her crazy. Stories tell that she held captives on top of Fajada Butte without food or water until they died."

Along with the others, Madison and Lonan looked toward the large jutting rock. It was just a shadow against the dark horizon.

A small boy jumped up. "Gol-lee, Mr. Spotted Elk. How'd she get them up there?" His mother grabbed the fabric of his coat and pulled him back to his seat. The children laughed, and it took a minute for their parents to quiet them.

Sam moved to stand before the child and shook his finger at him. "That is an excellent question, young man."

The boy gave his mother a "see" look. She smiled and put an arm around his shoulder.

"When Talking Bird lived, there were stairs all the way to the top. No one is allowed to try to climb them today, because it's dangerous."

Heads bobbed in understanding.

Lilly sat across the circle from them, her eyes enjoying the active interest of the children.

"In the meantime, Nukpana's evil spirit festered in his prison and hatred for his people grew. One day, he finally escaped and set in motion his plan to wipe the pueblo people and their history off the face of the earth."

Sam strode around the fire, his steps sure and purposeful, his feet keeping rhythm with the drums played by the teen boys. He stopped. The drumbeats gradually increased in volume, then fell silent. Sam raised his voice. "The gods could not let this happen. They joined together to stop him. They devised a Grand Plan that would take many centuries to fulfill."

Madison saw Lilly turn and cock her head in the direction of Pueblo Bonito. She appeared to be listening, but Madison didn't hear anything. She closed her eyes to concentrate. Then, there it was, a faint echo of drumbeats, so soft they were hardly discernable. The flute joined the music, and as it gradually grew louder, Madison could feel the rhythm in the soil beneath her feet, like a heart beating, working to maintain the life of the earth.

Lonan whispered in her ear. "Listen, can you hear it, feel it?" Chu'a whined in fear and Lonan leaned down to reassure the young dog.

Madison could only nod. He clutched her shoulder tighter as 'yip, yip, yip' tore the air. It was the call of a fox on the wind. She looked up to see Lilly smiling at her. The older woman nodded.

"Of course, Talking Bird knew nothing about her son's plans. But one day, a young woman with hair the color of fire walked out of the rock." Sam pointed toward the cliff drawings behind Una Vida and snapped his fingers. "Just like that, she appeared." He moved farther around the circle. "And with her came a mighty warrior with eyes of gold. They had been chosen to fulfill the gods' Grand Plan."

About the author...

Linda LaRoque is a retired teacher who loves West Texas, its flora and fauna, and its people. Her stories paint pictures of life, love, and learning set against the raw landscape of ranches and rural communities in Texas.

Linda is a member of RWA, her local chapter of HOTRWA where she serves as president, NTRWA and Davis Mountain Trail Writers. She makes her home in Central Texas.

Visit Linda at www.lindalaroque.com